Praise for *101*

"Tom Pitts is fast becoming the underworld bard of the Bay Area, and *101* is his best yet. The cast of characters is rich, and the subject matter—the marijuana biz in Humboldt County on the cusp of legalization—could not be more timely. Plenty of violent action, betrayal and tough talk. Reading *101* will give you a contact high. Get this book NOW."

—T.J. English, author of
The Corporation and *The Westies*

"Throw out everything you know about crime fiction. Tom Pitts, author of *Hustle* and *American Static*, returns with a plot stickier than an ounce of Humboldt County's finest. *101* is typical Tom Pitts, the kind of novel that proves he'll forever and ever have followers, trailing behind him begging for one more hit."

—Eryk Pruitt, author of *What We Reckon*

101

ALSO BY TOM PITTS

Piggyback
Hustle
Knuckleball
American Static

TOM PITTS

101

DOWN&OUT
BOOKS

Down & Out Books
3959 Van Dyke Rd, Ste. 265
Lutz, FL 33558
www.DownAndOutBooks.com

The characters and events in this book are fictitious. Any similarity to real persons, living or dead, is coincidental and not intended by the author.

Cover image © sgoodwin4813 / 123RF Stock Photo
Cover design by Eric Beetner

ISBN: 1-948235-38-2
ISBN-13: 978-1-948235-38-9

For the tough-as-nails women in my own life,
Lula and Cheryl

Chapter One

May 2016
(Six months before California voters legalize marijuana)

When her message came, Vic didn't hesitate. Ripper shook him from a dead sleep, apologetically handing him the blinking phone. He sat up in the darkness and didn't allow himself to think about why Barbara was reaching out. Even though it was pitch black outside, Vic dutifully walked to the only place he could get a signal—a fertilizer sack forty yards from the house. He shivered in the cold, wet predawn air and dialed.

"What's wrong?"

"Why does something have to be wrong?"

As soon as he heard her voice, the vision of her face lit his mind. He missed her. He hadn't realized how much. It'd been too long since he'd seen her. He used to call her his angel of Fulton Street, but he stopped because he didn't want to think about Fulton Street. He didn't even want to say the words. That day bonded Vic and Barbara forever. They both knew that. There was no reason to invoke the name of the street. The Fulton Street Massacre would live on in the imaginations of many, but there were only two survivors—the only ones who knew what really happened—and they'd worked hard over the last twenty years to block that day from their minds.

"Barbara, please. It's the middle of the night. What's going on?"

"It's Jerry. I think he's in trouble."

"Again."

"Yes, again. But it feels different this time. I don't know. He seems scared. He's not usually scared like this."

"What do you want me to do?"

"I want him to come up there, stay with you. Just till whatever is going on blows over. He's a good worker, you could use him up there."

"I haven't seen him since he was a kid. I don't know if I'd even recognize him."

"He's the same kid, Vic. And he needs help."

On his way up the 101, Jerry tried to count the aches and pains in his body. An itch above his eye, a lump of scar tissue that had been mashed into his forehead the week before. He'd taken a heel to the ribs that same night. It still hurt to breathe or stretch or cough. His elbow screamed from being twisted behind his back. He thought about all the scars and wounds he had collected over his twenty-five years. All the madness he'd wrought. He didn't have much to show for it.

Twenty-five wasn't old by most people's standards, but Jerry never figured he'd live past twenty-one. It was getting tougher and tougher to bounce back. Not only from a brawl, but from the booze, the blow, the skipped sleep.

Not that he was in the wrong that night. He was right, and he was justified. It'd started out as a small celebration, but it soured. The whiskey didn't help. More often than not these days, when he had a few shots, he ended up in a fight. He wasn't particularly good at it either. The drinking or the fights.

Everybody said it'd be Piper who drove him out of town, broke him. They said she'd get him deep into some sort of shit and she'd leave him to the sharks. But they were wrong. Sort of. Things didn't work out exactly as they'd planned, but these kinds of things never do. Sometimes you have to improvise.

The road had gone on for hours. It was mid-morning when he crossed the Golden Gate and slipped out of a fog bank, and he still hadn't checked his rearview yet. From the open fields outside Santa Rosa to the small-scale mountains of Mendocino County, the 101 rolled on, taking him farther and farther from the origin of his troubles. It felt good to be alone and on the road with a Marlboro wedged between his lips. The blacktop narrowed into a grove of redwoods and he rolled down the window to take in the lush forest air. Only two lanes wound through the wooded patch and RVs, semi-trucks, and hatch-backs overloaded with camping equipment forced him to slow. The highway shoulders suddenly trimmed so thin a passenger could reach out and slap the bark on the huge trees, if they'd wanted. If he had a passenger.

He broke past Richardson Grove and headed over the Eel River. He was maybe ten minutes away from Garberville, the proposed meeting spot. He hit the radio. Static. The scan button served up nothing, rolling on and on, the digits speeding by. Finally, it landed on a scratchy local station. He could barely make out the melody, but there was no mistaking that pearly electric guitar. The fucking Grateful Dead. Perfect. Hippy country indeed. Growing up in California with a name like Jerry had its drawbacks. He punched the power button with his index and returned to silence.

Pulling off at the Garberville exit, he was dumped right into the small town. No warning, no edge, and no residential border, just a short row of grocery stores, gas stations, and bars. And lots of dirty-looking kids. Railroad-hopping, dreadlocked kids. Most of the shops were painted with bright murals and signs in the windows promised deals on fertilizer and dirt and organic options for pest control. He knew it'd be a wait before they came to fetch him, so he pulled into a parking spot and climbed out of the car before pulling his cell.

Leaning back on the warm hood, he reached deep in his jeans and found the scrap of paper with the number and dialed.

No answer. He tried again. Nothing. He figured he'd give it a cigarette's time and give it another shot.

"You up here to trim?"

The voice took him by surprise. He was gawking at a pretty young—too young—girl exiting a bar and didn't notice the dirty man come up on him.

"What?"

"Trim. You know, are you hooked up already? Or still looking? I know some guys that still pay by the hour, but, you know, you gotta work. They let you smoke on the job, but no alcohol. That's why they let me go. But I bring somebody good back, they might change their minds, you know?"

The kid was filthy, stinking, caked with dirt. Hair more matted than dreadlocked. There were black spots on his cheeks. Jerry couldn't tell if they were moles or bits of dried food.

"I'm waiting for someone."

"Oh, no, I get it. Everybody's lookin' though. These guys are twenty an hour, old school. None of that pay-by-weight bullshit, you know?" The kid's smile revealed a row of chipped, yellow teeth. He'd taken his share of punches, that's for sure.

"No, man, I'm fine. I'm just waitin' on a ride."

"These guys have it together, dude. They feed you and everything. And if you wanna work all night, they got you." He stood bug-eyed now, waiting for this last comment to sink in. "You know?"

"Yeah," he said. "I get it." Jerry felt the clot of scar tissue above his eye twitch.

"You want my number or somethin'? In case, you know, you wanna hook it up?"

Jerry shook his head, slowly, so his position was clear.

"You got a number or somethin'? They might change their minds about the pay, maybe up it or somethin'."

"If everyone here is looking for work, why the fuck would they up their price?"

"Well...do you got a smoke maybe? I been smoking nothing

but rolled tobacco for days, I'm dying for a tailor-made."

Jerry reached in his pocket, shook out a Marlboro, stuck it in his mouth, and lit it. He blew smoke at the kid's face.

When the kid realized he wasn't going to pass the cigarette to him, he said, "That ain't cool."

"Fuck off." No more. No less. It took a moment for the comment to register, but then the dirty young man shuffled on down the street, hoping to coerce the next stationary citizen into God knows what he needed them for. As he watched him walk away, Jerry noticed the sidewalks were filled with these young kids. He saw them on the way in, but he now noticed there was no one else on the sidewalks. No middle-aged well-to-do types, no redneck want-to-fight types. No elderly errand runners. Certainly no police. Only dirty, sad-looking kids. The kind you see on the sidewalks of Berkeley—or any town that'll let them— begging for change and plotting their next high.

A gruff voice came over the line. It sounded distracted, annoyed. "Yeah?"

"This is Jerry."

"Who?"

"I'm looking for Vic. Tell him it's Juan's friend, Jerry."

No response. The street noise from the Garberville sidewalks made it tough to hear what was going on in the background. He should have made the call from inside the car. He got off the hood and moved to open the door and a sleepy voice came on the line.

"Hello?"

"Is this Vic?"

"Yeah."

"It's Juan's friend. He called you, right?"

"I know who you are. Where you at?"

The voice was dry and most definitely American. Jerry wondered if Vic would have an accent. But the rasp he now heard was Northern as a cowboy's. Jerry said, "I'm in Garberville. In front of a place called the Blue Moon Café."

Vic made a noise like a one syllable chuckle, but it came out as a cough. "All right. Stay there. I'll have somebody come down the hill and get you."

"Should I go in and wait?"

"Don't matter. It's gonna take about forty-five minutes, so if you wanna go in and have a beer, go ahead. Stay at the Blue Moon, though. I don't wanna come looking for you."

"Yeah. You know the place? Is the food any good?"

Jerry heard Vic's bronchial laugh once more and then the line went dead.

"You a cop?"

Jerry hadn't stepped away from his car and another kid was already on him, barely distinguishable from the last. Dirt caked on his neck so thick it cracked like plaster. A cigarette was stuck behind his ear, bent at the middle, damp with the oil from his hair. He kept his arms a few inches out at the side, not quite hanging, so if there were trouble, he was ready to spring.

"No," Jerry said. "I'm not a cop. What the fuck makes you think I'm a cop."

"You look like a cop. You're sitting here looking around, talking on your phone. Plus, look at your ride. That's a fucking cop car. You a cop?"

"Cops up here usually drive rentals?"

"Rental?" The new kid with the greasy blond hair leaned back and eyed the length of the car, huffing through his nose as though he were appraising it. "Fuckin' rental, huh? That's worse than being a cop. Means you're a cop magnet." He gave Jerry another once over, inspecting him from head to toe, then walked away without saying a word.

* * *

6

The inside of the Blue Moon Café didn't look like a café at all. It looked like a bar. A bar reeking of burned French fry grease and filthy hair, but still a bar. The kind of place you'd usually find old drunks and local geezers whiling away their borrowed time, but the Blue Moon had neither. It was packed with more of the same dirty kids who lined the street. Young men and women who looked like they weren't old enough to be in the place. But there they were, belly up to the copper bar, half-finished drinks and empties collected in front of them. Jerry squeezed through and tried to read the taps, all of them strange off-brand beers he didn't recognize.

The bartender wasn't clearing the bar, only taking orders. He looked overworked and annoyed. "What'dya need?"

"Uh...do you have an IPA on tap?"

The bartender rolled his eyes and turned to pull Jerry's beer. Jerry looked from side to side and realized he and the barkeep were probably the oldest people in the place. The bartender returned with his beer and sat it on a napkin in front of him.

"Is it always this busy?"

The bartender shouted over the din, "What'd you expect? It's fucking trimming season," and turned down the bar to take the next order.

Jerry took his beer and napkin and worked his way back toward the door. The place was full, not a seat in the house. Tables in the restaurant area, deuces and four-seaters, but those too were filled. No plates of food or people reading menus, only more dirty kids drinking. Jerry stood by the door looking through the smudged glass at the street, sipping his pint as slowly as possible.

"You Jerry?"

He was confused. He glanced over his shoulder to make sure the guy was talking to him and not someone behind him. In a bar full of rough and dirty characters, the man in front of him was rougher and dirtier than most anyone there.

"Vic?"

"Nah, fuck no. I'm Ripper. Vic told me to come down the hill and fetch you."

"Shit," Jerry said, "In the nick of time, too. This's my third pint. You parked outside? Do I follow you, or what?"

"We got a few minutes. I don't wanna go back up the hill just yet. Shit, I just got off that mother. Lemme get a pop before we head out." Ripper stepped past Jerry and elbowed his way to the bar. He was sleeveless and dirty and when he brushed by, Jerry caught a waft of his funk. His arms were covered in blurred blue tattoos that looked older than the skin sporting them. Some of the patrons seemed to know him and vied for his attention, but Ripper was focused on the bartender. He called out to him by name and the bartender stopped what he was doing and positioned himself to take the order. "What's that fancy fuckin' scotch I like?"

"Balvenie," the barkeep said without missing a beat.

"Yeah, that's the shit. Gimme two doubles and two of whatever my friend here is drinking." Ripper pointed back to Jerry, but the bartender had no recollection of what he was drinking. "What'd got, Jerry? What're ya drinkin'?"

"IPA."

Ripper grinned and said, "Two Grizzlies and two of them scotches."

After the drinks were poured and the shots thrown back, Ripper led Jerry to a table.

"So, what'd you think of Garbageville?"

Jerry laughed. The name fit perfectly. "I don't get it. Is it always like this?"

"Fuck no. It's trimming season and all these little fucks are up here looking for work. But shit is scaling back. It ain't the business it used to be." He took a deep pull from his beer. "It's all glutted out and it's only gonna get worse. We're fighting legalization, but it's gonna fucking happen. Soon too. Probably in November, that's what they say."

Jerry took a thoughtful pull on his own beer, but, really, he had no opinion on the shifting laws. He figured there'd always be laws, and there'd always be a reason to break them.

"To be honest," Ripper continued, "I'm not sure why you're here. I don't even know if Vic has any work left. We just had a hungry crew of six up there for ten days. Chicks, all of 'em. Talking sixteen hours a day. A real fucking henhouse. They knew their shit though. Trimmed something like a hundred pounds. Maybe more."

"Oh, I'm not here to work," Jerry said.

Ripper furrowed his brow.

"I'm just here to visit for a bit."

"Visit, huh? Visit a guy you never met?"

Jerry wasn't quite sure how to phrase it. He'd known about Vic most of his life, but didn't remember ever meeting him. His mother told him very little. Mostly stories of his heroics and Robin Hood-like criminal prowess. Vic was a dark mysterious force behind what drove his mother, and he was nervous to finally meet the man. Juan knew him. It was Juan's idea to call him. He was a little envious Juan got to do business with Vic, the legend, but that was circumstance more than anything. Juan was in the same line of work as Vic. Other friends in the marijuana game had met him too.

"I'm like a friend of the family."

Ripper eyed Jerry all over again, like he was seeing him for the first time. It wasn't a relaxed friend-of-a-friend scan either. It was a look of suspicion. Like Jerry brought a dark cloud with him. "One of them deals, huh? All right, I get it. Nice fuckin' shiner, by the way." He nodded his chin at Jerry's bruised eye and smiled. "Let's have another shot of that scotch and hit the road. C'mon. I'm buyin'."

Chapter Two

The road up the hill was long and dirty. Deep with ruts and lined close with trees whose branches reached out to scratch and scar the car. Jerry did his best to keep up with Ripper's four-wheel drive, but cursed as he was forced to a near stop over and over by the constant hazard that was the road itself. Must be impossible in the rain, Jerry thought. Then, announced by a high whining rev, an all-terrain vehicle passed him on a tight corner, the kind of ATV that looked like a motorcycle stuck between four ballooned tires. The man driving the ATV wore no helmet, but kept his face shrouded with a black handkerchief to filter out the dust.

"Motherfucker," Jerry said under his breath. He said it to the man with the masked face, to the ruts in the dirt road, to the jarring, failing shocks in his piece-of-shit rental, he said it to Juan for suggesting he come up here in the first place, but mostly he said it to Ripper. He wanted Ripper to slow the fuck down. Several forks and tributaries ran off the main path and he worried Ripper would pull on to one and he'd be lost out here in this spider web of unmarked roads. He'd never find his way back down the hill, let alone the freeway. He did his best to cling to the clouds of dust laid out like breadcrumbs before him.

Near the bottom there'd been gaps in the flora, breathing room where the road hairpinned and opened up into tiny meadows dotted with manzanita and madrones, but as they climbed, the woods became denser. Redwoods and cedars packed tight with huge prehistoric ferns and blackberry bramble.

He searched for signs of the industry around him. There were no patches of tall green cannabis sprouting up, no guarded greenhouses with shotgun-toting locals standing sentinel. Only fences. Some of them wire, some of them wood. Several with tall planked boards you couldn't see through. No mailboxes or nameplates adorned the openings where two-track paths led into private properties. He saw no more than the dirty mouth of the gate.

Ripper braked and pulled a hard right into a gap in the fence line and the road became more tortured than the one they'd just exited. Jerry's shoulder banged into the door as he heard the undercarriage scrape against dirt and gravel. The track shot upward and, through a cloud of dust, he saw Ripper's brake lights. He stopped short behind him and climbed out as the dust settled.

Three or four trucks stood parked in a loose semi-circle and, beyond them, a smattering of ATVs, enduro motorcycles, and two of what looked to be heavy-duty, off-road golf carts. Beyond the battery of vehicles, Jerry noticed the weed. Finally. There were patches of it, circled with meshed wire to keep out wild life. On the rise to their left, there were strange white open-ended tents, more like rounded greenhouses, bursting with budding plants. They reminded Jerry of small white airplane hangars. Four of these structures stood side by side and a wide path led to more in the woods.

Dogs barked and greeted them. Vicious barks with wagging tails. They were large mutts, black and tan.

"That's Lloyd, the black one, and the tan one is Mongo."

The barking stopped and there was another noise. A soft chugging. It was a generator laboring steadily and beyond it, a small rustic shack with a porch almost as big as the house.

"This is the place?" he asked.

"This is it," Ripper said. "This is where the magic happens."

"Is Vic here?"

"Oh yeah." Ripper was already heading toward a deep ice chest standing by the edge of the porch. He pulled two beer cans, both cheap American brands, and turned to Jerry. "Bud or Miller?"

Jerry said Miller and Ripper tossed him the can. They cracked the beers and stood on the dirt off the side of the large porch. After a deep pull, a silence welled between them.

"So you know Juan, huh?"

"Who's Juan?"

For one quick second Jerry wondered if he weren't here as some kind of fluke, some twisted case of mistaken identity.

"After you talk with Vic, I'll show you around," Ripper said. "I know you said you're just visiting, but there's always shit to be done around here. Fuck, I'm the only hired hand. Vic is just the whip cracker."

"You calling me a cracker?"

The voice behind them sounded as raspy as it did on the phone, like the throat that housed such a voice had to be painted with glue. Jerry turned to find a man standing on the porch in a bathrobe with a cup of coffee in his hand. His hair was mussed from sleep and his chin rough with grey stubble, but there was something presentable about him, something formidable, noble in the way he carried himself.

"Vic? I'm Jerry, I'm—"

"I know who you are. You're probably too young to remember, but I've met you before." Before Jerry could respond, Vic turned to Ripper. "Get up to number three and check the lines, would you? Cherry Bomb came by and said the bottoms of the plants are all browning. Fucking woke me up too."

"Sure thing," Ripper said and, without saying another word or taking a sip of his beer, turned and climbed into one of the four-wheel-drive golf carts and drove off.

Vic and Jerry stood there for a long moment, letting the silence pass between them. For Jerry it was uncomfortable, but Vic took in the stillness like fresh air. He put his hand on his hip and sipped his coffee. Slow, deliberate sips while he looked at Jerry over the rim of his cup. He seemed measured and relaxed. He was in his domain and wasn't holding it over Jerry, trying to intimidate, but that was the effect anyway.

After a few more loud sips, Vic tossed the remnants of the coffee in the grass. "Well, let's get you settled. You want a cup of coffee? I'm gonna have another. My machine's broken, so it's gonna be cowboy swill. That alright?"

Even though he wasn't sure what cowboy swill was, Jerry nodded anyway and followed him onto the porch and toward the cabin's door.

Vic stopped at the house's threshold and pointed to an old couch at the edge of the deck. "Here, have a seat, I'll get you a cup."

Jerry sat down on the dirty couch. It smelled of mildew. It'd probably been outside for years. He tried to take it all in. The surrounding nature, the echoing quiet. Vic took his time inside the shack and Jerry waited.

Vic returned with the second mug and a small carton of milk. He set them down without saying anything.

"I'm not sure what Juan told you about me being up here," Jerry said.

"Juan?"

"Yeah, when he called."

There was a flat silence before Vic answered. "Juan didn't call me. Your mother did."

Jerry let that sink in. He should've known better. Juan was in on the job. Sort of. He helped work it—pointing out risks—but he wasn't getting a cut or anything. Reflex had kicked in when things didn't feel right, and Jerry called Juan. He knew he'd been ID'd by the people he burned and he wasn't sure where to turn. So he called Juan. And it looked like Juan—who he trusted with his life, who he'd known since the seventh grade—called his mom. And his mom called her go-to knight in shining armor.

"You look like shit. What's that?" Vic said, pointing to his eye. "A fight? Is that part of why you're here? Or all of why you're here?"

"Yeah, well, you know, you shoulda seen the other guy." Jerry offered up a smile to frame the lame joke.

Vic didn't laugh, didn't smile, he only studied Jerry. He stood the mug and milk on a makeshift table made from a huge wooden spool that once carried fiber optic cable, then took a seat on a folding chair across from Jerry. The steaming mug sat untouched beside Jerry's open beer. Birds were chittering, but that was the only noise. That and the curious sound of nature, the sound of silence so full it's symphonic. Vic sipped his coffee, and Jerry sat.

Juan sucked for air but there was none. The plastic sealed his mouth and he felt his heart harden with panic. Every muscle, every tendon, ached for oxygen. His eyes bulged and black dots exploded in his field of vision.

They yanked the bag from his head and his lungs pulled for air. He leaned forward in the chair, hoping it would keep him from fainting. He wanted to hold his head with his hands, but his hands were zip-tied behind his back. His ankles, too, criss-crossed with duct tape and lashed to the chair's legs.

"Juan, you're going to have to tell us where he is."

Juan only shook his head. He wasn't able to talk yet. He needed more air.

Cardiff looked at Aaron Pullman and nodded. Aaron punched Juan in the temple with a gloved fist. Juan collapsed onto the floor, taking the chair with him.

"Why are you being loyal to him, Juan? He's not your friend. You know he wouldn't do the same for you. He's proven that." Cardiff squatted down and spoke more softly, his faint accent folding a melody into his voice. "You need to tell us where he went."

The hardwood floor rocked back and forth and Juan gulped in enough air to say, "I don't know where he is."

"Then you need to tell us what you *do* know."

"I don't know anything."

"Of course you do," Cardiff said. "You're friends. You're more than friends, you're *part-ners*." He sang the last word, twisting high in a mocking way.

"He's gone. I didn't talk to him. I haven't seen him."

Cardiff leaned in a little closer and said, "That's a goddamn shame."

He wound his index finger in the air, a signal for Aaron to wrap things up. Aaron bent down with the plastic bag again and hooded it over Juan's head, only this time he cinched it tight with one hand while he took a spool of duct tape and wrapped it around Juan's neck with the other hand.

Juan thrashed. His hands were tied behind his back. He tried to bite through the plastic but his teeth found no purchase. Panic set in, he knew what the duct tape meant. His lungs pulled and pulled, but it was over in moments.

Cardiff and Pullman watched till it was over, till the stench of Juan's bowels singed the air.

"Clean up," Cardiff said. "Make sure you get everything. Open some curtains in here too. Let in some light so you can see what you're doing. I'll get the car and meet you at the end of the block."

"Took you long enough."

Aaron Pullman squeezed into the front seat, he wasn't much taller than Cardiff, but he was thicker. It was never more apparent than when he tried to fit in to the front seat of Cardiff's car. "I wanted to make sure."

"Make sure? Make sure of what? That I get a ticket for double-parking?" Aaron didn't laugh, but Cardiff said, "You may think I'm kidding, but San Francisco meter maids are the worst. It's just that kind of breadcrumb we don't want to leave for some detective who decides to do his job." He started the engine and joined traffic. "Find anything interesting up there?"

Aaron hated Cardiff's accent. He was never sure where it came from. It sounded English, but also Southern at the same time. Cardiff was hooked up with the Russians, but the accent was something altogether different. He never bothered to ask Cardiff about his past, the less he knew the better. All he knew was Cardiff sounded condescending. He reached into his jacket and pulled out a small flip phone. "Burner."

"Hmmm. A disposable he forgot to dispose of, huh? Good, I'll check it in a minute. Tell me you left his personal phone in his apartment."

"I did. I left it."

"But you checked it first."

"I checked it first."

"All right then."

They sat silent for a few blocks while Cardiff worked his way through the late afternoon traffic.

"Where are we going?" Aaron asked.

"We're following the clues, Pullman. We're following the clues."

Chapter Three

Vic grilled some steaks for Jerry and Ripper. He took his time marinating the meat. While they waited, he soaked some potatoes and asparagus in the same concoction he used for the meat. The steaks were cheap cuts, but they smelled delicious as they cooked. Ripper hadn't returned, but Jerry figured the aroma would draw him back like a hungry dog.

"I noticed the wire you got wrapped around the plants," Jerry said. "You got wildlife troubles out here?"

Vic didn't look up from the grill. "Nothing I'm too worried about." He nodded to a .30-06 Springfield leaning against a railing in a corner of the deck.

Jerry hadn't noticed the gun before. It was tucked in with a few brooms and a shovel like any other household tool. "Damn."

"It'll stop most anything. Bear might be tough, but I've never seen one. Seen their shit—stepped in it—but haven't seen an actual bear." The steaks sizzled and the thick grey smoke blew up into Vic's face. "Plenty of deer though. They're the fuckers you gotta watch out for. They'll eat you out of business."

It'd been mostly silent since Ripper left and this was the longest Jerry and Vic had spoken all afternoon. Jerry decided to push the small talk. "How long you been up here?"

"Too long. Medium rare? Or rare?"

"Medium rare is fine."

The dogs sounded off in a chorus alarm. A cloud of dust rose up behind the vehicles already parked and a truck door slammed.

A woman's voice called out. "Vic! *Vic!*"

"That'd be Ghia," Vic said. He set down the tongs he was using to prod the meat and wiped his hands on his jeans.

"Vic!" The voice shrieked this time.

A woman rounded the ATVs and stepped toward the house. A wide brimmed hat shadowed her face and she wore big tan work gloves.

"That fucker Dan is messing with the water again." She noticed Jerry and took down her tone. "Oh, hello."

"Jerry, this is Ghia. Ghia, Jerry."

She pulled off her hat and shook down a mane of grey intertwined with chestnut brown. Her sun-kissed skin had the healthy tone of someone who spent their days working outdoors. Jerry started to get up, but she waved him back down. "That's alright, honey. Relax, I'm only here for a minute." Then she turned to Vic. "What are you going to do about it?" she said. "This affects you too, you know. Those lines feed right into the back five."

"Which Dan?" Vic asked. "Dandy Dan? Or Furry Dan?"

"Dandy Dan. Not Mister Clean, but the other bald one." She turned to Jerry. "Three Dans on the same damn mountain. Might as well live in Mayberry."

"All right," Vic said. "I'll go up and talk to him."

"Talk to him? He's stealing our water. I hope you'll do more than that. This is how it starts, Vic. This is how—"

"Ghia, I said I'd talk to him. I'll go up there after dinner. You wanna stay for something to eat?"

Her eyes passed over the smoking grill to Jerry. She raised her eyebrows and said, "No, not for dinner, but I'll have a beer if you got one."

Cardiff exited the 580 in Downtown Oakland and drove for a while under the freeway. He hooked a right on Broadway and pulled into the first metered spot he found. He threw the car into park and hit the stereo power with his knuckle, but left the engine running. "Okay, let's have it."

Aaron looked at him blankly.

"The burner. Let me see it."

Aaron reached into his pocket and pulled out the small flip phone. "I think the battery is real low. You may wanna charge it."

"Why didn't you plug it in while we were driving?"

Aaron's brow furrowed. He looked at the phone in his hand as though it may defend his inaction.

"Never mind. Give it here." Cardiff snatched it, flipped it open, and powered it on. He scrolled to the call log and studied it. "Aaron, get me a pen and some paper out of the glove box, will you?"

Aaron checked the glove box, found a pen, but had to search through the other debris for paper. "There's no paper. Only napkins."

"What are napkins made out of?"

Aaron didn't answer. He handed a sheath of white napkins to Cardiff. He felt like saying something. Or doing something. Instead, he handed over the napkins and kept quiet.

Ghia's one beer turned into three, or four. Ripper came back from his duties and two other spindly, spotted young men showed up. The one with the worst acne introduced himself as Cherry Bomb, the other as Jake. Vic cut the steaks in half so they all had a plate and they sat on the porch to eat and talk.

Jerry didn't understand most of what was said. There was talk of clones, hybrids, strains, soils, CO_2, nitrates, and manure. They used strange slang and other terms sounding far too advanced for his high school education. Stories and gossip eventually won over the shop talk and Jerry sat back and listened as the back-biting began. Who was fucking who, who owed money, and, again and again, who was siphoning water.

"Fuckin' Tipple got me these clones that'll shoot straight up, but they ain't got no hairs at four weeks," the one called Jake said.

"If you extend their light for an extra two hours and increase the carbon drip, they'll be fine," Cherry Bomb answered with his mouth full of steak. "Problem is, they're supposed to be purple, but no one's shocked 'em lately 'cause it drops the stickiness for real, then they cure too fast."

"That Tipple is a piece of work. He's been sending those sprouts all over the hill, but he hasn't given Ripper a damn dime," Ghia said. "A kid like that should know better. His mom had to bail him out last time with the Radleys down on the row."

"He's gacked up on the booger sugar," Jake said.

"That ain't blow, that's straight up crank. Dirty biker crank at that," Ripper said. "Fuck Tipple. And fuck his mom too."

And on it went, the conversation ricocheting back and forth across the porch. Jerry tried to join once or twice, but he was just being polite. He didn't know the players, or the game. Besides, the beer and the whiskey were beginning to dull his wit.

Vic sat quiet too, enjoying the banter from his guests, but never adding to it unless asked. A rumor would get passed back and forth, discredited or upheld, and eventually one of them would ask, "What do you think, Vic?" and he'd shrug his shoulders, noncommittal. But Jerry saw he was filing this information away, every bit of it.

At one point, after the liquor began to flow, Vic leaned over to Jerry and asked, "You doin' all right?"

Jerry nodded. He had a full stomach, a few shots of whiskey, and a cold beer in his hand. The best he felt since he left the Bay.

"I'm gonna clear these guys out of here in a few minutes. You want to take a ride up the hill with me? Talk to Dandy Dan with me?"

"Sure," Jerry said.

* * *

After the company departed, Vic told Ripper to clean up and do the dishes. He swept his arm over all the debris covering the porch, taking all the bottles, cans, and paper plates as well.

"You got it," Ripper said. He was used to the exchange of cleaning for being fed. "You going for a late night stroll or something?"

"Yeah, something," Vic said. Then he turned to Jerry. "You ready?"

Jerry nodded.

"Hang on a sec." Vic slipped into the house.

Jerry still hadn't been inside the whole time. When he needed to piss, Vic pointed at the endless trees in the darkness surrounding the cabin, so that's where he went. So far, there was no other reason to go inside. When Vic returned to the porch, he had a simple tan holster clipped onto his belt. Jerry saw the semi-automatic inside the holster. Probably a nine, maybe bigger, he didn't really know firearms. "You gonna need that?"

"Probably not. Better safe than sorry, though." Vic pointed to the off-road golf cart ATV. "C'mon, we'll take the Rhino."

"Rhino? Why do you call it that?"

"'Cause that's what it's called."

The darkness tightened around them as they pulled away from the cabin. The small headlights on the Rhino barely lit the path ahead, but Vic pushed the whining engine and they flew into the night, Jerry gripping the roll bars expecting to crash at any moment. The Rhino dipped and tree branches slapped at its sides, stinging Jerry's shoulders.

Barking dogs sounded over the engine and their barks grew louder as light appeared through the forest. They braked at a clearing before a shack. A cabin like Vic's but smaller. The dogs were tethered to a tree near the door, and they yapped and barked and pulled at their chains.

Vic drew the semi-automatic from his belt and racked a round into the chamber.

"What now?" Jerry asked.

"Now we wait for him to come out."

Jerry wasn't sure what this was, what he'd been drawn into. "Then what?"

"Then you watch and learn. You can see how a grown-up does business."

Chapter Four

"Shut up!" A deep voice shouted at the dogs from inside the tiny building. "Shut the fuck up!" A door swung open and a shadow crowded the entrance.

"That him?" Jerry whispered.

Dan's bald head shone in the glow of the shack; he looked big and brawny, like a clean-shaven lumberjack. There was nothing dandy about him.

"Dandy Dan? Yeah, that's him. He already knows we're here. You don't need to whisper. If this thing had a goddamn horn, we wouldn't have to sit here so long." Vic took a soft pack of Camels from his shirt pocket and shook one out. "You want one?"

Jerry did, but he said no. He was scared, unsure of what was going to happen. He wanted to be ready for anything.

"Who the fuck's there?" Dandy Dan shouted at the Rhino's headlights. The dogs kept barking.

Vic stayed silent.

Dan repeated his question and walked toward the vehicle. Jerry saw something in his right hand. At first he thought it was a bat or a stick, but as Dan stepped into the headlights, he saw it was a rifle.

"Stay here," Vic said.

Jerry was happy to stay put—he felt helpless—he was the only one without a gun.

Vic stepped in front of the ATV, nothing in his hands.

"What's that thing? A Red Ryder?"

"Vic, that you?"

"Yeah, Dan. What's with the gun?" Vic was walking straight toward him now.

"I dunno who the fuck is coming up the driveway. What's a Red Ryder?"

"Shit, you don't remember Red Ryders? I thought you were older than that." Vic was close to Dan now, standing with his back to Jerry in the Rhino. "I guess you're still a youngster."

"What's up, man?"

Vic punched him hard in the solar plexus. Dan dropped to his knees, using the gun to balance and keep him from falling all the way to the ground.

"You stealing water again, Dan?" Vic didn't move for the gun, he stood over Dan, waiting for a response.

Dan moaned and tried to get up, using the rifle as a crutch. Vic kicked it out from under him and Dan fell back to the ground with the rifle.

Vic leaned down. "I know it's you, so don't deny it."

"You're wrong, Vic. It's—"

Vic punched him in the side of the head. "I just told you not to deny it. You fucking figure out your own problems without making 'em someone else's. I don't want to come back up here." Then Vic got up and walked back to the Rhino without turning around.

"Water's a big thing up here," Vic said. "People steal it with trucks, they siphon it off with pipes, they suck it straight out the rivers. Without water, nothing grows. It's liquid gold on the hill. If you ain't got it, your plot is useless." They were heading back down the hill now, both of them with glowing Camels stuck in their mouths. "Last month, someone pulled up to the elementary school up in Fortuna—drained the reservoir tank on top of the school. Every last drop. Must have snuck by at night with a truck. Desperate times, desperate measures."

They pitched forward in the darkness, letting the cool night air pull the smoke from their faces. Vic drove slower on the way down the hill, pleased with how things had gone with Dandy Dan.

Cardiff stood in front of the desk with his arms folded. At the desk, a small man tapped phone numbers onto the screen.

"You know, you could've searched this shit yourself. It ain't that hard," Treaclie said.

"If it was so easy, why the fuck is it taking so long?"

Treaclie rolled his eyes and continued the search.

Aaron sat quiet in a corner, breaking small bits of chocolate off a Hershey's bar. He liked watching Cardiff be an asshole to someone else for a change.

Treaclie worked for a few more minutes, wrote some names on a slip of paper, and leaned back in his chair. "Well, I got a few names here. And if you consider them in the order of the calls he made, it's like a road map."

"That's exactly what I wanted to hear."

"If you give me a few minutes, I can firm up the information; maybe get a couple of actual addresses."

"Real minutes? Or the short hours you've been passing off as minutes since we been here?"

Treaclie sighed. He knew better than to get into it with Cardiff. The man could be snippy and snide, but it could turn ugly easily. He'd seen it happen. He glanced at Aaron who sat near the corner. He didn't know who he was, but he looked dangerous. Nothing scarier than Cardiff with backup.

From his chair, Aaron sharpened his focus, too, and readied his reflexes. He didn't want things to turn ugly either. He'd be the one cleaning up. He'd done enough of that for one day.

"Look," Treaclie said, "these things take time. I'm doing the best I can."

Cardiff drew in a deep breath, and let it out slow, like he was holding back something terrible. "You *look*, fuckface. I don't have time to sit here while you jerk off in front of your computer. Tell you what. I'm going to be back here at twelve noon sharp. You be here, *with* the information I'm asking for, or I'm going to scalp you, you understand?"

Treaclie looked at him confused.

"Yeah," Cardiff said, "you heard me, I said scalp. I'm going to take the sharpest knife in your kitchen and slice open your fucking forehead and I'm going to yank your hair right off your head."

Treaclie didn't say anything.

"Tomorrow, noon. Sharp. Sharp as that knife in your kitchen," Cardiff said.

When they returned to the house, the dogs greeted them without barking. They wagged their tails and jumped up at the Rhino.

"*Git.* Git on, Lloyd. Down, Mongo, down." Vic said, shooing the dogs away. The house was quiet and the lights were off save for one bare bulb glowing above the door.

"I just got that," Jerry said.

"Got what?"

"Mongo and Lloyd. Mongoloid. Pretty funny."

"Shoe fits."

They stepped onto the porch and the wood creaked under their weight.

"Where's Ripper?"

"Asleep."

"Shit, what time is it?"

"It's only nine. But out here, once it's dark, there ain't much to do. Besides, a full day's work, a few beers, that'll do it. I'm pretty beat myself. You need anything before you turn in?"

"A place to sleep."

Vic laughed at his own inhospitality. "Shit, I didn't even

show you your bunk, did I. I'm sorry, kid. Let's go inside for a nightcap first."

Jerry followed Vic inside the cabin. The first thing that hit him was the tang of green bud. The ceiling was sectioned off with rows of drying plants hanging from string. The string crisscrossed across the width of the room so there was a narrow path you could walk through without your head bumping into the stalactites of weed. The place was compact and cluttered, yet everything seemed to have a purpose and a place. Hammered together shelves were packed with supplies. Mostly nonperishables from the big box stores, but also scales, bongs, glass jars, and bags—turkey bags, garbage bags, sandwich bags, freezer bags, and paper sacks. Along the farthest wall were plastic bins stacked like mason's bricks all the way to the roof. And to the left of those, garbage bags overflowing with weed. And beside them, pounds of weed double-wrapped in turkey bags in a wide pyramid, at least fifty of them.

"Welcome to the factory," Vic said.

"Holy shit."

"Yeah, there ain't much room for anything else in here. You smoke?"

"Sometimes. I mean, I could, you know, sample the local fare."

"Be my guest. There's more here than you can smoke in a lifetime."

Jerry pointed to the open garbage sacks. "Just grab some from there?"

"Fuck no, that's the shake. I got a kid comes by and gets rid of that—turns it into hash, or dab, or whatever the fuck they're using it for these days." Vic moved to the food storage and pointed to the jars on the top shelf. "We got outdoor, indoor, the shit we're growing in the hoopers outside."

"Hoopers?"

"Yeah, those big white things we got lit up. We cover 'em at night and keep the lights on 'em for a few extra hours. Trick the plants into thinking they're indoors. Makes for great sensimilla without the headache of really being inside." He turned back to the shelf. "Let's see, we got hash, killer fucking keef. We got so much of this shit I can't give it away. It's mostly big bud, but hybrids of it—orange dream, strawberry sunshine, couple different strains of cookies. Lemon dream. Dragon berry. Shit, I don't know. Grab a jar and twist one up. I'm going to pour myself a bourbon. You want one?"

Jerry nodded and moved to the jars to finger through them. The large ones were marked with strange hieroglyphics differentiating the strains, the small ones were filled with chips of hash or fluffy yellow keef. Some of the jars in back held keef that'd settled and the sediment was darker and denser.

"Damn, this shit is crazy."

"Yeah, it's what we do up here. Grow a whole lotta crazy."

"I been on the wrong end of this business."

Vic took two short glasses from the cupboard and set them on the wood-planked kitchen counter. "Ah, it's over anyway. This business is done. It's gonna go all the way legal any minute. Then the big shots are going to be the only ones up here. All these mom and pop operations like us? We'll be back in the city hustling."

Chapter Five

Jerry woke up with a cold joint between his fingers. It'd extinguished itself after only a few drags. He was still in the plastic chair by the kitchen table. An empty shot glass beside a half-drained beer in front of him. His neck hurt and eyes burned. And his mouth tasted like shit.

"Hello?" His voice was raspy. He took a slug of the warm beer and forced it over his dry white tongue.

The room was empty and he guessed the rest of the house was too. He had to piss. He leaned forward and that familiar throb started to beat in his head. The dogs barked outside, and over their din, he heard women's voices. He stood and steadied himself and ran his fingers though his hair as the front door swung open.

A woman with blonde dreadlocks and tattooed sleeves sang out. "*Vic!*"

"I don't think he's here." Jerry's throat still coarse.

"Oh, and who are you?" Her tone was playful and flirtatious, but she walked right by him to the shelves and took down a tall glass bong.

Jerry introduced himself while she pushed through the jars till she found an appropriate choice to fill her bowl.

"Nettie, Carla, looks like we're working with someone new today."

Before Jerry could explain he wasn't working with them, the door swung open again and Nettie and Carla rolled in. Nettie

29

was tall and pale with oddly dyed hair that probably started out as green. Carla was older than Jerry, shorter than them all, and she wrinkled up her nose like she smelled something bad when she laid eyes on him.

Nettie said, "I hope you like shitty music, because Carla loves shitty music and that's all we're gonna listen to today, right, Carla?"

Carla said, "Is there any coffee made? Should I make some?"

"You know where it is, go ahead and make some. I think his machine is broken, so you gotta use that handheld thingy," Nettie said. "Trinity, pack me a bowl too, would you?"

Trinity asked Jerry, "You want a bong rip?...I didn't catch your name."

"Jerry."

"Jer-*ree*." She said it like she was considering its fit, whether he should go on using it or upgrade to another name. She reminded Jerry a little of Piper, the same fiery hair, the same cocky attitude.

"And no, no bong hit. Although, I could use a cup of coffee if you guys are making some."

"You trim before, Jerry?" Nettie asked. "I hope so, because we ain't teaching and it's tough keeping up. We've got kind of a system worked out and—"

"No, I'm not trimming. I'm just a visitor. You guys go ahead and do what you need to do. I'll stay out of the way." He picked up his cigarettes and headed for the door. A solitary piss in the woods sounded pretty good right now. "Any of you guys heard from Vic?"

"Vic? No. He's probably still asleep."

"How about Ripper?"

"He's up and out early," Trinity said with a chuckle. "He works for a living."

Jerry sat patiently on the porch for more than an hour. He didn't have a watch and his phone was dead. He guessed it was late morning. He wondered how long Vic was going to sleep.

He'd peeked in the cabin once or twice and saw the three girls hard at work—each hunched over their tray with spring scissors pinched in their hands. Music played and drowned out whatever they talked about. Jerry wasn't interested anyway. His head still throbbed. After the coffee, he switched to beer.

The voices inside the house rose to a crescendo, underscored by some friendly yapping from Mongo and Lloyd. Jerry realized he'd fallen asleep in his chair again. Early afternoon sun beat down on his face.

Ghia was in the doorframe, looking cheerful and flush and every bit the healthy granola-eating hippie woman Jerry judged her to be. "Good morning, young man. You're looking chipper."

Jerry moved to get up but was buoyed down by his sleep.

"That's all right, I was just leaving," she said.

Vic appeared behind her and didn't say anything. He walked her to the edge of the porch and waved her off. She turned and blew him a kiss. He didn't blow one back. Instead he bent down to scratch Mongo's head. When she was gone, he turned to Jerry. "She stopped by after you passed out. Wanted to thank me for helping out with Dandy Dan."

Jerry said, "Nice." But Vic only shrugged. "So he turned the spigot back on?"

"Dan? Yeah. For now." Vic took a chair from the picnic table on the porch and sat across from Jerry. The kid looked terrible. Just like someone should look after passing out in a chair and sleeping till morning with their chin on their chest. "How you feeling?"

"All right, I guess. Still a bit hungover. What the fuck is in that weed?"

"You wanted the best, you got it." Vic leaned back and reached into his pocket for his Camels and shook one out. He offered it to Jerry, but Jerry shook his head. Vic put the cigarette in his mouth and dug for a light while Jerry watched him. He lit the smoke and took a few long, slow drags before saying, "You remember what we talked about that night?"

"About the weed?"

Vic shook his head.

"The water?"

"No."

"The guy in San Francisco?" He was guessing now.

"No. Your mother. You remember us talking about her?"

Jerry scoured his brain. The cannabis had erased everything. "No. What about her?"

"Never mind, we'll talk later." Vic got up and stretched and his ankles and wrists crackled and popped. He looked down at his guest and regarded him. Jerry reminded Vic of himself at that age. Looking tough, acting tough, but still a naïve young man inside. Vic spent many years wearing the mask of toughness—until fate stepped in and forced the reality of toughness upon him. He wished he could go back to being that young man, that foolish kid, and make some different decisions. "I'm going to make some lunch for the girls. I'll fix you a plate. It'll make you feel better."

Vic's entry into the house signaled a break for the trimmers and Jerry listened to the increased commotion as they got up and moved about the tiny house. Trinity exited and dug sodas out of the cooler for the others.

"You want another beer?" she said.

Jerry tipped his can. "Naw, I'm good."

With three cans cradled in her arms, she turned to him. "How're you doing? You holding up?"

"Yeah, just taking it all in. Loving being out of the city, you know? Fucking beautiful place Vic's got up here, huh?"

"Oh, this isn't Vic's place. It's Big Man's. Vic's only the caretaker."

"Caretaker? Who's Big Man?"

Trinity looked at him. If he didn't know Big Man, she'd said too much. She smiled, but it was more of a wince. "You sure you don't need anything?"

Jerry smiled and shook his head and Trinity went back inside.

* * *

"Who the fuck is Barbara Bertram?" Cardiff was turning over the scrap of paper in his hand as though it would reveal more on its backside. The late morning sun was heating up the car. He could smell his own freshly soaped skin, but overpowering that familiar scent was the unshowered funk of Aaron, who sat in the car next to him.

Aaron wasn't paying attention to Cardiff. He was staring back at the doorway to Treaclie's apartment building. Treaclie had acted tough, but when Cardiff and Aaron showed up in the morning, he had everything ready, a complete list of all the contacts in Juan's phone and as much personal information on them as possible prepared in the order in which they'd been contacted. Cardiff patted Treaclie on the head, then grabbed his hair and yanked it upward in a mock scalping. Cardiff thought it was hilarious, Aaron barely cracked a smile. Treaclie didn't think it was a joke and came very close to soiling his pants.

Aaron said, "You want me to drive you up there?"

Cardiff squinted at the address below the name.

"Citrus Heights? Where the fuck is that? Sounds like some place in Florida my grandmother would go to die."

They'd switched seats when they came out of Treaclie's, but they remained parked in front of his building. Aaron pulled a pack of Marlboro Reds from his jacket pocket and cupped them in his hand.

"What are you doing?" Cardiff said.

"Nothing. I'm just holding them. I wasn't gonna, I was going to stand outside and—"

"We don't have time. Let's go, let's go. This fucking place is two hours away. You and your goddamn cigarettes."

Chapter Six

Roland Mackie didn't hate his job, he hated the procedure. Not the antiquated methods policemen have used for decades, but the conformity of thought, the narrow process through which most officers' thinking must be channeled. If it was *this* kind of crime, it must be *that* kind of perpetrator, thus only such-and-such department may handle the case. He knew bureaucracy demanded as much, but he couldn't help but believe these ideas boxed in their thinking. Where it was a criminal's job to think as far outside the box as possible, law enforcement had trained themselves to sit squarely and comfortably inside said box.

Mackie had been on the scene for about twenty minutes. That was all he needed. He saw the body, peeked around the apartment. He saw it was a violent execution via suffocation, but he also saw the trappings of the victim, the small but quirky life choices the victim had made—what kind of movies sat on his shelves, the pictures on the walls, even the food in the fridge. Somehow, the minutia didn't add up to what the homicide team was leaning toward. They wanted to paint the victim as another casualty in the drug wars. Mackie wasn't buying it. Neither was his gut.

Now it was a question of information, of investigation. He didn't need CSI to figure out what'd happened. He needed raw data. He ran the kid's name through the system, but none of the usual bells sounded, so Mackie took a closer look at the arrest record of Juan Jiménez and a name jumped out at him. Jiménez had been arrested with a man named Gerald "Jerry" Bertram twice. This was more than a coincidence, it was fate. Mackie had his radar tuned for Bertram's name for years. He knew what Bertram was into, and knew—mostly likely—who it was with. It wasn't that he had a hard-on for the kid, but Mackie figured, if the kid popped up, that'd lead him to the mother. Barbara Bertram. And if she was in the mix, chances were, Victor Thomas wouldn't be too far behind. And a chance for Mackie to set his sights on Vic was too good to pass up.

Mackie stepped out of the small apartment into the hallway and pulled his cell. He made sure he was far from the door when he dialed.

"Why am I calling? Because I need a hand here. A little info, that's all I'm asking."

Tory Nagle laughed into the phone. He regretted it as soon as he began. Even though Mackie was an old friend, it still sounded condescending. It was exactly what was expected from federal officers when they dealt with local PD. He hated being that stereotype.

"You think this is funny?" Mackie said. "I'll tell you what's funny. Fucking homicide pulls me in here because they think it's a MS-13 thing. They think everything is a MS-13 thing, ever since that double last year. This kid's not even Salvadoran, he's Colombian. And as far as I know, he ain't the kind of Colombian they think he is. He's just a kid fucking with the wrong people."

"And you don't think those people are MS-13."

"No, I don't. It just doesn't fit."

"What does fit?"

Mackie peeked over his shoulder to make sure none of his colleagues were listening, then plugged a finger into one ear and said, "Bikers."

"Bikers?"

"Yeah, you know, outlaws, one percenters. Guys like the Dead BBs."

Nagle breathed loudly into the phone before speaking. "Isn't that still under the purview of SFPD's gang task force?"

"C'mon, we both know the feds have had ears up on the big bike gangs for years. All we do is arrest 'em when they crash into civilians. There's no investigative work being done. The task force is for street gangs. Norteños Sureños stuff."

"Mexican stuff."

"Yeah, that's what I'm saying."

"Why the fuck they got a Mick on the team?"

"Fuck you, Nagle. I'm asking for help here."

"So you don't think a Colombian kid, killed in this manner—suffocated with a bag over his head—has anything to do with drugs and gangs? Sounds like MS-13's M.O."

"No. I think it has everything to do with drugs and gangs, just not the kind of drugs or the same gangs the task force deals with."

"All right, tell you what. Let's do lunch tomorrow. You're buying."

"Tomorrow? This is kind of pressing. I'm standing here at the crime scene now. Can we do it today?"

"Jesus, Roland, I don't know. It's already eleven-thirty. I kind of had plans for lunch."

"Well, cancel 'em. I can be there in an hour."

"All right, all right. Tell you what, I'll meet you downstairs here at one."

"Ha! Perfect. Now you can see what it's like to eat on a real cop's budget." Mackie laughed and started to say goodbye, but realized Nagle was already off the line. He slipped his cell back into his hip pocket and ducked under the yellow crime scene tape, back into the apartment.

Vic sat on a fertilizer sack outside one of the white hooped tents. The afternoon sun beat down on his face. It was one of the only spots near his cabin he received any cell phone signal, a thin strip of service they'd mapped out over the last few years.

The fertilizer sack was moulded and concave from so many hours of use.

"Barbara, it's me again. Call me back."

He stared at his phone a moment, then hit redial and left another message. He watched Jerry wind through the assorted trucks and ATVs on his way up from the house.

"How ya doin'?" Vic called out.

Jerry waited till he was a bit closer before he spoke. "All right, I guess. A little bored. I was hanging with the women, but they're pretty focused on what they're doing."

"Good. That's what I'm paying 'em for."

Jerry stood examining the marijuana in the hooper. The plants in the low makeshift building were so full they pushed out the ends of the structure like a Thanksgiving cornucopia. "Damn, this shit looks good. How long till it's ready?"

Vic tucked the cell back into his pants pocket. "Jerry, what are you doing here?"

Jerry looked from the plants to Vic, not sure if he'd heard the question correctly.

"I'm visiting."

"You're running."

"Look, I don't know what Juan told you."

"Juan didn't tell me nothing. I barely even know that little fucker. It was your mother who called me, remember? Not Juan. When's the last time you spoke to Juan?"

"Day I came up—before I left."

"You called him since?"

Jerry shook his head.

"Your mom mentioned something about a girl."

"Yeah. Piper. Fuckin' firecracker."

"This is all about a girl?"

"Is all *what* about a girl?"

"You show up here all beat up. Now your mother—who I've known for twenty fucking years—ain't picking up her phone. Your friend Juan can't be reached. It's time to tell me what the fuck is going on."

"This is like the third time you've brought up my mom. Maybe you should tell me what the fuck is going on."

Vic stood up and stepped toward Jerry. He was at least two inches shorter than the younger man, but the look in his eye evened them out. "You maybe wanna watch your tone with me. Remember, kid, you're a guest in my home."

"Yeah, Trinity told me, this isn't even your place. You're like the caretaker here."

Vic used three fingers and jabbed Jerry underneath the sternum. Hot breath blasted out of Jerry's mouth before he dropped to his knees. Vic didn't step back, he towered over Jerry now. "You give respect where respect's due. When you're ready to talk about this, we'll talk."

Jerry gasped for breath. "You fuckin' told me—"

Vic used the same three fingers to jab Jerry in the throat, ending his sentence. "You're not ready to talk," he said, before walking back to the cabin, leaving Jerry on his knees in the dirt with his hands wrapped around his own neck.

Vic walked into the kitchen, bending his head to avoid the drying plants hanging from the ceiling. The three girls sat bent over their trays. "Trinity, you know what talking out of school means?"

Trinity looked scared. Something in Vic's tone. She shook her head.

"I didn't think so. You're done for today. Stick your shit in a bag and I'll weigh it and pay you tomorrow."

No one spoke. No one moved.

"Go on. Get outta here."

Nettie finally spoke. "What happened to your friend?"

"Jerry? He'll be down in a few minutes. He's getting some air. Why don't you two set him up with a spot and teach him how to trim. We're going to put him to work."

Trinity fought back tears. She grabbed her bag and bolted

straight through the door. She'd driven Nettie and Carla there today, but she didn't care, they could find their own way home. She knew she'd been wrong to mention Big Man to Jerry, but she was still pissed, embarrassed, humiliated. On the short path to the truck, she saw Jerry walking down from the hooper. She tried to keep her head down and step around him.

"What's up?" he said. "Where're you off to in such a rush?"

Trinity sucked in a breath, knew she shouldn't say anything, but let it all out in a burst of emotion. "Fuckin' Vic fired me. Fuckin' asshole."

"Fired you? For what?"

"For telling you about Big Man. Goddamn it, I got such a big mouth. I'm so fucking stupid." She clenched her fists and squeezed them so hard they shook.

"Hey, hey, now. Calm down. Don't talk like that. You want me to speak to him?"

"No. What's the point? He's doing it to punish me. Once his mind is set on something, that's it. You don't know him. He can be a cold motherfucker."

"No, no, no, I'll talk to him. Stay here a minute."

Trinity grabbed him by the shirt. "*No.* It's not that big of a deal. I don't need the money that bad. Don't piss him off any more than he already is. He's scary. Even Big Man is scared of him. Please, don't drag me in any farther. Fuck it, I'll come back and kiss his ass later. Tell the girls to call me if they need a ride out of here." She spun on her heel and walked to her truck, got in, slammed the door, and spat gravel behind her, leaving only a cloud of dust.

Citrus Heights was a small suburb outside of Sacramento, indistinguishable from the others that bordered it. Carmichael, Roseville, Orangevale, they all ran into each other and the only thing that changed was the color of the street signs. No downtowns, no civic centers, nothing but a homogenous blanket of suburban banality. Even with the help of GPS, Aaron and Cardiff had trouble finding the house. It, like the neighborhood, was indistinguishable from the others surrounding it. A small blue stucco one-story with a lawn turned brown. A Honda Civic stood in the driveway.

"Fucking depressing," Cardiff said.

Aaron didn't say anything. He thought it looked nice. Idyllic. It beat the hell out of the place he grew up.

"Don't just sit there," Cardiff said. "Let's get this done."

"What is it we're supposed to do here?"

"You know what we need to do. Let's find out what she knows. Maybe it's nothing and we can all sit down and have cookies and milk. Jesus, Aaron, what the fuck's gotten into you? You forget how to do your job?"

Aaron reached over and grabbed Cardiff's forearm and squeezed it. Cardiff winced. It got his attention. Aaron glared at Cardiff. "No. I ain't forgot nothing. And I hope *you* ain't forgetting why I got this job."

Cardiff gnashed his tiny teeth together. He wanted to smack Aaron, but he wouldn't do it. They both knew that. Aaron was bigger, stronger, and a better fighter. Everything but meaner. But that counted for something, Cardiff thought. That counted for a lot.

But Aaron had the entire weight of the Dead BBs motorcycle club behind him. That counted for something. Something else, but something.

"All right, tough guy," Cardiff said. "You made your point. Let's go inside and you can make your point in there."

Aaron released him and Cardiff got out on the passenger's side and, without waiting for Aaron, walked straight to the front door.

Cardiff knocked. He stood off to the left of the peephole and waved Aaron behind him so, if she looked out, she'd only see his smiling face. He was clean cut; he could pass for a bible salesman. He knocked again and pressed his ear to the door. He turned and smiled at Aaron, barely able to contain his excitement.

A melodic voice called out from behind the door. "Who is it?"

Cardiff said her name, then something else, not an actual word, a few syllables mixed up but with a tone that sounded official.

A woman opened the door. "I'm sorry, what did you—"

Cardiff pushed the door with the heel of his hand and shoved the woman back with the other.

Aaron checked over his shoulder before following Cardiff in.

"Get the hell out!" She was shouting, brave and bold, but she was clearly terrified. With no chance to arm herself or even grab a phone, she was helpless.

"Sit down and shut up," Cardiff said.

"I don't know who you are or what—"

Aaron stepped around Cardiff and wrapped his large hands around Barbara's biceps and lifted her off the floor. She swung her legs and tried kicking him in the groin, but it had no effect. With her feet thrashing in the air, Aaron walked her backward into her house and dropped her on the couch. He bent down and placed a huge palm across her mouth and said, "Shut up and listen." Then he pulled the palm away before she bit him.

From the couch, Barbara sneered at both of them, her mind working fast. This was no robbery, this was no home invasion. This was about Jerry. Whenever trouble found its way to her front door, it seemed to be Jerry. This time she spoke slow and even. "What do you want?"

Cardiff nodded, a smirk on his face. "You already know why we're here, don't you?"

Barbara set her teeth together and tightened her lips. She placed her hands on her knees like a petulant child.

Aaron walked into the kitchen and opened the fridge. He pushed past the milk and juice, hoping for a beer, but settling for a soda. Store brand diet cola. Yum. He straightened up and walked back into the living room and sat on coffee table so his knees were almost touching Barbara's.

Cardiff was saying, "Look here, Babs, we don't want to make it weird. We don't want to fuck up you or your house. You know this kid of yours is always in trouble. Just tell us where he is. We're going to find out anyway. If we can get to him before the cops do, he's definitely got a chance to make things right." Cardiff paused and looked at Aaron. "Right?"

"Definitely," Aaron said.

"But if someone gets to him before us? He's going to have problems that won't go away." Cardiff paused and waited for an answer. Nothing. "You know what I mean by a problem that won't go away?"

Barbara stared straight ahead.

Cardiff leaned in and whispered, "That means he's going to die."

Aaron held the soda can out in front of her face. Without moving her head, she glanced down at it. Aaron popped the top. Barbara flinched.

"Barbara," Cardiff said, "where's your cell phone?"

She held fast, still refusing to speak.

"Aaron, find the phone."

Aaron took a long pull off the soda, belched, and got up to search the house. He walked to the bedroom and returned in seconds, a cell in his hand with its charger dangling like an umbilical cord.

Cardiff held his hand out without taking his eyes off Barbara. "Thank you, sir. Okay, now." He powered on the phone. "Let's see who you've been chatting with." He fingered through to the call logs in the cell and scrolled through. "Who's Cindy? She must be a good pal. Nine-one-six, huh? I guess she's local. Is she one of Jerry's whores? Or one of your bingo bitches? Shall we pay her a visit too?"

Aaron sat back down on the coffee table and finished the soda, crushed the can and set it down on the floor.

Cardiff continued, "Two missed calls from Vic. Incoming, Jerry. Outgoing, Jerry. Incoming, Jerry. *Twice*. Outgoing, Jerry.

Here we go. Outgoing, Vic. Then outgoing Jerry. Hmmn. Middle of the night? Who's Vic? Is that a Vic or a Victoria? Somebody who's a confidant, no doubt." Cardiff's voice went up a notch, got a little louder, got a little meaner. "You call 'em up to cry on their shoulder? Weep about your miserable thief of a son. You tell 'em he's gone and done it again? You tell Vic you don't need bail money this time, just a place for the miserable piece of shit to hide?"

Silence. Cardiff was expecting Barbara to cry. She didn't. The central air whirred and the refrigerator motor powered up. No one spoke.

Cardiff bent over so his face was close to Barbara's. He was sure she felt his hot breath, could smell its foul odor. "Barbara. Who the fuck is Vic?"

Chapter Seven

Vic was sipping his third cup of coffee, a pair of dollar-store readers resting on his nose and a dog-eared paperback in his lap. He'd read the same paragraph at least three times and it still made no sense. The girls were quietly working. After they showed Jerry the basics, they all settled back into the mundane chore of trimming the buds. Jerry was a quick learner, but there really wasn't much to it. Take off the excess leaves, don't trim too close, drop the finished product in a bucket. Repeat. That was the difficult part, the endless repeating. Still, it brought a smile to his face when Nettie called Jerry Edward Trimmerhands.

His phone buzzed. One ring and they hung up. He didn't even need to look at it. He knew who it was. Vic got up and walked out of the house and up to the hooper where he'd have a strong enough signal to talk. He plopped down on the sack of fertilizer and looked at his phone. Missed call: B. He swiped the number to return the call and waited for an answer.

Big Man's voice came on the line. "Hey."

"Howdy."

"We need to talk."

"Everything okay?"

"Do we ever talk when things are okay?"

"All right. You coming by?"

"Um...no. How 'bout we meet by the bridge. You know the place I mean?"

"Sure. When."

"An hour."

Vic said, "All right," and hung up. If Big Man was ready to meet in an hour, that meant he was already in Humboldt County. Usually when he came up north, Big Man let Vic know ahead of time. Usually it was menial business. Picking up money, checking on his property, or to hang out and do blow and drink whiskey for three days straight. But from the tone of his voice, Vic knew it was none of the above.

It would take him a half hour just to get down the hill, then another ten minutes to the bridge. Vic stood, squinted at the midday sun, then reached into the makeshift greenhouse and touched the soil in one of the large pots. It stuck to his index finger. Moist enough. He stretched and walked back to the house.

He watched Big Man squeeze out the cab of his Ford F-250. He made it look like a toy truck. To say Big Man's name fit would be an understatement, and an underassessment. Big Man was huge. Sheer bulk. He looked every part the bearded biker he was. No colors, no Harley, but the second you saw him, you felt like an entire chapter of the Cripplers were riding right at you.

The Cripplers were mostly local older guys. They weren't the Dead BBs, but they were respected. They enjoyed a symbiotic relationship with the bigger club without the law enforcement scrutiny that went with being a bigger club.

He lumbered toward Vic's truck. He walked with a limp. Probably because his knees were close to buckling from carrying around that load, Vic figured. He opened the door to Vic's Toyota Tundra and pulled himself in.

"Is this about Dandy Dan? Because that fucker was stealing water just as sure as I'm sitting here."

The man across the seat from him filled the cab. Barely any daylight filtered over his massive shoulders.

"Hello to you too, Vic." Big Man coughed and it sounded

layered like a bronchial accordion. He kept coughing until his face was crimson. He pulled a pack of Marlboro Reds and jammed one in his mouth. He held out the pack to Vic, but Vic shook his head.

"I got my own."

Big Man still coughed while he lit the cigarette. It wasn't until he'd sucked in a few lungfuls that the hacking slowed.

"Shit, you all right? That sounds terrible."

"Oh yeah, I'm fine. The only thing that stops it though is a coffin nail." He took another deep pull and stifled another cough. "Just give me a second."

Vic waited as the cab of his truck filled with smoke. Finally, he cracked his window and lit a Camel of his own. When Big Man regained his composure, Vic started in again. "Ghia asked if I'd go talk to him. I know for a fact—"

"Fuck Dandy Dan. He's a fucking punk. I don't doubt for a minute he's tryin' to siphon offa us. I'm here 'bout somethin' else."

Vic sat back and waited.

"You got a kid up here? Guy in his twenties. Fuckin' half-assed in the wind?"

"Yeah. His name is Jerry. He's the son of a good friend of mine. Why?"

"Seems everyone in the club knows right where he's at. This little fuck screwed over some friends of mine. Not that I give a shit how the guy makes a buck, but I got a relationship with these people and that shit is a two-way street. Know what I'm sayin'?"

"What people?"

"Dead BBs."

"Fuck."

"That's right. Fuck. Fuck me, fuck you, and fuck him."

Vic smoked his Camel. He waited for Big Man to say more. Big Man didn't do anything but blow hot air out of his nostrils. He was out of breath just sitting still.

"What'd he do?"

"Seems he hooked up with a girl named Piper. He mention her?"

"Yeah, he said something about her."

"Oh please God, tell me she's not up here with him."

"No, I ain't seen her. He just mentioned her."

"Good. She's the daughter of their club's president. Not the local guy, the main guy. This fuckin' Jerry is banging her. Dangerous enough spot to put yourself in, but then—get this—he convinces her to fucking burn a club bank."

Vic said, "Club bank? What'd you mean? Like the BBs' clubhouse?"

"No, the weed clubs, the dispensaries. They back a chain of medicinal shops in Oakland and SF and they collect their dough from all of 'em and keep it at one store in Oakland. They can't stick that shit in the bank, you know. It's a lot of fuckin' money."

"The BBs have their own chain of pot clubs?"

"Sort of. They back a Russian dude named Vlad the Inhaler. He's the face, they're the back office."

Vic smiled.

"You think this shit is funny?"

"No," Vic said. "Vlad the Inhaler, that's fuckin' funny."

Big Man didn't smile back. "It ain't the name on the marquee, it's just what we always called him."

Vic shook his head, repeating the name for his own amusement.

"Glad you find some levity in our situation here." Big Man cleared his throat. "Vic, you're my friend, my brother, and I respect your judgement, but I don't care if this kid is the son of the pope, you gotta give him up."

"I can't. She's a friend. I made a promise."

Big Man sighed. He knew better than to argue with Vic.

"Then I can't have him on the hill."

"Look, I said I'd—"

Big Man cut him off. "I made promises too. I can't have this."

"They're not Cripplers. What's it to you?"

Big Man drew in a patient breath. "You know better than that. We got an affiliation. We got a tight relationship with these guys, a working relationship. No way I can cover on this shit. No way. These guys ain't gonna let this go. It's two hundred grand he took. Maybe—*maybe*—they forgive the girl, but I doubt it. But two hundred large? Forget it. Your friend's boy is done."

"All right."

"All right, what?"

"All right, I'll get him outta here. Just give me a day or two to figure out where to take him."

"You ain't got a day or two. They already know he's up here, man. They're coming for him. You know these fuckers, they don't play."

"It'll be fine. I'll have him out by tomorrow."

The phone signal was still pretty strong down by the 101, so after Big Man pulled away, Vic dialed Barbara's number. No answer. He didn't leave a message this time. She'd never gone this long without returning a call. Something was wrong; he felt it in his gut. He decided to go back up the hill and clear out the girls. He'd weigh out their work, pay them, and tell them to hit the road.

On the way back he pondered the odds. The Dead BBs were a small but far-reaching outfit. Any beefs that came out of this weren't going to go away. Big Man pretty much said not to expect any help from him or his crew. He thought about Jerry, what he knew about the kid—which wasn't much—and how deep he was willing to go. Jerry was a nice enough guy, but he wasn't blood, not really. That made him remember Barbara. What she'd done for him. She was family. Maybe not blood, but family just the same.

No, he had to do what he could for the kid. He promised

Barbara. He kept his word, always. It's who he was. Who he is.

As he pulled off the gravel road onto the rutted tracks forming his driveway, he saw an unfamiliar parked car, a red Ford Focus pulled to the right of the fleet. It was wedged in between Jerry's rental and the dead trunk of a mammoth oak. He stopped and killed his engine. The Ford looked like a rental too. Vic pulled his Glock 19 from the Tundra's glove box and slipped out of the cab. The air was still and quiet except for the chittering of the birds. He stepped toward the house, aware of each crunch the gravel made under his feet.

Vic paused to count the voices inside. No signs of terror, no signs of violence—in fact, it was the opposite. Sounds of laughter jostled out of the shack. Didn't even sound like the girls were working.

Vic stepped onto the porch and, with the pistol in front of him, slowly opened the door.

"Vic!" Nettie said. "There you are. We're taking a break. C'mon in. You want a hit?" Nettie held out a thick joint and raised her eyebrows. "Whoa, what's with the gun?"

She must have been high, because she'd forgotten he didn't smoke that shit. He let the gun drop down to his side and entered the room. The air was thick and the girls stood in a semi-circle—as best they could with the drying plants hanging by their heads. There was a jovial mood in the room, they were drinking beer and passing two joints back and forth.

Vic was about to ask where Jerry was and whose car was parked in front when Jerry stepped into the room from the kitchen alcove with an unopened beer in his hand. Beside him was a young pretty redhead. Vic knew instantly who she was.

"Vic, I want you to meet Piper. Remember? I was telling you about her."

Chapter Eight

Vic nodded, smiled. "How'd you find us up here?"

"Oh, easy. I been coming up here with my parents since I was a little kid. I know this hill better than most people on it."

"That so?" Vic felt the smile on his face freeze. It must have looked more like a sneer now. The room cooled a little. The trimmers quietened down. "Nettie, Carla, bag up your shit. We're closing early today. I'll pay you out and give you each a fifty-buck bonus for the trouble. Sound fair?"

The girls both smiled and nodded, but it was out of politeness. They knew something was up. They gathered their stuff, poured what they'd trimmed into turkey bags, and avoided eye contact with Piper or Jerry.

"I want to talk to you two." Vic pointed to the porch. "Lemme finish up here and we'll have a beer and figure this out."

"Figure what out?" Piper said.

This time, Vic knew his smile had deteriorated into a sneer. "Let me finish up with Carla and Nettie, then we'll talk."

Jerry plucked one of the burning joints from an ashtray and pinched it between his lips. "C'mon, babe. Let's have a smoke in the sun."

Vic's formula for trimmers was simple. Fifty cents a gram. It came out to about two-twenty-five a pound. Seemed to be the going rate and nobody complained. Not to him anyway. He tossed the girls' turkey bags on the big chrome kitchen scale and subtracted the weight of the bag. He doled out the cash from a

50

roll he kept in a cookie jar on the middle shelf behind the break-fast cereals.

When Vic was done counting, Nettie asked, "You gonna want us back tomorrow, Vic?"

Carla elbowed her in the ribs.

"That's all right, Carla," Vic said. "No big deal. Shit just got weird with the extra guests. Just call me first. I'll know early. If I don't call you back in a few minutes, we're off. You guys did well today. It ain't you guys, it's just..." He nodded his chin toward the porch where Jerry and Piper sat smoking. "You know. Shit came up. Nice work. Like always, thanks."

They both stood for a moment. They glanced at each other and then at Vic.

Vic said, "Did I forget something?"

"Trinity's gone. You fired her, remember? She was our ride."

"I didn't fire her. I gave her the day off." Vic scratched his scalp. "Ripper back yet?"

The girls shrugged their shoulders.

"I'll call Ghia. Maybe she can give you guys a ride down the hill." He pulled his cell from his pocket and started to dial, but stopped. He knew better, he couldn't get a signal inside the cabin and Ghia had no signal at her place either. She only called him when she was down in Garberville getting supplies. "I'll drive you two over to her place. Let's go."

Nettie said, "Jesus, Vic, rush much?"

Vic turned and looked at her. She didn't say another word. He ushered them out to the truck and, on his way past Jerry and Piper he pointed a stern finger. "You guys stay right where you are. I'm going to be back in ten minutes. Don't move."

Piper shrugged. "Where we gonna go?"

Ollie Jeffers was a team player. When he was told to do something, he did it. He was a fuckup most of his life, so when he finally found something he was good at, he wanted to be the best. For Ollie, that was being a biker. And not just an outlaw biker. And not just a man who loved his bike, wrenched it to life, and rode it the whole way to runs—not lugging it along on a trailer like a lot of pussies and poseurs—but someone who showed up for church every week, prospected without a hiccup, and patched in loud and proud. He excelled at all the high points of being a Dead BB. Not just an outlaw, but a fucking criminal. That's what Ollie really loved. After all, isn't that what this life was about? It was with no small sense of irony Ollie had spent his whole existence swimming against the stream only to discover things finally clicked when he started following orders. Things made sense when he became a Dead BB. He knew exactly what was expected of him.

He liked where his life was at now. He knew it wouldn't last. It was the nature of the lifestyle. He knew he'd most likely end up dead or in prison. But, he decided, if it was prison, he was going to walk in there with a reputation that'd carry him though till the day they pulled a blanket over him. And if it was the graveyard, he knew his brothers would throw him one hell of a wake.

He mused over these things while he sat in the front seat of his white panel van. Technically, not his van. It was registered to the recently deceased mother of a girlfriend of one of his brothers in the Oakland Chapter of the Dead BBs. It was a work van. Only to be used for clandestine operations.

He reached over to the passenger seat and picked up a cold slice of pizza from an open box. Hawaiian with jalapeno. His favorite. Still hot when it was ice cold.

A rustling rose from the back of the van. It was empty, no seats, no equipment. Only a dirty mattress and a woman in her fifties bound and gagged. She was awake again. Or maybe she never really fell asleep. It was Ollie's job to make sure she stayed alive. Make sure she didn't choke on the blood possibly gathering in her mouth. She'd taken a beating. Quite a beating. It wasn't Ollie who beat her. He would have though, had he been asked. Often, when he was brought in after the fact on jobs like this, he felt a little jealous, a little left out. He could've handled the whole job, if they'd let him.

She grunted, tried to cry out behind her gag.

"You're fine," Ollie said.

She was trying to say something. No way he'd be able to understand her unless he removed the gag. That wasn't going to happen. He got out of his seat and knelt down beside the hostage. He didn't hit her, he didn't touch her. "You're gonna be fine. It's my job to make sure you're okay. Just shut up and wait. You ain't gettin' up right now. You ain't leaving this van."

She said something else into the gag. Her eyes bulged with the earnestness. She had a lot of verve for a woman her age.

"If you gotta piss, just piss your pants. Go ahead, I've smelled worse. If you gotta shit, you're outta luck. Pinch that shit up. Otherwise, just try to sleep or somethin'. This'll be over soon. I'm waitin' on a call to see where I'm supposed to take you. We'll get you fixed up there, get you a beer or whatever, let you use the bathroom."

Barbara Bertram fell backward on to the mattress and stared at the roof of the van. It was hopeless, this guy was an idiot. *This'll all be over soon* didn't sound like a bathroom and a beer, it sounded like a bullet.

When Vic returned from dropping Nettie and Carla, the first thing he saw was the empty space beside Jerry's rental. The red Ford was gone. He stared at the patch of gravel where it'd sat.

"Shit."

He climbed out of the car and the dogs waggled up to him, happy and excited, tongues flapping. No sign of Piper or Jerry. No point in calling out their names. He went straight to his room and bent down in the closet. He spun the dial on the old safe bolted to the floor. He pulled his Glock 19, along with three boxes of ammunition, his laser-sighted .38, two boxes of

Speer Gold Dot hollow-points, and a million-volt stun gun he'd never used—just in case he was faced with hand-to-hand combat. A rifle seemed too cumbersome, but after a heartbeat of reflection, he grabbed some .30-06 ammo and went to where he'd stood the rifle on the porch. He set the firearms on the kitchen table and cracked the fridge. Energy drinks, protein bars, and two beers. The beers were for immediate consumption. He turned to the makeshift bar beside the pots and pans at the far right of the sink and he picked up the one-point-seven-five-liter-sized bottle of Jim Beam. He hooked a finger through the handle, lifted the jug straight to his mouth, and took a solid pull before filling up two small stainless-steel flasks. When he was finished, he cracked one of the beers and took a drink. He looked around the kitchen for what else he needed. He remembered his sheathed Bowie knife, found it hanging off the back of a chair, and fixed it to his belt. There was most of a carton of cigarettes sitting between the flour and sugar on the food shelf and he tucked it under his left arm.

The light was just beginning to fail outside. Long shadows from the redwoods stretched across the cabin, cooling the air and quietening the birds. Vic sat down the beer can and listened. Nothing. He'd grown used to the sounds of silence during his stay on the hill. He knew what nothing sounded like, intimately. It was quiet, but this time, somehow, different. It took a moment to process what it was. The unheard sound was his instinct, his intuition. There was something coming. Something terrible.

He overflowed the dogs' bowls with food and topped off their water. He stared at them a moment, wondering if he should take them with him. They'd kill any advantage of surprise he may have, but they'd probably guard the shack with their lives. Definitely with their lives. He decided to drop them at Ghia's and let them lounge with her pups. They'd stay there at least until dark.

He gathered up his portable arsenal and lugged it to the

truck. Except for the Glock already in a clip-on holster on his belt, he left the rest on the seat of the Tundra. Then he went back for the food and drink. As an afterthought, he grabbed a gallon jug of water and a six-pack of beer. He locked the door, and told the Lloyd and Mongo to get in the back of the pickup. He listened hard one more time, heard that same ominous nothing, and started the truck.

Cardiff was in the passenger seat shouting into his cell. "Yeah, we're almost there...We've already passed Garberville. What exit is it?...No, I can't, the fucking GPS keeps cutting out up here... What did Ollie find out?...Are you sure? Have someone else talk to her, I'm telling you, she knows more than what she told us."

Aaron was behind the wheel asking what exit. Cardiff was waving him off and plugging his left ear with his finger. "Aaron, roll up the goddamn window, I can't hear a thing."

Aaron powered up the windows and took the speed down to sixty-five. They had enough felonies in the car to put them both behind bars for a long time. Guns for the hunt and drugs to keep them going.

Cardiff covered the phone with his hand and said, "We're coming up on it. Get over."

When they hit the frontage road, Aaron slowed to a crawl. "Now what?"

Still holding the cell, Cardiff said to Aaron, "I don't fucking know. We should have brought an Indian guide." Then into the cell, "What? No, I was talking to Aaron...Fuck, yeah we're going to need a hand...Who?...You're kidding...No, that's perfect. How do we find him?" Cardiff plugged his ear again so he could hear the directions. Then, after a moment, he turned to Aaron and said, "Hit the brakes. We got ourselves some help."

* * *

On Larkin Street, across from the monolith that houses San Francisco's FBI offices, there were three Vietnamese sandwich shops. Each specialized in *bánh mì,* delicious hoagies stuffed with sweet shredded carrots, cilantro, jalapeno peppers, and a variety of meats. When Mackie joked with Nagle about lunch on a cop's budget, he was already thinking of his beloved barbequed pork. They were quick, affordable, and popular with the cops, lawyers, and various civil servants who worked in and around the federal building.

The small shop they chose was busy with the lunch rush, bright noise filled the place and Nagle and Mackie had to strain to hear and be heard. After ordering and waiting for their food, Mackie started in with his theory on Juan Jiménez. The theory was based on the tie-in of Jerry Bertram's name and criminal history. Mackie knew Jerry sometimes acted as a wholesale supplier to the pot clubs, but as a novice in the weed game and an incorrigible thief, he'd probably made some enemies too. It stands to reason, he said, there's a connection between Jerry and the biker gangs because of recent shift in the pot clubs and their ownership. It was common knowledge a third of the city's marijuana dispensaries were fronts for the Dead BBs, but it was the feds who were supposedly putting together a racketeering case against the motorcycle club.

"C'mon, Roland, even if that were true, you know I can't talk about an ongoing investigation."

"*If?* Even *if* it were true? Everyone knows you guys are looking at the BBs for a big RICO case, and I don't think you're going too far off the reservation if you do a little consulting with a friend." Mackie took a break to bite into the *bánh mì.*

"You want to know what I think?" Nagle said.

"Yeah," Mackie said with a mouth full of meat. "That's what I'm fucking here for."

"I think you're putting too much in the 'where there's smoke there's fire' theory. I think maybe your vision is blurred by your past experiences with this Jerry fella. I think you got a conflict of interest going here."

"Christ," Mackie said. "You sound like my ex-wife."

"You talk to her about cases? No wonder she's an ex."

They both laughed at that one.

A man with close-cropped grey hair and a dark mustache approached their table. Mackie stopped laughing.

"Nagle, how you doing?"

"Fine, Bill, fine. How're you?"

The man didn't answer, instead he held out his hand to Mackie. "I'm Special Agent Forrester. And you are?"

"Roland Mackie."

Mackie extended his hand and Forrester gave it a firm shake. After he let go, Forrester stood at the table, waiting. Mackie raised his eyebrows a touch.

"Who are you with, Roland?"

Nagle cut in, "I'm sorry. Roland's with SFPD's gang task force."

"Oh, SFPD. So this is a work lunch then?"

"No, Bill, this is a *lunch* lunch. I've known Roland for years—since college."

"Well then..." Forrester smiled. "I'll let you two get back to it." But he didn't move. He stood there another moment, surveying them both.

After a few beats of silence, Nagle said, "I'll see you upstairs, Bill." And he lifted the hoagie to his mouth to signal the end of the conversation. Bill Forrester turned and walked out of the shop empty-handed. He hadn't even placed an order.

"What the fuck was that?" Mackie said.

"An asshole, that's what."

"Please tell me he's not your superior officer."

"Technically yes, but he doesn't head my case files. He's just another Machiavellian opportunist climbing over the backs of his fellow agents. He's got some sort of fierce loyalty to the bureau, thinks they're going to make him a director one day."

"So, what's that got to do with me?"

"Two things—he thinks if he catches me sharing information, he can serve me up to the bosses and better himself."

"What's the other thing?"

With a mouth full of Vietnamese sandwich, Nagle said, "He's scared I'm going to stumble on to a big case without him and suck up some of his glory."

Chapter Nine

Piper had known Meth Master Mike since she was a kid. Her father—actually her stepfather—used to warn her to stay away from him. "He's a slippery fucker and you don't need to know no more than that." She saw him at some of the club functions, at least the ones she was allowed to go to. He was fast-talking and funny. She didn't know why they called him Meth Master Mike. She was just a kid, she didn't know what meth was. One thing stuck with her though—her stepfather's insistence she stay away. Nothing like a stern warning to burn memories into a child's head. To her, even then, Mike was mysterious, alluring with his forbidden charm.

She remembered Mike, his scrawny wife, his crazy dogs he used to take everywhere, and most importantly—for now— where he lived. His tiny compound was close to the 101, at the bottom of the hill—the mountain they all affectionately referred to as the hill. It was lodged behind a curious row of mobile trailers along a paved frontage road lined with potholes and sprouted with weeds. Piper and Jerry crawled along the unlined pavement at ten miles per hour. Each lot they passed more cluttered and chaotic than the last. Skeletons of cars, dead washers and dryers, waist-high weeds listing lazy in the breeze. Strange makeshift antennas sprouted up from the dwellings like rusted beanstalks. All of the places seemed deserted. Plenty of fallout, but no human survivors.

Dogs barked and strained on chains as Piper and Jerry rolled along the row. She was trying hard to remember which spot was Mike's. It'd been years since she'd been here, and even then she had to wait in the car while her stepfather conducted business inside. Alone. Her mother was long gone, so there was never anyone to wait with her while her father conducted his business.

Mike seemed like such a friendly man, she didn't understand why she wasn't allowed any closer. "You'll figure it out when you're older," her stepfather would say. He said that about so many things, and he was right. Being her father's daughter was an education. Her mother disappeared before Piper hit four. Mom was just a faint memory. The way old Dad told it, between the speed and the vodka, she was never really there anyway.

They reached a solitary mailbox painted red, white, and blue hammered to a rotted fence post. "This is it," she said.

"You sure?"

"Yeah, I'm sure." She'd spent hours as a child waiting by the mailbox, playing with Mike's Presa Canarios—two massive brindle dogs with wide jaws and squared heads—who terrified everyone who came near them, but seemed to love little Piper.

She stopped the car and climbed out, waiting to be greeted by the dogs. Some kind of dogs. Everyone up here owned dogs. Yet none came.

"What're you waiting for?" Jerry asked.

"I just figured he'd have some dogs. I don't wanna walk in without meeting them, in case they're new ones."

"When's the last time you were here?"

Piper thought about it. "Shit, maybe ten years."

"Then I'd say they'd have to be new ones." Jerry scanned the gravel drive, saw and heard nothing. "Hey, what's that in the tree?"

He pointed at a small camera that twisted its tiny white plastic orb to peer back at them. They heard the small hydraulic sound of its lens trying to focus and shift its point of view. Then they noticed another in a lower branch, and one on the tree opposite.

Five cameras in all were watching them. Five independent robotic eyes peering at them.

"Jesus, that's fucking creepy," Jerry said.

Piper squinted into them, then waved. She stepped out from behind the car and stood, waiting to be appraised. After a moment, when nothing happened, she took a few small steps toward the tree with the most eyes.

"What now?" Jerry said.

"I guess we go in."

"I'm not leaving the car out here."

"Why not?"

"You know why not. What we got in the trunk, I ain't leaving it alone on the road."

"What's gonna happen out here? There's no one around. C'mon, let's go in."

"Fuck that, we might get shot." Jerry spoke from the safety of the car. "Any fucker with this much security is paranoid and I don't feel like pissing him off."

"We're not going to piss him off. I've known him since I was a kid."

"You haven't seen this motherfucker in ten—"

A voice called out, crackling through an unseen intercom. "Who's that?"

"Hello," Piper said to the tree.

"Piper Tribban? That you?" The voice sounded decrepit, ancient, as though it were calling out from another time.

"Mike? It is. It's me."

There was silence.

Piper said, "Mike, can we come in? We're..." She thought about how to phrase it. "We were in the neighborhood."

Mike's voice crackled back. "Hang on, stay there. I'm coming out."

After a minute, a short frail-looking man with a ratty beard and long hair came trotting toward them. His shirt and pants were mismatched flannel and Jerry was pretty sure they were pajamas. He was carrying something in his right hand, and although it was hard to be certain, it appeared to be a large handgun.

"Fuck, what's he holding?"

"Don't worry," Piper said. "It's fine. Everybody's got one."

"We don't," Jerry said. As the man got closer, the object became clear. "Jesus, look at the size of that hand cannon."

Mike's voice crackled almost as much as it did through the intercom. "Piper! Goddamn. You're a sight for sore eyes. What the hell? Lookit you. All grown up and shit."

Jerry opened the door and climbed out of the passenger seat. Mike stopped, lifted the gun, and pointed it at Jerry's head. "Who's your friend?"

Jerry froze. He waited for the man to lower the gun, but it remained pointed at his head. The thing looked so heavy and Mike's hand quivered under the strain, but he kept the barrel trained on his head. Jerry felt his heart pounding against his ribs. "Piper?"

"No, no, Mike, it's cool. That's my boyfriend, Jerry."

"Jerry." He said it in a flat tone. Seeing if it sounded authentic if he said it aloud.

"Yeah," Piper said. "Jerry."

This time Mike said it to Jerry. "Jerry?"

"Yeah. Jerry. That's me."

"Like Jerry Garcia?"

"Yeah, something like that."

The inside of Mike's place was a tiny area cordoned off by sheets acting as walls. When Piper reached to pull at one of the sheets to find a bathroom, Mike held up his hand, with the gun still in it. "Whoa, don't go back there. Out of bounds. Ten-yard penalty."

Piper looked at the gun and Mike apologized and set it down. "It's a real fucking mess, this place. I'm sorry." He pointed to a cluster of old kitchen chairs covered with papers and unopened bills. "Have a seat, I'll get you what you need."

"I need a bathroom," Piper said.

A look of pain crossed Mike's face and his tone softened. "Shit, um...give me a few minutes." He disappeared behind the curtain on the left while Jerry and Piper sat on the chairs and waited. They didn't bother moving the debris off the seats, there was no place to set it. There was no table in the room, only the chairs. Five in all. There was a dirty framed window that looked painted shut, the glass panels clouded with filth. A tight moldy air almost clung to them, as though it'd been stuck circulating in there for years. A faint note of industrial chemicals cut through the mildew, like paint thinner or engine grease.

Mike pulled back the curtain and waved to Piper. "C'mon, c'mon, I'll show you. Let's go. Nature calls, but it don't wait. I know, I know." He ushered her past, but before he let the curtain fall he grabbed the enormous handgun, gave Jerry a dour look, motioned him back to the seat with the barrel of the gun. "You sit tight, Jerry Garcia."

"Ghia!" Vic called out her name, but was sure she wasn't home. Her two dogs, Stanley and Possum, leapt at Mongo and Lloyd in the bed of the Tundra. Their excitement always brought Ghia out if she was home. He called her name again, half-wondering if Piper and Jerry might be hiding in the nearby woods.

He let down the tailgate of the Toyota and his dogs hopped down, licking and sniffing their greetings with Ghia's dogs. He walked to the porch and filled both the water bowls to the brim, making sure they had enough in case it was a while before anyone returned. She was probably off watering her patches. She tended at least a dozen plots of varying size dotting their side of the hill. Some as small as ten plants, some as large as fifty. Ghia was a prodigious grower and had been up there for years. The secret, she always told him, was consistency. Find the routine that works and stick to it, she'd say.

Vic found an old lawn chair, positioned near the east side of the cabin to catch the morning sun, and sat down. He shook out a Camel and smoked while he watched the dogs play. Where the hell did those kids get to? Where would they know to go? Jerry knew no one on the hill. So it had to be the girl, Piper, leading the way. He stubbed out the cigarette on his boot and stood. The bigger question, at least in his mind, where the hell is Barbara?

They'd been sitting in the van so long. Ollie needed to piss. He set the burner phone on the dash and stared at it, willing it to ring. Like all things in his life involving his will, it failed. The woman in back feigned sleep. He knew she was faking because her breathing never got heavy. She was lying still, not moving, with her eyes squeezed shut. Maybe she was trying to will something of her own.

Barbara lay in the fetal position. Her arms had been wrapped round the front of her then taped and tied. Straight-jacket style. She was glad they weren't still pinched behind her. When the two goons—the assholes who'd pulled her out of her own house—snatched her, they bound her wrists behind her back. They pulled their car into her garage so they wouldn't be seen stuffing her into the trunk. It was blindingly painful. Two hours she bounced in back like a sack of dog food before they passed her off. She begged the third man—the one they handed her off to, the stinking hulk she was lying in a van with right now—to retie her. She had arthritis in her shoulders and was losing the circulation in her hands. He must have had a mother somewhere on the planet, because, once they were alone, he peeled away the duct tape and fastened her arms around her chest, roping them tight in sleeves then tape. Unfortunately, he also had the bright idea of taping her ankles together, so making a run for it was out of the question. Along with the tape securing the gag in her mouth, she was completely inert. No more ability to act or communicate than a lump of meat. She stayed in a fetal position with nothing to do but think.

One thought kept floating to the surface of her consciousness. How long would it take Vic to find her? And would he find her in time? She was certain Jerry made it up to Humboldt. There was no way to know if he was still safe. But Vic, he'd know what to do. There weren't a lot of breadcrumbs on the trail, but it'd be enough, she was sure of that.

She smelled his awful breath before she opened her eyes. She felt the sudden rip of tape being yanked from the edges of her mouth. He mumbled an apology while he plucked out the gag.

"You gotta piss?"

Not sure if it was a trick question, she nodded.

"Me too. Me too. I been waiting on a call for over three hours. I can't stand it no more. I got no bottle, no bucket. I can't leave you in here alone. That's what they said. Not for a second." With deftness, he waved a knife in front of her face, the quick-release blade flipping open under her nose. "You're gonna come with me. We're gonna piss."

She stared at him, unsure of what to say.

"Right?" He gestured with the knife, not in a threatening way, but casually. But it was still a knife, inches from her face.

"Okay."

"I got orders to kill you if you try to run."

She didn't say anything.

"So don't try to run." He bore into her eyes. The most serious look he could conjure. "Okay?"

"Okay."

Chapter Ten

Mike drew back the sheet and Piper walked back into the room. She didn't try to signal Jerry, she didn't make any eye contact at all. Jerry watched her as she took the chair across from him.

"You alright?" he asked.

"Of course she's alright. What kinda shitshow you think I'm running here?" Mike still held the sheet open with the barrel of the gun while he reached through his pajama shirt and scratched at his navel with his free hand. "Goddamn, son, I been knowing this kid since she was...a kid. If there's a place in this world for this child, it's here in my arcade. This's my compound, my castle with no towers. And if a man can't be king in his own tower, then the tower crumbles, doesn't it? Shit rolls downhill, am I right? Tell me if I'm wrong. Shit, even a broken clock is right twice a day."

Jerry wasn't sure if Mike was on the defense or if he was teasing. His manner shifted from jovial and gregarious to obtuse and threatening. He loomed above their seats, waving his arms and speaking to a blank spot in the walls instead of looking into their faces. He went on for a few more moments, revving up, making less and less sense as he spoke. Then he stopped and regarded his guests. "Can I get you two anything?"

Piper and Jerry looked to each other for confirmation.

"No," Piper said.

Mike looked at Jerry and Jerry shook his head.

"No? You sure? Maybe a little pick-me-up? A little go-fast.

Just a wee hit off the pipe? Or I can cut you a line? Little bump-a-bump?"

Again, they both shook their heads.

"Not your flavor, not your speed? Excuse the pun." He paused to snicker at his own joke. "I probably got some beer in back, soda for sure. I got those orange flavored vitamin packs, just mix 'em with cold water. Let's see. I got potato chips, some cookies—but they're kind of old. Oh, hey, I got weed, of course. Maybe some hash, I dunno. I got—"

"We're fine, Mike. Really." Piper wanted him to sit down, to slow down. "Hey, what happened to your dogs? I remember them so well."

"Aw, shit. The grey one got a tumor, big fuckin' lump, right in the chest, so I hadda put him down. But the brown one, Rick James, I use to call him, remember? He was a mean fucker and he turned on me. I hadda shoot him, right in the fucking mouth. Clamped on the barrel of my gun. That's how close he got to taking off my hand. I loved that dog, but it turned. Like a demon got in him. I could see it, the demon I mean. It'd rise up and Ricky's chest would puff out. His eyes, you know, you could see it in his eyes too. I fucking shot that goddamn thing. And I'm glad I did it too. Thing was a true hound of hell—a demon dog."

Jerry knew coming here was a bad idea. As soon as he heard Mike's name. Meth Master Mike. Was that a name, or an occupation? What good could come from a guy with a name like that? He wished he'd stayed in the car. With the air conditioning and the money.

Mike took one of the empty chairs and spun it around. At first he tried sitting on it with the backrest facing his chest, but he couldn't settle into a comfortable position, so he stood and set his foot on the seat and leaned on his knee. "So what is it you told me in back? What are you doing here? Did you say someone was looking for you?"

"Mike, I know you know my stepfather, and you know how

he is, but you can't let him know we're here. Can't we make it our little secret?"

Mike's thin wet lips curved up into a smile. "Oh, I'm good at keeping secrets."

Piper quaked at the comment. Mike may not have noticed, but Jerry did. He wondered what Piper had seen behind the curtain.

A phone rang from the back, a metallic ring from an old rotary phone.

"Shit," Mike said. "What the fuck?"

It kept ringing. Three, four, five more times.

"Betty!" Mike shouted. "Ain't you got fuckin' ears?"

The phone kept ringing.

Mike finally straightened up and said, "I guess it ain't gonna stop. I gotta get that." He disappeared behind the curtain.

They heard voices, but the phone was still ringing. Jerry started to say something, but Piper shushed him. They heard Mike pick up the phone. His voice filtered back from behind the sheet. "What? Now?...Holy shit. You bet I do...Oh, and I got some news for you too...What? Right now?"

They looked at each other, trying to siphon meaning out of Mike's words.

"All right. I can meet you quick." They heard Mike say. "Lemme put some pants on and I'll get out there."

They listened to some clatter and the slamming of drawers, then the sheet flew back again and Mike appeared slightly more dressed than when they'd arrived.

"I got a quick piece of business to attend to. I'll be back in like, oh, twenty minutes. I wanna hear all about what you're telling me, girl, but I gotta do this thing. Both you two don't go nowhere. You need something, you holler out and Betty will come out the back and get it for you." He held his palms out as if to tell them to stay, to hold them there, then he turned and went out the door, leaving it swinging in the open air.

"Betty?" Jerry said.

Piper leaned in and whispered, "It's a boy—at least I think it's a boy. He's back there in a dress and really bad makeup. It's fuckin' weird, dude."

"You're kiddin' me. What do you want to do? Should we wait for him?"

Piper bit her bottom lip. "I dunno. Who do you think he was talking to?"

"How am I supposed to know? Some fuckin' speed deal, I guess."

"You think it had something to do with us?"

"No." As soon as he said it, Jerry second-guessed his answer. It was beginning to dawn on him that traveling all those miles wasn't enough. Would never be enough. The trouble he left behind was nipping at his heels. "I don't know. Do you?"

Piper looked at the sheet, then at the open door. She didn't know either.

Jerry looked at her. She seemed smaller in that moment, more childlike. What had he dragged her into? What had she dragged him into?

A pale arm reached around the sheet and drew it back. A skinny boy in a dirty denim dress stood there gawking at them. His lips were slashed with bright red lipstick and gaudy blue bolts of eyeshadow rested above his eyes. "He'll be back. Don't worry. He always comes back."

After pulling out of Ghia's driveway, Vic stood his truck in the center of the road. It was more of a trail. Three dry ruts winding their way up and down the hill. Rowed with sprouting grass and often narrowing to a width barely broad enough for a single vehicle to fit through, Vic knew the road well. In the years he'd been up on the hill, he'd gotten to know every bend, dip, and driveway. He stared down it now like he was staring into the abyss.

They wouldn't have gone farther up. Probably not. There

was nowhere up there for them to go. The denizens of the hill were well-armed and violently protective of their privacy. With good reason, too. Most unwanted visitors were thieves rather than law enforcement. Smart money said the kids went down the hill. Jerry was lost up here—he knew no one. But Piper, she knew the place, knew it well enough to remember where Big Man's shack was. It'd be a biker's place they'd run. Or a friend of a biker. Vic had to assume they weren't stupid enough to go to Garberville. If they burned the Dead BBs—like Big Man said—they might as well have their pictures on wanted posters on every fence post along the 101—from Garberville to San Francisco.

He stuck a cigarette in his mouth, rolled down the window and listened to the wind for a moment. He put the truck in drive and headed down the hill.

Jerry and Piper sat waiting while Betty fixed them tea. They didn't ask for it, they didn't want it, but young Betty banged around behind the drawn sheet preparing it anyway. Like some twisted version of a child's tea party the boy insisted on playing out. He brought out two TV trays and covered them with mismatched placemats. After several minutes, he appeared again with sugar, a small carton of milk, saucers, but no cups.

When Betty disappeared behind the hanging sheet once again, Jerry said he wanted to smoke. Instead of sitting in the gloom of Mike's shack, he stepped into the daylight of the doorway and lit a cigarette. The same industrious sounds of Betty's tea brewing, the banging and the clumsy clanking, could be heard outside. Jerry smoked and listened. He peered down the short driveway to the car. That's what was on his mind. The car. The trunk. The money. Then he heard something else. The throaty burr of a Harley. He swallowed hard and took another hit from the smoke. More than one Harley. At least one more.

He leaned in through the open door. "I think we should go."

Piper frowned. "What about Mike? I thought we were waiting?"

"Bikes, Piper. Listen."

Knitting her eyebrows together, she stood and bent her head around the doorway. "Fuck. What a prick."

Jerry agreed. "Let's go."

Cardiff and Aaron were flanked by four Dead BBs on their motorcycles. The guttural roar of the squadron made Cardiff feel strong and undefeatable, but Aaron was used to it. He knew three of the guys, older brothers from the Nomad Chapter. The BBs had a widespread chapter intended to encompass all the Northern California cities too small for their own chapter, but their official clubhouse was in West Sacramento. There were so many Nomad members in Humboldt that they became the only chapter who didn't hold church weekly. After the strain of having to fulfill the promise of punishing members absent from the mandatory weekly meetings, they decided to loosen the reins. The Humboldt guys were too old and held too much juice to make them ride all that way once a week. Besides, a few had gotten popped for DUIs on the way home and that made for an unnecessary risk.

One of the BBs on Cardiff's left roared up and hooked his thumb, telling Cardiff to turn at the next intersection. The whole congregation made the turn, then, a few seconds after, Meth Master Mike brought up the rear with his tired-looking white Ford Taurus.

The sound of a squadron of Harleys wasn't unusual in Garberville, and it didn't turn any heads as they proceeded to the squalid row of shacks where Mike lived either. They wore no colors or vests. Other than the small "property of Dead BBs" stickers on their engines, they had no insignia. But they didn't need it. Anyone who saw them knew exactly who they were, what they were. The roar of the bikes was enough. They had no intention of intimidating or surprising anyone; it was business as usual, and the bikers were deaf to the din they created.

"Fuck yeah, they're close. Goddamn it, I can practically feel the ground shakin'."

"Stop it, Jerry. You're making me more nervous than I need to be." Piper stomped on the gas and they spun around and fishtailed on the gravel lining the sides of the narrow, paved road.

"Where're we going?"

"We got no choice. We gotta go back up the hill. There's only one way to the freeway and that's the way they're coming." She watched the rearview mirror while she drove. No bikes. Not yet.

"We can't go back to Vic's," Jerry said. "That's the first fuckin' place they'll look."

"I know, I know, I know." She pulled the wheel to the right and took the main road up the hill. She was forced to slow as soon as they hit the primitive track and they bounced in the car, their shoulders hitting the doors as the wheels banged into the deep ruts. "Let's just get out of sight for a while. Gimme some time to think."

"How well do you know this mountain?"

"I know this road goes up, and they're behind us. What else do I need to know?"

Her voice clipped with irritation. Jerry didn't respond. Instead he gripped the dashboard with both hands and clamped together his teeth.

The first of the Dead BBs hooked a left into Mike's driveway. Roger Rocket hit the kill switch and let the last coughing chug out of the engine. Roger Rocket is what he called himself. It never stuck. Everyone else, at least the brothers, called him Doughboy.

If you weren't a member and you called him Doughboy, you better be packing.

A second bike roared up behind him. The rider twisted the throttle once before killing the noise. "Eh, Doughboy. You ever fuckin' change your oil? You got black smoke coming out your pipe."

"It's fine," Doughboy said. He was fat. Big and fat. It took a grunting effort for him to swing his leg over the back of the bike. By the time he was off his bike, all four of the Dead BBs and both cars were fanned out in Mike's yard.

Terry Naughton stayed on his mount, lighting a cigarette before turning the engine off. Terry was the Nomad president and the others deferred to him, waiting for some sort of tacit approval to keep moving.

"What the fuck is that?" Terry said. He pointed to the right of the shack where Betty was bent over a freestanding sink doing dishes.

Meth Master Mike was out of his old Taurus now, loping up toward Terry. "What'd you mean? That's my girl."

"That ain't no fuckin' girl. Jesus, Mike, you're standing too close to the fucking beakers. That's...I don't know what the fuck that is. It ain't right, I tell you that."

Mike seemed unperturbed by the bikers' repulsion. "Want not, judge not. That's what they say."

"Nobody says that," Doughboy said.

Another Dead BB yawned and stretched. "Is there anything going on here, or what? You got some hospitality to show us? A beer maybe?"

"You want a bump?" Mike asked.

"Fuck no. I don't do that shit. I got the real thing." He patted the breast pocket of his leather vest. "I am thirsty though, Mike."

"Suit yourself," Mike said. "Cocaine is for losers and snoozers. I got the best glass this side of..." He was at a sudden and rare loss for words. "California."

Cardiff sat in his car during the whole exchange, watching the bikers, calculating time.

From the passenger seat, Aaron asked Cardiff, "You ready?"

"Ready to leave? Yeah. You get out and make sure things keep moving. I'm not about to sit here for an hour while these assholes work on their buzz."

Aaron opened his door, but before he got out, he leaned over to Cardiff and said, "Careful now. You're talking about my brothers."

Chapter Eleven

Vic heard the Harleys. Hell, they rattled the whole valley. The rattle of the Thunderheaders cut through the crisp air and rolled up the hill with thick resonance. If they were planning on coming up here with those things, they weren't going to surprise him. He pulled as far as he could to the right, far enough to where the branches of the poplars squeaked against the Tundra. He turned off the motor and listened. There was something else. Above the distant roar of the bikes at the base of the mountain, he heard something closer, something moving. It was the crunch of gravel, the more subdued grind of a sedan's engine. Vic fired up the truck and drove down about forty yards to an old fire road entrance. Barely visible, two grown-over tracks led off the main road behind a thicket of trees. Vic pulled the truck as deep as it would go. The fire road led nowhere, the path covered with thorny raspberry bramble and blocked with a fallen tree. Vic killed the motor once more and listened to the approaching car.

He had no vantage of the road, the clump of brush too thick to see through. He waited as the car approached. It could be any one of the residents of the hill. There was never what you'd call traffic on the road, but it was traversed all day long by growers coming and going, getting supplies, commuting to their patches, or visiting their neighbors. He lifted the Glock 19 from the seat beside him and racked one into the chamber.

* * *

Barbara and Ollie were sharing a gas station restroom when Ollie's phone rang. He was trying to piss when it began vibrating in his pocket.

With his dick in one hand and a handful of Barbara's shirt in the other, he said, "Shit."

She thought about clocking him and making a break for it, but factored in his size, weight, and reach, and realized it'd only earn her a beating. The man had kindness deep in his eyes, but he seemed determined to follow through on whatever plan they had for her.

The buzzing from Ollie's pocket stopped, then began again. His stream continued unabated. "Goddamn it," he said. "Just lemme finish."

Barbara kept her eyes averted while he shook off his penis and tucked it hastily back in his jeans. He pushed her back against the wall while he dug in his pocket for the phone.

"I know...sorry, I was taking a piss...no, she's right here with me...what'd you mean, I'm in—" Ollie caught himself, he wasn't supposed to reveal their location. He looked at Barbara, making sure she didn't somehow divine any information from his truncated sentence. "I'm right where we're supposed to be."

Barbara'd seen enough when he pulled her from the van into the gas station bathroom. She guessed it was Oakland, but it could've been Berkeley or Richmond. Somewhere in the East Bay. Her captor had been careful to pull the van as close to the bathroom door as possible before cutting her loose. But even in those few steps in the open sunlight, she recognized the air, the flat surroundings, the overcast sky. She'd spent enough time there, it felt like Oakland. "Don't do nothing stupid and make me do nothing stupid," is what he'd told her. Her captor was dumb and dangerous. There may be a softness, a childishness underneath his exterior, but his desperate need to please his overlords made him volatile.

"You want me to bring her?"

Barbara tried to discern the voice on the line, some kind of address, landmark. She heard nothing.

"Yeah, okay. Not the main place, right? The other spot?... You got it."

With his pants still undone and his fist still twisted up in Barbara's shirt, Ollie pulled her out of the restroom and back into the van. It took several minutes to secure her again. He apologized several times for winding the tape too tight, or bumping her against the inside of the van, but was otherwise quiet.

So was she. Patient. Helpless.

The ride was short. City blocks, rights, lefts, no U-turns or evasive maneuvers. She tried to count and memorize the maze, but realized there was no point. She didn't know where they began. She listened for identifying sounds, anything that'd help map her position, but he had the radio on. Bad classic rock drowned out any clues from the street.

The van stopped. Her captor climbed out and a heavy gate scraped across asphalt. He got back in, moved the van forward, then he got out and dragged the gate closed again. It was quiet. She was in the van alone.

After ten minutes or more, the van's back door swung open. She felt two sets of hands lift and pull her out. Two new men. She smelled them. Beer and sweat and stale smoke. They didn't speak. They dragged her across the pavement and inside a building. A door slammed shut behind them. The smoke was thick and music played quietly, perhaps in another room. The two men held her, propped up, blind and immobile. She heard voices, but not close to her. They whispered.

"All right. Drop her."

Both the men on either side let go and she crumbled to the floor. With no limb to break her fall, she fell hard and it hurt.

"Roll her over and take that shit off."

The tape and blindfold were ripped from her face, but they

made no effort to remove her other bindings. She looked face-up at a high ceiling with fluorescent lights hanging from bare rafters.

Then a face leaned into view, above her head to the left, upside down.

"Barbara Bertram."

It wasn't a question and she didn't respond.

"You know who I am?"

He was ugly, weathered. His skin was dark with age, but he was white, crystal blue eyes. The awkward position of his face upturned in her line of sight making him all the more grotesque. She shook her head.

"My name is Eric Tribban." He waited a second. When the name got no response from her, he continued, "Your son. Your piece-of-shit son—that waste of fucking space you shit into this world—has two hundred thousand dollars of mine." He let that hang in the air a moment. When she didn't flinch, he added, "And my daughter."

That registered. Barbara tried not to let it show.

"That's right. You know exactly who I'm talking about. She been by your place?"

Barbara shook her head.

"You sure? I'm gonna find out. We already know where they are."

She tried to speak. Her throat was dry, raspy. "Why don't you ask her then?"

The man raised his eyebrows and grinned. His teeth were yellow and spaced wide apart. "Tough mamma, huh? I respect that, okay, you want to protect your cub and all. But the kid's fate is pretty much sealed. I want the money."

"I don't know anything about any money."

He laughed. "That's what we're gonna find out, honey. That's what we're gonna find out."

He straightened up to walk away, and Barbara said, "Please, I'm thirsty. Can I have some water?"

With his back turned, he stopped. He reached out to one of the other men who handed him a can of beer. He walked back to Barbara and poured the beer out onto her face.

He heard them bickering. Sniping at each other like an old married couple lost in foreign land. Their windows were down and after they'd passed by, he smelled their cigarette smoke too. He threw the truck in reverse and wedged out of the pocket behind the trees.

"Stupid fucking kids," he said to himself, craning his neck around, eyeing the fresh cloud of dust hanging above the gravel. He righted the truck and sped after them, spitting rocks from his own tires. They'd gained a quarter mile by the time he had the Ford in his sights. He increased his speed, not wanting to sound the horn. They tried to speed up too, but the rough road wouldn't allow it.

"Jesus Christ, who is that?" Piper glared at the rearview while trying to keep the car on track.

Jerry turned in his seat and saw the truck. Hard to make out the driver through the dust, but there was only one person in the cab. "It's Vic. Slow down, he's waving at us."

"Fuck that guy. I don't know who the hell he is, I ain't slowing down for shit."

"Piper, slow down. He's my friend."

"Your friend? You said you barely even know the guy."

"He's a friend of my mother's. He's trying to tell us something."

She relented and slowed down, pulling slightly to the right, then stopping. Vic pulled up beside them.

"You got heat on your tails."

Jerry leaned between Piper and the steering wheel and shouted up to Vic. "I know, we heard 'em. That's why we're going up instead of down."

"Yeah, but this road goes nowhere. If they're coming up, you're fucked. There's an old horse trail about two hundred yards up on the right, pull in there and get as far along as you can. I'll be right behind you."

"Then what?" Piper said.

"Then we hide."

Chapter Twelve

The horse trail twisted and dropped sharply off the main road, submerging the two vehicles in foliage so they weren't visible to anyone driving by. When they parked, Vic grabbed two warming beers from the six-pack in his truck and walked them to the Ford. He passed one to each of them and pulled his flask of bourbon.

"Here's to high times in low places." He took a short pull off the flask and offered it through the window. They both shook their heads. "Now that we got a minute, why don't we finish that conversation we were having back at my place."

Piper and Jerry looked at each other, silent, like reprimanded children.

"You got a herd of bikers coming up the hill looking for you. Jerry, your mother is missing, and God help you if anything happened to her. And, both you two, you're hiding in the woods with me like scared baby deer. Now it's time to tell me what the fuck is going on."

Piper, petulant, said, "Look, man, it's not like that. We just—"

"Bullshit. Piper, I already know who you are—*and* who your father is—so don't act like those Dead BBs down there just materialized outta thin air"

"Stepfather," Piper said.

"What?"

"Stepfather. He's not my father, he's my stepfather."

"Father, stepfather, uncle, I don't give a shit. It doesn't really change the situation. I know what you did with the pot club, I know you two burned some fucking Russian who's connected to the BBs, but what I don't know is the details—how we're going to make it right. And most of all, I don't know if you two put your mom in danger. That's something we need to find out right now."

"I can call her," Jerry said.

"No, you can't, because we're out here in the fucking bush and we got no signal. But I've been calling and she ain't calling back. And that *never* happens. Ever." Vic pursed his lips together trying to keep from losing his temper. He lowered his voice. "Something's wrong. You know it, and I know it."

They told him. With Vic leaning into the window and them staring straight at the windshield. They told him about Vlad the Inhaler, about casing the club. They told him how they got in through the back. It was an easy job to disable the electricity. All they did was open the fuse box and throw a switch. The fuse box was on the outside of the building, for Christ's sake. The alarm, the motion detectors, the cameras, nothing worked after that.

"How'd you get into the safe?"

Jerry chuckled. "They're fucking stoners, man. The safe was never locked. Maybe no one could remember the combination. You could see it from the front counter during the day. It was always cracked. There was dust on the top of the door because they never shut it. They figured no one would dare break in, and, if they did, they'd never get by all the alarms and shit. And anybody that's a pro should've known it was a Dead BB joint."

"And that was enough, huh? Professionals—real criminals—knew better than to rip 'em off?"

"Yeah, I guess."

"You know why that is?"

Jerry didn't answer, but he knew what was coming.

"Because people who fuck with the BBs end up dead. Because

that's what they do. The people you burned, the ones who are down the road right now loading up their guns, the ones who are about to be hunting us like dogs? They *are* the professionals. Your girl here, she's blood, she'll be fine. The man ain't going to off his own daughter. Probably not, anyway. But somebody's going to pay for this, and it's gonna be you. You and anybody who stands in between them and that fuckin' money. Speaking of which, where is it?"

"Where's what?" Jerry said.

"The money you stole. Where's it buried?"

With his thumb, Jerry pointed behind him, indicating the trunk.

Vic said, "Jesus fucking Christ."

Piper started the car. "Fuck you. I don't have to listen to this bullshit."

Vic drew his Glock from its holster. It only took him a second. He kept it at his side. "Turn off the engine. I let you leave and you're putting us all at risk."

Jerry held up his hands. "Hey, whoa. Slow down. Nobody's going anywhere. Relax, Vic."

Vic didn't ask again. The gun stayed ready at his side.

Piper turned off the engine.

Vic leaned in the window and spoke in an even voice. "I know this may all seem like fun and games to you kids, but let me assure you, I ain't a kid. I been around these people. They don't play games, and neither do I." He looked directly at Piper. "I am a very serious man." He straightened up, listened to the woods, and pulled the flask from his back pocket. He took a quick swig and offered it through the window. "Thought you might've changed your mind."

Terry Naughton asked Mike if he had the keys to his second car, the Toyota Celica sitting near the corner of the house.

"What for?"

"Your back seat is all fulla shit and we can't very well take these things up there, can we." He gestured to the Harleys behind him. "They'll hear us coming as soon as we start 'em."

Mike sucked a long breath through his nose. He counted the bikers; he counted the space in the clean-cut stranger's car. "Can't y'all fit in there?" He pointed at Cardiff.

Terry looked at Doughboy, then back to Mike. "Are you fucking kidding me? Give me those keys."

No threats necessary. Mike reached into his dirty jeans and held out the keys. Terry didn't take them. "Now what?"

Terry said, "Now you get in and do your Indian scout thing and drive us up the hill. You gotta show us where these fuckers are."

"How do I know where they are, I mean, they know you're coming, they could be anywhere. I don't even know if they're up—"

Terry stepped toward him and Mike stopped talking. "We called you for a reason. Get moving."

Terry made a round-'em-up motion with his hand and the whole party filed into the vehicles. Doughboy and another climbed in behind Cardiff and Aaron. Terry got into the passenger seat of Mike's car while the last biker jumped in back. And Meth Master Mike slowly made his way to his car, looking scared, brain racing, tweaked out of his mind.

"Get her up."

Ollie and another biker clamped their meaty hands around her biceps and yanked her to her feet. Barbara wasn't sure where the third henchman was. She wondered if he was standing behind her now with a gun in his hand. Eric Tribban was seated at a small folding table across the room. There was a big window behind him, but it was covered in sheets and assorted flags to obscure any view from the outside and daylight filtered down on him and the table. Barbara noticed two coffee cups and a sugar bowl sitting in front of him.

"Siddown, Barbara. We're waiting."

She didn't move. She couldn't move.

"Cut that shit off her, Ollie."

The cups were empty. Barbara wondered why a kidnapping was turning into a tea party.

The third man, the one she'd feared was the executioner, stuck his head around a corner far across the room. "He's here."

"Finally," Eric said.

A short man in a mismatched track outfit was ushered into the room. He was shorter, older, didn't fit the combination of the other men. Gold chains and slicked back hair, he reminded Barbara of the East Coast gangsters she saw in the movies, the stereotypical Italian hood.

Eric stood up to greet him. "Dmitri, how're you doing? Where's he at? I thought it was gonna be him?"

Except he wasn't Italian.

"No. Not yet. He wanted me to come have a look. See what you have cooking."

His accent rolled, his voice low and melodic. He was Russian, Barbara guessed. Or Ukrainian, or Serb, or Croatian, or Armenian.

"This her? This the lady?" He squinted at Barbara as though she were a dog at the pound.

"The mother? Yeah, that's her. We were just gonna have coffee. You want some?"

Dmitri considered the question, like it was his most important decision of the day. Finally, "Sure. Why not."

Eric snapped his fingers at Ollie and hooked a thumb at the staircase behind him.

The flask was getting light. They'd all had a few tugs and the beers were about gone too. No one had spoken for at least ten minutes. Vic still stood at the Ford's window, Piper and Jerry sat inside. The nature felt close to them as they hid. It enveloped them. The smell, the sound, it was so serene, belying the danger they knew they were in.

"My stepfather's an asshole."

"That so," Vic said.

Jerry put his hand on Piper's forearm as if to quell her speech. Like the barbs would somehow hurt him too.

"No, Jerry. You know it's true. Fuck him. That's why we did it. Well...that's why I did it."

Vic said, "If you wanted to piss your father off, you could've just dated a black guy."

Piper smiled, but she didn't laugh. Jerry wasn't sure if he was the butt of the joke or not.

"He's my stepfather. He'll throw me to the wolves, just like anyone else."

"Why do you say that?" Vic dropped his cigarette into the dirt and crushed it with the toe of his boot.

"It's just the way it's always been. The club first. Business first. Fuck the family."

"I think he may surprise you. When a man's family is threatened, it tends to make 'em a little more sentimental."

"You don't know my father."

"Your stepfather," Vic corrected.

"Whatever."

Chapter Thirteen

Vlad the Inhaler's real name was Vladimir Lysenko. He was about as American as any landed immigrant from Russia could hope to be. Technically Belarus, but Americans considered Belarus part of Russia. They thought anything east of Berlin was Russia. He'd been in America most of his adult life. He loved California. He loved the lifestyle, he loved the women, and he loved the weed.

He'd always considered himself a connoisseur. He drank the best vodka, snorted the best cocaine, but it was the cannabis he really had a taste for. From the day he landed at SFO in the early nineties, he sought out the best smoke possible. When Prop 215 passed in ninety-six, he figured that'd be the end of the good stuff. Medicinal marijuana would lower the bar for pot in Northern California. He was wrong. It only got better. The opportunities opened up for him. He was early on the scene with his dispensary, and, when the field busted open after the turn of the century, he was poised to run the biggest chain in the Bay Area. When legalization happened, and it would, he'd be poised to go legit in a big way. Prop 64 was already on the ballot, and this was the year they thought weed was going to win. Most of the guys he dealt with didn't like the idea, but not Vlad. He only had to hang onto his fiefdom till the proposition passed. Thing was, pot store monopolies were frowned upon—by the local government, the authorities, and the consumers. So he had to build a network of buffers, owners in name only. That created a complicated web of deceit and money laundering, and before long he needed help—both with the cash and the supply.

This is how he came to be partners with the Dead BBs. A deal with the devil, he understood, but a necessary one. What he didn't realize is they were just as adept at worming their way into a situation as the people he was already trying to avoid doing business with. People like the Armenians, or the Russians, or the Ukrainians, or, shit, even the Italians. The outlaw bikers, though, they had something Vlad wanted. They were hip, they ran in the circles he wanted to run in. They weren't out at overpriced restaurants wearing gaudy suits. They were at rock concerts and clubs with dangerous, sleazy-looking women. They had an edge Vlad coveted. They were his people. Or at least that's what he thought at the time.

Vlad leaned into the mirror and scraped the razorblade across his cheek, careful to avoid the line of beard he'd sculpted along his jawbone. He stood back, studied his eyes, and let his gaze slip down to his midriff. He wore an outsized black heavy metal shirt, a familiar band's logo blown up to cover the entire front side of the garment, but it didn't entirely hide his growing paunch. More visits to the gym and more cocaine. And less ice cream. Ice cream was an occupational hazard to anyone who loved cannabis.

He toweled the excess shaving cream from his face and left the bathroom. Tatiana was waiting for him, looking bored and annoyed. A look she cultivated and wore every moment she could.

Without looking up she said, "Dmitri called. He said to tell you he just got there."

"And?"

"And what? He doesn't say anything else. He never says anything. He treats me like a child."

"Tatiana..."

"What? It's true. I hate that little worm. You should see the way he looks at me."

"I do see the way he looks at you. What do you expect? With what you wear? You're going to get looks. I thought that was the whole idea."

Tatiana flipped him off. He didn't understand his sister. She wanted everything two ways. She wanted to live the high life, but she didn't want to work. She wanted to dress like a hooker, but not have men ogle her—at least not the men she detested. She didn't like being judged as a Russian Mafia princess, but she wouldn't stop hanging out with gangsters. Vladimir never understood that saying about having cake and eating it, but he was sure it applied to his sister.

"Since he's not here, I need a ride to the Walgreen. Dmitri said he'd take me, but the little pig left before I was ready."

"Oh, he's a little pig, but you can deal with that little pig if you need a ride somewhere?"

She stood staring at him, hands on her hips. Waiting for a different response.

Eventually, he said, "We'll take the BMW. Right after I load a bong rip."

Vlad's schedule that day was simple. His biggest chore would be to stop by the main warehouse near the waterfront. It was where they did the buying for all the stores. They had growers coming in from all over California, all of them thinking they had the best deal to offer. It was Vlad's job to break their hearts and tell them what they had—the harvest they'd poured their blood, sweat, and tears into growing—wasn't good enough for the price they were asking, even though it often was. He'd cherry pick the best buds and tell them to take home the rest. He'd also do some bickering with the individual club owners. Sometimes these guys were shills for the Dead BBs too, so it was very political. You had to be careful whose toes you stepped on and how hard you ground your heel.

Today was a little more delicate than usual. Vlad was focused on recent developments with one of the San Francisco clubs. One larceny was exposing another. An unfortunate

downside to being in the drug business. He wasn't looking forward to dealing with the troubles over at Eric's. It'll be nice, he
thought, when all this is legal and there won't be the need for
such cloak and dagger affairs. He needed to expedite this afternoon's warehouse stop and rubberstamp a few purchases to
keep things at the clubs moving.

First though, he had to drop Tatiana, if nothing else just to
shut her up. Hopefully his sister wouldn't tack on any extra
stops, but with her, you had to be ready for surprises. He knew
he was expected at Eric's ASAP, but it wasn't life or death.
Well, not for him anyway.

He had no idea they'd locate and secure the woman so fast.
He preferred not to be there while the interrogation was going
on, that's what Dmitri was for. He trusted Dmitri to make sure
it was done properly and, to keep his name out of it in case they
should choose to let the woman live. Vlad wasn't squeamish, far
from it. But he knew when to keep his distance.

But first, before any of this could happen, Vlad need to inhale.

The conversation ebbed confessional. Taking turns, the two of
them told Vic what'd actually happened, and how Jerry caught
a beating at the Haight Street bar. Some half-assed biker spotted
him, recognizing Jerry from a photo a friend of a friend of a
Dead BB showed him. A photo the BBs had been circulating like
a twenty-first-century wanted poster.

He was lucky his attacker was brave, Vic told him, because,
had the guy not mustered the nerve to kick Jerry's ass, he probably would've dropped a dime instead. And that would have
meant three or four Dead BBs showing up before Jerry finished
his beer.

Jerry said. "That's when we knew it was time to go."

Their plan had fallen apart, like they always do, so the two
lovers thought they'd split up and meet in Oregon in a month or
so. But Jerry didn't know anyone in Portland, and he needed a

place to lie low.

So, like a frightened child, he ran home. Barbara knew there was something wrong, something that eclipsed the usual kind of trouble he brought to her front door. That's when Barbara called her son's old friend, Juan Jiménez. And then she called Vic.

"She called Juan and told him what to say, I think. And then she told me to call Juan—saying he'd know what to do—just to get me out of her house. I call Juan and sure enough he's got an idea for where I can lay low, and that idea is you. She knew I wasn't going to take her advice in a situation like this, so she made it look like it was Juan's idea to hide out with you."

"She's a smart lady. She knows you well."

Jerry smiled. "Well, when I see Juan, I'm gonna kick his ass for being a shill for my mom."

"I don't think you're gonna see Juan no more."

"Why?"

"All that calling back and forth you guys did. It led them from Juan to your mother or your mother to Juan. Either way, you can bet your last dollar they had a little visit with your friend. Otherwise they wouldn't be barking up our tree right now."

"You think they killed Juan?" There was a quake in his voice, suddenly realizing how far in they were. He'd known Juan since he was twelve. He considered Juan to be his best friend. A nervous wave of nausea squeezed around Jerry's guts.

"I think there's a pretty good chance, don't you? That's why we need to make sure your mother's okay. What'd you think was gonna happen when you steal that kinda money?"

"I didn't think they'd start killing people over twenty grand."

Vic looked at Jerry, studying him for tells and ticks. "Twenty? Word is you got two hundred."

"Two hundred what?"

Vic smiled. "Two hundred thousand."

Jerry blanched. His mind raced trying to understand what

this meant. He couldn't. His synapses misfired, he scrunched up his nose, and he looked like he smelled something sour.

Piper cut in. "Where the fuck did you—"

Vic held up his hand to silence them. There was a crunch in the trees, the familiar sound of feet trampling the forest floor. He drew the Glock from his holster once again. The footsteps were coming from beyond the cars, deeper in the woods, not from the road. As they approached, Vic was certain it was only one pair of feet.

If the BBs were scouting the woods on foot, it was too dangerous to retreat in one of the vehicles, and too risky to start firing off rounds. And it was too late to get back to the Tundra for his buck knife. Vic steadied his aim on the hood of the Ford while Jerry and Piper slid down in their seats. The heavy footfalls continued unabated. Whoever they belonged to wasn't slowing for caution or to take aim.

"Vic! That you?" Ghia's voice cut through the silence. "Are you pointin' a gun at me?"

"Jesus fucking Murphy," Vic murmured.

Ghia's volume was earthshaking after their sub-rosa talk. "What the hell are you doin'?" She clomped toward them, her steel-toed work boots heavy with mud. "Is that the kid? Hey, Jerry. Oh, who's this?"

Vic spoke softly, "Ghia, this is Piper. Piper, Ghia. Me and the kids were just having a little chat."

"Odd place to do it. I thought you were hunting rabbits or some shit. Huntin' with a Glock, that'd be you all right." She laughed and sighed. "Why the hell aren't you having this little pow-wow at your place?"

"Somebody's on the hill, looking for these two. We're thinking they may be on the way to my place, if they ain't already been there."

"I just saw Ripper up on the sunny-side patch, he didn't say anything."

Vic hadn't considered Ripper. He was usually gone till just

after the sun went down, and he never carried a weapon—no need to. He needed to flag him somehow and keep him from returning to the house. "Well, he's not at the shack, so how would he know?"

"No, he said he had to go back and get gloves, it was all quiet. I mean, he said it was weird there was no one there. Not even the girls. He asked if you were at my place."

"What'd you tell him?"

"I said, I hope so." Ghia raised her eyebrows a bit, but the flirtation was lost on the seriousness of the moment.

Vic took this in, trying to arrange the information in a way that'd be helpful to him, but it didn't tell him anything.

Ghia said, "I think you should be."

Vic was looking at the two silent younger people in the Ford. He lifted his head. "Should be what?"

"At my place. They ain't gonna find you there. Let's go, have a drink, eat some lunch, then you can figure out what to do."

Vic shook his head. "No, too risky. They're coming up the hill loaded for bear. I don't want to drag you into this. It might end up messy."

"You kiddin' me, Vic? Messy is what I do. You know that. C'mon. We'll load up and get the hell gone. You can use my ATVs and get down the backside. If they're coming hard like you say, sitting here has got to be the stupidest thing you can do."

It'd already occurred to Vic to use the Rhino to get himself and the kids off the hill, but he cut himself off from his cabin when he chased Piper's Ford farther up the hill. Getting back to his spot was an unnecessary risk. And Ghia was right, the long twisting driveway to her place was close. They could make it there, suit up in the off-road vehicles, and take the only other exit off the hill—through the bush.

"All right," he said, "My truck is packed, we'll take that one. You two can ride in the back. Leave that red piece of shit here."

Jerry looked confused and Piper was about to speak, but Vic cut them off. "The Ford is too easy to spot. If they see that thing sitting in Ghia's driveway, they're just gonna draw and start shooting. Grab that goddamn money out of the trunk and bring it with you." He clapped his hands. "Let's go, we've got to make it quick. Those bastards are already on the move."

From his silent spot inside the car, Jerry asked, "How do you know?"

"Because I can feel it."

Chapter Fourteen

Ripper was more hungover than usual. He blamed it on Vic's Jim Beam. He was convinced what you didn't pay for up front with your dollars, you paid for the next day in pain. He always teased Vic about drinking the cheap shit, but when the evening wound down, he'd thrown it back like he bought it himself.

He'd already gone back to the house once, telling himself it was to get better gloves, but really it was just to down a couple beers to fend off the rest of the hangover, the part he hadn't sweated out. Ghia ran into him while he was checking the lines on the sunny-side patch. She took one look at him and laughed. She made a crack about the brown liquor, and that's when he decided he needed some hair of the dog. The beer just wasn't cutting it. But now, with the sun well past its arc and his chores mostly done, he was ready to call it an early day. He couldn't keep his mind off that cooler. Perpetually stocked and packed with ice. One thing about old Vic, he never let his workers go hungry, or thirsty.

He mounted the ATV, the squat older one, his favorite among the off-roaders available, and headed down the hill.

He parked and dismounted, noticing nothing but the film of alcohol sweat on his skin the wind failed to dry during the ride. His first stop, the cooler. After plucking a Coors from the deepest recesses, he stood and drained nearly half the can. He stepped onto the porch, wondering why the dogs weren't there to greet him. Then he saw the window on the front door had been broken out.

"Hello?"

There was no response. No dogs, no TV, no radio.

"Hello-o?"

Ripper opened the front door and swept away a little of the glass with his foot.

"Siddown, partner." Doughboy was across the room at the table in front of Vic's pantry shelves. A shotgun rested in his lap and one of the biggest guns Ripper'd ever seen in his hand.

"Nice gun." Ripper tried to keep his voice steady, but it cracked and shook all the same.

"Yeah, it is." Doughboy held it up, admiring the long barrel. "It's a stainless-steel, rubber-gripped .357 magnum and I'm gonna stick it right up your ass if you don't do exactly what I say."

Before Ripper could answer, another man stepped out of the kitchen alcove. He recognized him from the bars in Garberville. A biker named Billy, a Dead BB. This meant the fat man at the table was also a Dead BB. Billy didn't have a weapon, but he didn't need one. Neither did the fat man at the table. They were both BBs and Ripper was fucked.

Vlad hushed his sister as they sped along the Oakland side streets. The day had slipped away from Vlad and he was running late—later than usual. He gripped the wheel with one hand while his phone was pinched between his shoulder and ear. With his free hand, he slapped away his sister's hand while she tried to raise the volume on the radio. Normally, he'd have the phone tapped into the Bluetooth so he could speak freely and openly, but he didn't want Tatiana hearing what was being said.

"I can't hear you. Say that again." Vlad listened for a moment, then spoke. "I don't understand. Why is it they cannot call? It's a simple thing. These guys always want to play their games. Is the other guy there? The main guy? Yes? Put him on." While he waited for Dmitri to put Eric Tribban on the phone, he said to Tatiana, "Don't touch the radio. I can't hear my friends. If you don't like the station, turn it off."

She ignored him and punched the preset station and an even electronic beat burst from the speakers. Vlad jabbed the power button—ending the debate. "Tatiana, where can I drop you?"

"The same place I told you to drop me an hour ago. Walgreen. Why you being such a bitch today?"

"I told you, I have—hello? Eric? This is Vlad. I know, I know. I'm coming right now. Have you heard from our friends up north?...No? Why not?...I see...I see." Vlad's tone was patient and understanding, but he wrinkled his face and curled his lip. "Okay, no problem. I'm about ten minutes away."

He hit the end-call button with his thumb and threw the phone to the floorboards at Tatiana's feet. "Fuck, shit, piss. Stupid fucking animals."

Tatiana didn't say anything.

Stanley, Possum, Mongo, and Lloyd gave them a frantic greeting. They were all bull terrier mixes, except for Stanley. He was an old retriever who got pushed around by the excitement of the other dogs.

"Alright, alright, alright," Ghia said, "settle down." She held her hands out to keep the dogs from jumping up. That seemed to work for her and her alone. The others were pummeled by the pups. Thankfully they weren't barking at the newcomers, Jerry and Piper, only leaping and lapping at them. Vic knew they didn't need the extra noise.

Ghia hustled them into the tiny house, the pack of dogs and the three guests. Jerry and Piper took it in, the post-hippie décor, the cozy cottage in sharp contrast to Vic's utilitarian shack. There were worn patchwork quilts thrown over the furniture, random mismatched frames of black-and-white photos sandwiched between old concert posters from Winterland and the Fillmore. The obligatory bong sat atop a small kitchen table. Other than that, there were no other trappings of the weed factory that filled Vic's shack. It was cute, quaint, and decidedly feminine. Unlike Ghia herself.

"Nice place," Piper said.

"Thanks. I like it. Y'all want anything? I can make a pot of coffee, or tea. A beer, maybe?"

"I'll take a beer," Vic said. "But I don't think we should be staying too long. Those guys are on the hunt for us. There's no telling how quick they're going to piece you and me together."

Ghia reached out and brushed the back of her hand across Vic's face. "Sweetie, that may've been the most romantic thing you've ever said to me."

Doughboy stood over Ripper with the .357's barrel pressed into the kneeling man's forehead. "There's only so many times I can ask you, then I have to shoot you. You get that, right?"

Ripper would have gambled on grabbing the barrel of the gun and going hand-to-hand with Doughboy, but he knew the other BB, Billy, stood behind him with a shotgun aimed at his lower back.

"Look, we're not going to kill you if you tell us where he is. We know that piece of shit is with him. We just want the kid, not Vic. That fucker can crawl back under whatever rock he's hiding. We just want the kid and the girl."

"What girl?" Ripper asked. He saw Doughboy's nose wrinkle with confusion before he felt the butt of the shotgun slam against the base of his skull. He saw white and tasted familiar copper in his mouth, but he held on to consciousness as he crumbled to the floor. He stayed there, curled into a fetal position, waiting for the next blow. It came. The butt of the Remington smashed into his ribs causing him to cry out. "What girl? What girl are you talking about?"

"Fuckin' shoot him," the BB with the shotgun said. "Just give him one. Cap him in the knee or something—let him know we're serious."

Doughboy grunted as he squatted down. He pressed the magnum's barrel into Ripper's thigh. "Last chance, fuck face. Where the fuck did they go?"

Between the pain in his head and his ribs, Ripper barely heard the question. "What girl? What are you talking about? There is no girl."

"Who is Vic with?"

Ripper was confused, delirious with agony. "Ghia? She barely even comes around."

Doughboy snapped his fingers and Billy plucked a small two-way radio from his belt. Doughboy snatched at it and keyed the mic. "Hey, hello? You guys listening?"

Cardiff's voice came back buried in a burst of static.

"The old man has a girlfriend. Somebody named Ghia. That sound familiar to anyone?"

Another shock of static came through the tiny speaker and Doughboy squinted as though it'd help him decipher it.

Ripper heard the other man set the shotgun on the floor, resting its butt down, probably hanging on the barrel for support. He felt the pressure of the .357 lighten off his thigh. He made his move. He grabbed the barrel and yanked it away from Doughboy, who, still squatting and focused on the radio, lost his balance and fell onto Ripper. At the same time he was getting crushed by Doughboy, Ripper tried to reach back and chop at the shotgun, but he was too slow and Billy the biker had already yanked it from the floor and was pointing it at the both of them. Ripper punched at Doughboy and tried to grab the pistol.

"Hold him down, Doughboy, I can't get a shot at him." Billy shimmied left and right, trying to get an angle he could shoot Ripper and not his friend.

Doughboy only grunted while Ripper rabbit-punched him in the stomach. His right hand—the one holding the .357—was stretched far from their melee. Ripper squeezed Doughboy's right wrist, pinching his nails into the fat man's skin.

"Let go of the gun, let go of the gun," Doughboy's friend

yelled. If he could use the Magnum instead of the shotgun, Billy's chances of catching Doughboy with friendly fire went way down. But Doughboy wasn't letting go. He clutched the .357 like his life depended on it.

The sound of the revolver going off was like a cannon. The large caliber in such a small room shook the walls. For one split second, all three of them froze. Ripper, realizing he hadn't been shot, head-butted Doughboy. Then there was another loud bang, a deeper boom. Ripper felt a terrible pain in his hip and leg, his whole right side began to burn. Doughboy's weight seemed to increase on top of him and he heard the other man shout, "Fuck!"

Doughboy cried out, screaming from the pain of buckshot that'd torn through his ample flesh. An unintelligible curse rang out and he rolled off Ripper.

Aaron asked Cardiff what he'd heard over the radio, but Cardiff couldn't tell.

"He said something and dropped the radio," Aaron said. "It sounded like someone punched him, right? You hear that? What the fuck was that?"

"I don't know, but we're pissing in the wind up here. Let's turn around and see what they got." Cardiff lifted the radio to his mouth. "Terry, you listening?"

After a moment, a voice came over the air. "Yeah."

"Ask that creepy fuck driving if he knows someone named Ghia?"

There was a brief silence, then Terry's voice came back again. "Yeah."

"Yeah, you'll ask, or yeah he knows who she is?" Cardiff took his thumb off the mic button and said to Aaron, "What the fuck is wrong with your people? They don't know how to communicate?"

Aaron didn't reply and focused on making the three-point

turn on the narrow road. As they descended, Cardiff drew his semi-automatic 9mm from his jacket and cradled it in his lap. Finally, Terry answered Cardiff's question.

"He says he knows her."

Cardiff keyed the mic. "Well, get over there and see what you can find out."

The voice came back. "Yeah."

Chapter Fifteen

Roland Mackie didn't get home till sunset. He felt rushed and anxious to get to his couch so he could do nothing. It wasn't unusual for him to be late, but if it were dark when he got there, it seemed like the evening—*his* time—was clipped. Ever since he and his wife split, Roland made a ritual of his solitary time. He cherished it. He'd walk in the door, pop open a bottle of Budweiser, and sit in the middle of his couch. No TV, no radio, no computer, just silence. His wife always had the TV on, even when she wasn't watching anything. The computer monitor would be up, the TV on, and she'd be talking on the phone. A constant static chaos he was never able to decompress in. He felt he was exorcising the heartbreak by defeating the memory of that steady noise with silence. Anything to not relive those moments with her.

He grabbed the obligatory beer from the fridge, turned up the thermostat, and sat down. His phone rang as he took his first sip and he quietly cursed himself for not remembering to silence it. He picked it up and saw Nagle's name flashing on the caller ID.

"Hey, what's up? Long time no see."

"You know that case you were asking me about today?"

"Yeah."

"Well, guess what? I go back upstairs and I get pulled into the SAC's office. I'm thinking Forrester ratted me out and I'm in deep shit, right?"

"Did he?"

"Yeah, sort of. I mean, he meant to fuck me up, but then the SAC asks me about your guy."

"Jerry Bertram?"

"No, the other one. Vladimir Lysenko. The pot club guy."

"I told you, he's up to his tits with bikers."

"It wasn't the bikers he was interested in. It was the Ukrainians. I guess Vlad is from Belarus, but he's tied up tight with the badasses from the Ukraine and some very shady folks from Armenia. Basically he paints it like Lysenko's a freelancer for all the Eastern Bloc bad guys. This Vlad's got an OC file on him since the nineties."

"So this is good, right? He wants you to come onboard."

"No, he wants *you* to come on board with *us*. He says he'll consider an exchange of information with SFPD on our biker case, if you'll help him nail down Lysenko."

Mackie sat in the silence of his apartment a moment, thinking about his boss, the man who headed the gang task force, the protocol and procedures he'd need to follow to make an interdepartmental—an inter*agency*—investigation work. He thought about the hoops he'd have to jump through with homicide too. Just getting permission to start the process would take time.

"Tell him I'm in."

"You sure you don't need to—"

"Yeah, I'm sure. Tell him I'm in. Where do you want to start?"

By the time Cardiff and Aaron pulled up to Vic's place, Doughboy had already dragged himself out to the porch and was sucking on a fifth of Jack. Cardiff got out of the car holding his Glock at his side. He took long, quick strides toward Doughboy.

"What happened?"

"Billy shot him, but I got caught in the crossfire."

Cardiff looked down at the big man's side, assessing the

damage. "Doesn't look too bad."

"Well it fucking hurts like it is."

"Next time don't let yourself get shot."

"Let myself? Listen you Russian piece of shit, I don't know—"

Cardiff leaned in a little and lowered his voice. "I'm not Russian." He turned, racked one into the chamber, and walked into the cabin.

Cardiff entered the shack and found Billy BB standing statue-still with the Remington pointed at the wood planked floor. He held it ready and sighted, as though his target lay only a few feet in front of him. Cardiff saw his eyes were unfocused.

"Where is he?"

"Who?" Billy said.

"The guy that shot your friend."

It took a moment, but Billy said, "I shot him."

"You shot who?"

"I shot Doughboy. I shot Ripper too. That's his name, the guy that was here."

"Ripper," Cardiff said to himself. "Okay, so where is he?"

"I dunno. I guess I freaked after Doughboy got shot. He got outta here somehow. It was confusing. Doughboy was flopping around like a fish."

"I thought you said you shot him?"

"I did. I shot him. I shot 'em both. It's a fuckin' shotgun. You fire and you're gonna hit whatever's in front of you." Billy turned toward Cardiff, the barrel of the Remington swinging round like a boom mast on a ship. "They were fighting. All twisted up on the floor. Doughboy told me to shoot."

"Whoa, hold the gun down, soldier." Cardiff held his hand out. "I don't want you to shoot me too."

"I'm not gonna...I didn't mean to shoot Doughboy. They were all tangled up."

Cardiff surveyed the flecks of blood on the floor. Droplets, smears, and specks of rusty red everywhere. "Where'd you shoot this other guy, Ripper?"

Exasperated now, Billy said, "Right here on the floor."

"No, where on his body? Where'd he get hit?"

"In the leg, same as Doughboy."

"How the fuck you let him get away then?"

Billy moved his lips, but didn't say anything. His shoulders shrugged upward.

Cardiff felt the weight of the gun in his hand. He tapped the barrel lightly on his leg. His first instinct was to shoot this stupid son of a bitch. If he had his way, he would have already dropped three of these bikers today. But they were the power here, he was working their side of the street. He pursed his lips till they curved in to a smile. "Well, I guess he didn't get too far then, eh?"

Billy nodded.

Cardiff spotted the .357 laying on the table beside the enormous bong. He sat down his gun and picked up the magnum. "This thing work?"

Billy nodded again.

Cardiff fired a shot to the right of the biker's feet. It was deafening. "Yeah, you're right, it does. Next time, try shooting him with this. That way he won't walk away when you're done."

"You hear that?" Vic said.

"Hear what, hon?"

"Where's Lloyd and Possum?"

They did a silent roll call and shrugged. Only two dogs remained in the small room. Vic held his finger to his lips and they all stood still in Ghia's cottage.

"There's nobody out there, the dogs'd be going crazy." Ghia resumed dropping supplies inside a shopping bag. Sardine tins, juice boxes, canned chili.

"Stop, Ghia, we don't need all this, I already put some shit together."

"Yeah, I saw. Guns and booze. It's already getting dark out there. If we get stuck on this mountain overnight, you're gonna thank me." She turned to the cupboard above her sink and tossed bandages and peroxide into the bag.

Stanley, the old retriever, began to whine, a high-pitched single note that sounded like a tea kettle starting to boil.

Jerry looked at the dog, then at the door.

"Don't worry," Ghia said. "She just thinks we're packing for a trip and we're going to leave her."

Mongo, the only other dog inside, barked. The brass bark of a pit bull, startling as an alarm.

"Jesus," Piper said.

Vic shushed them all and pulled his gun. He stepped to the door. He pressed his ear against it, hoping to glean a signal from one of the other dogs, but he heard nothing.

"It's time to go. Ghia, where's the key?"

Ghia reached for a single key hanging on the side of a pantry and stretched to give it to Vic still at the door.

"You ready?"

The three silently nodded.

Meth Master Mike parked his car at the start of the driveway, the pitted and rutted road no different from the wider road they'd pulled off. He sat, both hands on the wheel, feeling his heart rap against his ribcage.

"This it?" Terry asked.

"Yeah, this is it. I know cause I 'member a few years back she had a Thanksgiving thing and I wasn't invited, but I showed up with a buddy of mine and he got really drunk and threw up in her bathtub and she fuckin' blamed me, the fucking bitch. And then this other time I needed to borrow—"

"All right, enough. I get it." Fifteen minutes in a car with Mike and Terry's head was starting to pound. "Turn off the engine." Mike's car was so old, Terry had to actually roll down the window. He listened to the forest. "She got dogs?"

"Sure, I guess. I mean, everybody's got dogs, right?"

Terry cracked his door. He heard the padding of the paws, the sniffing of their snouts. "Shit."

Mike reached over and squeezed Terry's forearm. "Ssh," he said. "Let me." He reached down into his right boot and pulled out a nine-inch Bowie knife, the sheath glued onto the boot's leather. He started to make a quiet clucking sound with his mouth as he opened the door. He crept out of the car slowly, all the while making that clucking sound. Soon, Terry saw the dogs, two pit bulls. They weren't barking. They made their way toward Mike, curious and playful, sniffing at the air, getting closer. Mike kept clucking with his tongue, interspersing the sound with soft-sounding kisses. When Possum, Ghia's dog, reached Mike, it slowed—caution and instinct factoring into its approach. It sniffed at Mike, a low growl curling from its maw. Then, too fast for any of his companions to see, Mike stuck the knife straight into the dog's larynx. Possum made an abbreviated yelp, then succumbed to shuddering and collapsed on the forest floor.

Lloyd was near enough to snap at Mike, a single high-sounding bark the only warning, but Mike was ready and leapt at the dog, stabbing it over and over.

"Holy fuck," the biker in the back seat said. "Meth Master Mike's got some skills."

Mike stood, brushed off some leaves and pine needles, and returned to the driver's seat. "You wanna walk down, or you wanna drive?"

Terry nodded at Mike's arm, which dripped blood.

"Damn," Mike said. "I wonder which one o' them fuckers nipped me."

Chapter Sixteen

"Look, I got things to do," Eric Tribban said. "I can't be sitting here babysittin' all day."

Dmitri smiled and took another sip of his coffee. "This is delicious. Do you think I could get a fresh cup? This one's gone a bit cold."

"I'm serious, man. This ain't no little thing. I don't like this set up. This is my place. Having her here is an unnecessary risk."

Dmitri lowered his voice and when he did so his accent thickened. "What risk? What are you scared of? A woman? He said he'd be here, and he'll be here."

"It's been over an hour. Shit like this ain't a priority for him?"

"He wanted me to talk to her first."

"You haven't said a fucking word to her since you been here. She's right there. Talk to her."

Dmitri set down his mug and swiveled in his chair. "Barbara."

Barbara had been sitting on a plain wooden chair, hands on her thighs. She'd spent the last hour holding still and keeping quiet while letting her eyes dart around the room, looking for an escape route, some way she could fight back, some weapon she could seize, but there was nothing. She leveled a gaze at Dmitri, letting her eyes do the talking.

"Barbara Bertram." Dmitri smiled now. He knew she wasn't going to respond. "You notice you are not tied, not anymore. And no one has hit you. Not while I am here. And I haven't

108

asked you any questions. I think, if you have something to say, you will say it. No?" Dmitri paused to draw a cigarette from an exotic-looking black pack. The cigarette, too, was black, with a gold tip.

"I don't have anything to say because I don't know anything."

"I know, and—unfortunately for you—I believe you. You see, if you knew something, maybe you would have some value, you could help yourself. But, as it is, you're just one big mistake, you see? Why go through all the questions over and over when I can just cut to the part where I can have my fun."

Barbara knew what he was doing. He wanted to see her weep with fear. She wasn't going give him the satisfaction. Not even a lip quiver. "I can't tell you what I don't know."

"Okay, okay. But, for the formality of this situation, so I can tell my boss I tried before..." he held up open palms in a gesture of futility, "...you know. Let me ask you one more time." Dmitri stood, pushing the chair with the backs of his knees. "Your son, Jerry. Jerry Bertram. He stole a lot of money from me. Well, I shouldn't say only me, but from me and my friends. Now, Barbara, this is a lot of money, you understand. And it isn't just the cash—he discovered a hole in our security that we have to now plug. We can't have others finding out about the hole in our defense, yes? We know Jerry came to see you. We know this, Barbara, for a fact. He came to your nice peaceful little house and he brought with him our money. Now, what is your opinion—since you say you don't know anything, let us just have your opinion—what do you think? Does Jerry still have our money with him? Or did he leave it at your home?"

"I told you, I have no—"

Dmitri held up his hand. "Okay, okay, I understand. Maybe he didn't hand you a suitcase full of cash, but—what is your opinion—did he maybe hide something at your house? In the garage? Do you two have a special spot, a secret spot? Maybe this boy of yours, this boy who knows to lie, knows to steal, maybe this boy didn't tell you. Maybe he just hides what isn't his because he doesn't want *you* to be in trouble—doesn't want you to die." Dmitri took a long and deliberate drag off his black cigarette and added, "Die for *his* mistakes."

"He didn't have anything, didn't hide anything, didn't give me anything. He showed up empty-handed and left empty-handed. He slept on the couch and left first thing in the morning." Now her lip was quivering. She thought of how Jerry looked that morning, stoic but scared, his little boy eyes belying his poker face. She knew he was in trouble, and knew he wouldn't ask for help. He wasn't there to hide, she thought, he was there to say goodbye.

Dmitri turned back to the small table where his coffee mug stood and stubbed out his cigarette. To Eric, he said, "See? I told you. Useless. I should have cut right to the fun part."

Mongo began to bark. Quick, rhythmic yelps directed at the front door. Stanley joined in with his own aged, throaty bark. They both focused their attention on the door and whatever was beyond it.

"What is it, boy?" Ghia said.

"That'll be our guests," Vic said.

"It can't be. What about the dogs?"

"I think the dogs are gone." Vic tossed Ghia back the key for the ATV and pointed for Jerry and Piper to squat down near the table and for Ghia to take cover behind the fridge. He cursed himself for leaving his arsenal in the truck. It was dusk now, with night approaching fast. "I'm going to see what's out there. If they're not in the front yard, they're close, so I'm gonna try to lay down some cover. Ghia, you run to the Rhino and fire it up, I'm going to try to get my bag of tools out of the truck. Jerry, you get your ass in the back of that ATV and soon as I hand you those tools, pop a few rounds into the woods."

"Wait, what about me?" Piper said.

"You don't get shot. Just follow Jerry and keep your head

down."

Jerry said, "You're just gonna walk out there?"

"If we stay sitting here, we're fucked." Vic turned the door knob and cracked the door, tipping it open with his boot. No gunfire. Stanley and Mongo kept barking, wild and vicious, but they held their ground and didn't try to nose out the door. Jerry reached out and grabbed Mongo's collar, and the dog's paws began to scrape on the hardwood floor.

"Stanley, get back here," Ghia said from behind the fridge. The old retriever ran at the shaft of light coming in the door from the porch, pushing his way through. His hips banged on the jamb, but he didn't let it slow him down. Stanley disappeared into the darkness. Ghia called after him, but the dog didn't stop running.

"Goddamn it," Vic said.

Stanley's barking lessened with distance, but didn't stop. Jerry yanked on Mongo's collar and told him to shut up, but Mongo kept barking. Stanley was gone. His barks now drifting through the woods.

"You hear that?" Vic said.

"I can't hear shit over your dog," Jerry said.

Mongo kept barking and Vic poked the barrel of his gun out the door.

Terry, Mike, and the other BB were outside the old Taurus at the top of Ghia's driveway. Terry had his gun out and Mike had his Bowie knife in his hand, still slicked with dog blood.

"We going down there, or what?" Mike said.

"Sssh. I'm trying to hear what's going on." Terry tilted his head a little. "You hear them dogs? The barking? It just got louder. Maybe they're outside now?"

The BB said, "The little guy said to wait for them."

Terry swiveled his head and glared at the biker, curling his lip at the insubordination. "We ain't waiting if these fucks are leaving. I say when we go. You think that little fucking weirdo is in charge here?"

"Sorry, Ter."

"You're fuckin' eh right you are. This is all just a favor for Eric and Vlad. We're treating that guy right as a courtesy for them. I don't know that fucker and he's definitely not calling the shots on *my* hill."

"Yeah. I wasn't ready, that's all. I'm ready now."

Terry held a hand up to silence them while he tuned back in to what he couldn't see in the failing light down at Ghia's cottage. The BB took the opportunity to pull a small baggy of coke from his vest and tap a mound out on the pad of flesh between his thumb and index finger and lift it to his nose. Mike saw him and followed suit. He took a soot-blackened glass pipe from his pocket and held a lighter under it and inhaled deeply, the pipe sizzling and bubbling above the flame.

Terry heard the crackling of the meth pipe and turned to see what Mike was doing. "Are you fucking kidding me? Jesus, have a little self-control. Put that shit away."

Mike thought about pointing out what the BB was doing directly behind Terry's back, but thought better of it and returned the hot pipe to his pocket while he let the acrid smoke seep out of his nostrils. "I just didn't wanna die straight."

Terry wrinkled his nose in disgust. "Mike, you're a long fucking way from straight. And nobody's dying today."

They all took a few cautious steps down the driveway toward the house. Then they heard the deep barks of another dog.

Vic kicked the door wide and swung around with his pistol raised to eye level. Silence. Over his shoulder he called, "Let's go, let's go, let's go."

The three in the cottage scrambled. Ghia grabbed the shopping bag and ran, Jerry twisted his hand in Mongo's collar and dragged him toward the ATV, and Piper snapped and shouted for them all to hurry the hell up.

Vic heard Stanley's bark getting farther away, sounding like the dog was at full gallop. There was a flat *pop*, the unmistakable sound of a medium-caliber handgun. And no more sound from Stanley. The only bark now was Mongo's. Vic stuck to his plan and fired two rounds up the driveway as he raced to the Tundra and yanked what he could from the front seat.

All four of them squeezed onto the tiny ATX, the four-wheel golf cart, with Mongo still yelping and trying to jump off the back. Ghia pulled forward and they lurched down a two-track path, all the passengers grabbing onto the roll bars for support.

Moments after Terry shot the dog that came at them up the driveway, they heard two more shots. Neither shot came close to hitting them, but they fanned out anyway. Obviously someone was there, someone was waiting for them. They crept along the sides of the drive, trying to see what was obscured by the fauna and the blanket darkness night had thrown over them. They heard another dog, voices, then a whir—the vibrating buzz of an ATV's engine.

"Get on the fucking radio, tell those fuckers we're going in. Tell 'em to hurry up too."

Chapter Seventeen

"Where do we start?" Mackie said.

Mackie and Nagle sat in Nagle's cubicle on the twelfth floor of the San Francisco Federal Building. When Nagle called, Mackie convinced him to wait at the office while he raced back down to Civic Center from his apartment in the Sunset District. After meeting in the lobby, the two returned upstairs where they could sit and wind through the labyrinth of data only accessible from the FBI's computers.

"Your premise is the victim is tied to the weed clubs, right? That's how you pull Jerry Bertram into this."

"I don't pull him in. He's already in. It's his M.O. He's been preying on the clubs."

"Jesus Christ," Nagle said. "All this trouble over pot. What are these fuckers going to do when it goes legal this November?"

"If it passes."

"Oh, it'll pass. The only people opposing it are criminals."

Nagle took a loud sip from a cup of coffee. On the mug was a big heart with "Mr. Right" written in fat black letters. The mug reminded Mackie how alone he was, how desperate he must seem to his happily married friend. Mackie changed the subject. "You say the clubs are backed by the Dead BBs through this Russian guy."

"He's actually not Russian. Not technically."

"Whatever," Mackie said. "This homicide has all the earmarks of a gangland hit. You know, if it walks like a duck and talks like a duck."

"So you want to connect Juan Jiménez to Vlad Lysenko."

"No, I wanna connect Lysenko to Bertram."

"But if they're not known associates, if the pot club was just a target, a place for him to burn, then we're not going to find anything. It's just a heist, that's all. They didn't need to be partners for your boy to pull off a burglary."

"There's got to be a connection. Some way Bertram found to weasel his way into the dispensary. Some way, or someone."

Nagle sighed. He sensed Mackie's stubborn refusal to face the facts head-on. His friend wanted to steer the case in a direction he wanted it to go, he needed it to go. Nagle just wasn't sure which direction that was. "What's your obsession with this guy?" he asked.

"Who? Jerry?"

"Yeah."

"I been waiting a long time for his head to pop up." Mackie adjusted himself in his chair. "It's not really him I'm trying to tap into, it's his mother."

"His mother? Who's his mom?"

"Barbara Bertram."

"Okay. What the hell does she have to do with any of this? If she's not tied to Lysenko, then we're not interested in her. It's the rules of engagement. The bureau is already going out on a limb here."

Mackie winced a little, like what he was about to say might hurt him. "She's tied in. Maybe. If her kid's involved, then she fits in somewhere, trust me."

Nagle didn't speak. He crossed his arms and waited for the rest of the confessional.

"A known associate of his mother's. A guy named Victor Thomas. That's who I'm after."

"Jesus Christ, Roland. Are you kidding me? You got me up here going through files and chasing my tail and you're on some fucking secret mission? I put my reputation on the line when I told the SAC we were throwing in together."

"I thought you knew."

"Knew what?"

A silence fell between them. Mackie waited for the realization to dawn in his friend's eyes, but there was none. The buzz of the fluorescent lights hummed quietly over their heads. The office was empty. No straggling agents, no janitorial workers. Just Nagle and Mackie. "You remember the Fulton Street Massacre?"

"Sure. What was that, like ninety-four?"

"Ninety-six," Mackie said. "I was there."

"You kidding?" Nagle laughed. Then he did a quick calculation. "Shit, Roland, you been on the force that long? I didn't know."

"I finished with the academy in ninety-five. I was definitely still green. Hungry, but green. I was one of the first on the scene."

Nagle raised his eyebrows and nodded. "Wow. Scary. Big case."

"Wasn't mine, obviously. I was just first officer on the scene. It made an impression though. When they figured out Vic was the guy, I buried it deep, but I wanted him. I saw those bodies, what he did to them, the bullet holes in the walls. Didn't matter who the victims were, it was an atrocity. I mean, they were all scumbags, sure, but...I'd never seen anything like it. Before or since. Blood everywhere, torture. Fucking atrocity. A kid, Tory, a goddamned kid. I'll never forget it. I swore he'd pay for what he did, one way or another."

"How do you know this Barbara Bertram was involved?"

"Shit, both Bertram's and Victor Thomas' wallets were found at the scene. Homicide said they were being tortured, interrogated, whatever. I didn't see it that way. I think their IDs were left behind in the struggle. It was obvious to me, but it wasn't my call to make. The crew that caught it, they fucked it up. Homicide in the late nineties was a clusterfuck."

"I remember. Hawkins, Purcell, that whole fiasco. Quite a scandal. They wanted to bring us feds in, call the gang problem a RICO and stick all those unsolved homicides under one roof."

"Wouldn't have helped. Not with Fulton Street anyway. Those were different players than the street gangs." Mackie blinked away visuals forcing their way into his memory, rising like bile. He continued. "Vic put some distance between him and whatever circumstantial evidence there was and then disappeared."

"How'd he manage that?"

"The old-fashioned way. Killing witnesses. Or in this case, partners." Mackie cleared his throat. "At least three of his old pals from his high-roller days went M.I.A. and two more were found one-hundred percent K.I.A. Couldn't tie him to any of it."

"So what happened to him?"

"Nothing. He took his lifestyle down a few notches and got in the wind. First he was out in the desert near Joshua Tree, then, supposedly, somewhere in the Central Valley. One of them gas stops off the I-5 is what I heard. Then a whole bunch of rumors. The guy started his own franchise on misinformation. Last I heard he was either in Arizona or moving meth ingredients by the truckload from Mexico to some bikers in Riverside County."

"Until now."

Mackie nodded. "Until now."

Piper watched the forest pull away from her as she bounced in the shallow metal bed of the ATV. The rear storage was designed for coolers and camping equipment, not two people and a dog. There were no seats or safety belts and they rattled loose like forgotten trash. She and Jerry pressed against one another, watching their collective fate unravel in the darkness behind them. She squeezed Jerry's thigh as the small vehicle pitched side to side. She squeezed it for balance, for security, and because she loved him. She was scared, she knew she'd gone too far, but it was too late now. She couldn't undo what she and Jerry had done, they were powerless to halt the chain of events they'd set into motion. She had no way of knowing they'd come at them this hard. She expected trouble—that's why they fled—but this? No. Then she thought about what Vic had said. Two hundred grand. That's how much they were supposed to have taken from the safe that night. According to who? Vic? Her stepfather? Vlad, that asshole who ran the pot club? And if they didn't have it, who did? She felt the paltry girth of the leather pouch pressing against the small of her back. Two hundred grand, my ass, she thought.

A sour pit grew in her stomach. She should have known not to go up against her stepfather. Every time she tried to beat him, she failed. Law enforcement failed, his enemies failed. It made no sense to her that someone so callous—*so evil*—could be blessed with such good luck. It was as though the devil himself was his guardian angel.

The ATV had slowed considerably. The path they'd started out on had split, narrowed, and all but disappeared a quarter-mile from Ghia's cottage. They navigated through the forest floor now, working their way around stumps and fallen trees and sudden, steep drops in topography that yanked the vehicle down like an old-time rollercoaster. The darkness didn't help either. The cart was equipped with headlights, but the light traveled a short distance, illuminating only the obstacles and insects. Moths and mosquitos flitted and danced in the beams, mocking their slow progress.

"Jesus H. Christ, I can't see shit out here," Ghia said.

Their descent slowed to a crawl. As darkness set in, the ground became moist, the smell of moss and wood thickening with dew. The small patches of sky they could make out through the tops of the huge redwoods glittered with starlight, but very little of the glow made it down to the saplings and shrubs. The Polaris had rutted out twice and was once more stuck in a deep hole Jerry guessed belonged to a badger. "What the hell else would live down there?" he asked.

"You don't wanna know," Vic told him.

Reversing had no effect, so Jerry and Vic had to physically pull the cart from the hole while the balloon tires spun and spat earth at them. In another hundred yards, they were stranded again when they struck a fallen tree. The ATV's undercarriage scraped till it ground to a halt on the horizontal trunk, this time leaving the tires spinning in mid-air. Again they had to climb out and rock the vehicle's frame until the wheels found purchase.

Before they got back in the vehicle, Jerry asked, "What's that smell?"

"What smell?" Vic said.

"You don't smell it? It smells like, I dunno, a fuckin' hobo's dirty boots."

Vic paused and lifted his head and sniffed at the air. "Maybe, something."

There was a sound behind them in the darkness, a crunch of footsteps on brittle twigs and pine needles. Vic drew his gun. Silence. Then the sound of more footsteps.

Ghia leaned out from the ATV. "That's a bear, that's what that is."

"Holy shit," Jerry said. "They stink like that?"

Piper gripped the roll bar beside her. "Jerry, get back in. Hurry."

"It's alright, baby. It's alright."

"Ssh!" Vic said. He thumbed the hammer back on his Glock and inched his way counterclockwise, trying to get a position on the bear, but it was useless. There was nothing to see in the blackness. The animal's scent had increased, the stale pungent rank hanging on the air now, so strong it seemed to be warming the temperature.

Ghia stepped from the ATV. "That's not how you deal with a bear. This is how you deal with a bear." She stepped out in front of Vic and hooted into the blackness. "*Git!*" she hollered as she clapped her hands. "Git on, get outta here!"

They heard the bear's heavy footfalls breaking away in the woods.

"See?"

Vic smiled at her in the moonlight. "I knew we brought you along for a reason."

"Yeah," Ghia said. "To save your lives."

When he got back into the passenger seat, Vic asked, "You want me to drive?"

"What difference is that gonna make?" Ghia said. "You want to stop? Make camp?"

Piper leaned in from the back. "Camp? What? Those guys are after us. We can't just sit here in the bushes, we gotta keep going."

"She's got a point," Vic said. "We certainly can't make a fire, and every noise we make travels."

"Oh, c'mon. They'll never find us in here. Shoot, I can't even find us in here. They probably gave up and are sitting at the top of the hill waiting for us to crawl home. I say we wait 'em out, stay safe."

"No," Vic said. "I think we better keep on moving. We camp out now, we're going to end up living out here. My only question is, where're we going? You even know where you're at?"

Ghia turned the ignition and the Rhino leapt forward a few feet. "Not exactly, but I think we're getting close to Dan's."

From the back, Jerry asked, "Dandy Dan?"

"No, not him," Vic said. "Another Dan."

"Another bald Dan. Mister Clean we call him," Ghia said.

"Because he's bald?" Jerry asked.

"No, because he's lemony fresh—yes, because he's bald." Ghia shot Vic a look that said, where'd you find these two? Vic allowed himself a shallow smile and gripped the dash as the ATV banged into another turn.

They worked their way down the back of the hill, dodging marijuana patches, fences, trees, and bramble. Other growers' dogs would announce their arrival and departure as they passed other dwellings—something Vic knew their pursuers would use like radar to triangulate their position. And Mongo would answer from his spot in back where Jerry still held on to his collar. Whether the bikers were chancing it through the forest—unlikely, given the rough path they were traveling—or flanking wide on established roads, he was certain the group that shot at them were doing their best to cut them off before they reached Highway 101.

Cardiff leaned on the hood of the rental, his legs crossed at the ankles, arms folded across his chest. He peered up at the stars and pondered his next move, chewing softly on his bottom lip. Doughboy was curled up in the passenger seat, some torn bags, newspaper, and paper towels laid out to soak up the blood that refused to stop flowing from his shotgun wounds. Aaron, Terry Naughton, Meth Master Mike, and the other two BBs all stood in a semi-circle in Ghia's small driveway.

Aaron spoke to the open air. "Can we beat 'em down the mountain?"

"Fuck, yes," Mike said, suddenly animated, thinking the question was directed to him. "They're tripping on the woods in the dark. You kiddin'? They may be stuck in there for hours, days even. You don't even know. It's fucking bramble in there. Bramble. You know what bramble is? They might not ever make it out."

"We want 'em to make it out, Mike," Terry said. "We need to talk with them, you know?"

Mike smiled at Terry's euphemism. "Oh yeah, I know."

Cardiff said, "What I think Aaron means is, are we going to

sit here on our asses and wait to see if they come crawling back, or are we going to take some action and root them out?"

"Shit," Mike said, pointing with authority at the dense foliage in front of him. "I dunno if we *can* get 'em outta there. They was fools to go in there in the first place. At *night*? In the dark? I always say don't throw bad money after good, you know what I mean?"

Cardiff lifted himself off the car. "No, Mike, I have no idea what you mean. Most everything that comes out of that stinking hole of a mouth makes no sense whatsoever."

"Look," Mike said. "I ain't one to—"

"Save it." Cardiff held up a hand in front of Mike's face. "I'm sure you think this is your turf, and that these boys here are your friends, but I assure you, I have no problem gutting you from your balls to your chin and leaving you right here on this cunt's doorstep. And they'll have no problem cheering me on."

Mike screwed his face into a scowl, but something about Cardiff's tone, his candor, told him the man was serious. He didn't say another word.

Cardiff turned toward Terry. "And what do you think? You're the head man here. This is your turf. What are they trying to accomplish?"

Terry didn't move his head as he spoke, he kept his eyes trained on the black woods in front of him, as though they might divine some secret. "They're trying to get out the back door. There's only two ways down the goddamn hill. One's the road, the other's the bush. If they head down, straight down, I think I know where they're heading."

"Well then, what are we waiting for?"

"You want somebody to hang here?" Aaron asked. "In case they do come back?"

"Nah, fuck it," Cardiff said. "Torch this place."

Aaron asked, "You serious?"

"Yeah, light it up."

"Whoa, whoa, whoa," Terry said. "You can't start a fire up here. You're in the middle of the redwoods, the whole fuckin' place will go up."

Cardiff looked disappointed. "Well, damn it. Leave the fat one with the buckshot in his ass. And somebody to drive him back. The rest of us should get going. The sooner I'm off this fucking mountain, the better."

The forest floor abruptly flattened out and the trees grew sparse. Ghia picked up what speed she could as they slalomed through the redwoods toward a soft yellow glow. As they neared, a small cabin took shape. Like most of the shacks on the hill, it was utilitarian and Spartan in its design.

"Is that the place?" Vic asked.

"That's it. Glorious, isn't it?"

As they neared the cabin, they heard the chaotic yips of tiny dogs. Chihuahuas, Vic figured. It sounded like there were a dozen of them. In the back, Mongo started to ebb and tug. Then they heard a deep, booming voice telling the dogs to shut up. Lights clicked on and illuminated the small building, and the furor of the little dogs continued.

As they pulled up to the spot, a hulking presence filled the door. A six-foot-five man, whose bald head was shaved so clean the light from the house shone off it like a beacon, stood a shotgun in his right hand and—just as Ghia killed the engine—he shook the gun with one hand and pumped a shell into the chamber. Mr. Clean. "Who's there?"

"It's me, Ghia, and I got Vic with me. Don't shoot, big guy."

Dan didn't lower the gun, he leaned into the darkness a little, trying to see past the headlights of the vehicle. He lifted the shotgun up, the butt seated in his shoulder and the barrel pointing at the headlights. "Who's that with you?"

"Jesus Christ, Dan, put down the gun. It's Ghia and Vic."

Dan lowered the shotgun and held it at his side, and the dogs reappeared at his feet. It turned out there were only three of them making all that noise. He shooed them inside, closed the door behind him, and turned back to the ATV. "Turn your lights off. Who's that with you?"

"Just a couple of friends of ours." Ghia killed the headlights and climbed out of the driver's seat. "What's with all the precaution, Dan?"

"It's late, you come rolling out of the backwoods. What the hell's going on?"

Vic climbed out more slowly, keeping an eye on the house. "You alone, Dan?"

"Yeah, pretty much. Why?"

A door behind Dan opened and the volume of the small dogs rose once again. Vic brought up the barrel of his .38 and sighted on the block of light filling the door jamb.

"Whoa, whoa, whoa. Vic, hold it—there's someone in there."

Vic didn't say anything or lower his gun. A shadow filled the door, followed by the slight figure of a woman.

"Trinity," Vic said. "Step out here, please."

"Hey, Vic." She sounded sheepish, embarrassed. She'd heard his voice and didn't want to come outside. Getting fired by Vic earlier that day still stung. But now, with a gun pointed at her, she looked confused, scared. "I don't know what you think, but I didn't say anything else, I wouldn't do anything to mess you—"

"Is there anybody else in there?"

"No, it's just me and the dogs."

"Dan, is there anyone else in there?"

"No, Vic. Fuck, put down the gun. What're you doing?"

"That's what you said last time. I'm asking you—is there anyone else in the house?"

Mongo's steady barks rose in intensity and frequency as the exchange continued. Trinity stood frozen beside the open door while the three small dogs yapped wildly at Vic, but maintained their stance at the cabin's threshold.

"Vic, nobody's here."

"Everybody in the house. Jerry, Piper, you too. And grab that bag." He took several long, steady strides to Dan's cabin, past Trinity, past the dogs, keeping his weapon raised the whole time. He stopped at the door and swung the barrel in first, securing the main room, then entered and did the same for the bedroom and bathroom.

Chapter Eighteen

Cardiff and Aaron leaned on the front hood of the rental in the Merkels' driveway, the well-armed neighbor. Aaron was smoking a cigarette and Cardiff swatted away wisps of smoke as they drifted into his face.

"Do you have to do that?"

"We're outside."

"I know, but if these hillbillies were watching, they'd see the glow. God knows they can probably smell that shit. Seriously, if you have that much of a death wish, I can just save you the time and put a bullet in your head right now."

Aaron looked at him and took a deep pull on the cigarette and let the smoke slowly spill past his lips. "Delicious," he said.

"You want to call Eric?"

"What are we going to tell him? It's not like we have good news."

"What are you talking about?" Cardiff said. "Of course we have good news. They're not here. That means we have them on the run. Practically cornered."

"Cornered somewhere on a mountain? Trust me, he don't wanna hear that shit. And don't mention the kid in the shack and Doughboy, that ain't good news either. Not everyone is turned on by a body count like you are. What he wants to hear is Jerry is dead and his little girl is in the trunk of our car and on the way home."

"You're in the wrong fucking business, Aaron." Cardiff drew a cell from his pocket. "I'm calling him."

* * *

Their interrogation had spun into the night. After the initial questioning, not much happened. They seemed to be waiting her out, or waiting on another member of their party. Barbara watched the two communicate, the old school biker and the Eastern Bloc gangster. They seemed ill-at-ease, both of them. Their awkwardness augmented by several rounds of coffee. Sometime, shortly after dark, Eric Tribban switched to beer, but Dmitri, the short, thick, greasy man, stuck to coffee. Twice their conversation became so embroiled they felt the need to step outside. A good sign, Barbara thought. If they didn't want her hearing information, maybe they were considering letting her live.

Barbara was having trouble keeping her head up. The intensity of keeping on high alert since she was taken from her home that morning was wearing her down. No food, no rest, and now she found herself in what was essentially a staring contest with her captors. As she began to blink, and those blinks morphed into nods, a pounding of footsteps thundered down the stairs. The biker without a name stuck his head around the corner.

"Eric, you got a phone call."

"I'm busy."

"It's from our friend up north."

Upon hearing this, Dmitri first squinted at Barbara to see if her eyes brightened, then he checked his phone. Barbara assumed he was a little hurt or troubled his phone didn't ring first.

Eric stood, stretched, and exited to take the call upstairs. He probably didn't want Dmitri hearing what he said either. He left Ollie standing between Dmitri and Barbara.

"Ollie?" Dmitri said. "May I please get one more cup of this delicious coffee?"

"I don't think there's any more. You drank it all."

"Perfect. Perhaps you could make me a new pot, yes?"

Ollie shrugged and strode across the room toward the corner door that led to the stairs. When he got close enough, Dmitri reached out and grabbed his forearm. "Take your time, eh?"

Ollie turned back and looked at Barbara, then at Dmitri. He was leaving his watch, but under the direction of someone superior. Not a direct superior, but someone he'd recognized today as being farther up the food chain than him. He left the room and started up the stairs.

"How old are you, Barbara?" Dmitri's accent curled now, lilting upward as though he spoke to a child. "Sixty? Sixty-five?"

Barbara offered a thin smile, not taking the bait. Eric had gone upstairs to deal with his underlings, intentionally leaving Barbara alone with Dmitri. They'd played good cop/bad cop for a while, but threats weren't working.

"You cut a fine figure for such a...matronly woman." Dmitri pushed himself up from where he sat, exaggerating a groan of exhaustion. "You are still *active*, aren't you? You know what I mean by active, don't you, Barbara?" He rapped his knuckles on the table. "Sex-u-ally?"

"So that's it? I'm supposed to be scared of you raping me with that tiny Russian dick of yours?"

"First of all..." Dmitri chuckled. "I'm not Russian. But that's okay. I believe ignorance is you Americans' chief export. And secondly..." He picked up a well-worn Louisville slugger that'd been leaning on the front window. The kind so many people have hidden behind their front door—the welcome bat. "It's not my tiny dick you should be worried about."

"Hey, before you and your posse get all settled in, I think you better tell me what the hell is going on." Danny Clean tried to slow the parade of intruders, but they paid no mind to his concerns and followed Vic into the cottage's main room.

Vic moved to each of the three windows on the walls of the tiny enclosure and checked them, then he returned to the bathroom, this time stepping in the tub and looking out the tiny porthole there. The small window looked like it hadn't been cracked in years. When he came back into the room, he said, "I need to borrow your ride."

"You've got to be kidding me. I'm not letting you take my car. Trinity told me about what happened today up at your place. I dunno what's up with you, Vic, but you're acting like an asshole."

"I'm taking your car. If you're smart, you'll come with us."

"I ain't going nowhere with you." Mr. Clean was big, thick, and tough-looking, but he was clearly shaken by Vic's presence.

"Then follow us in your truck. You won't be safe here."

"I'm not playing with you, Vic. What the fuck is happening?" He threw a thumb toward Jerry and Piper. "Who are these assholes?"

"Where are your keys?"

"Fuck you, man."

Vic lifted his .38 and pointed the barrel directly between Mr. Clean's eyes. "Keys."

"You gotta be kidding me."

Mongo let out a low growl. The little dogs stayed quiet.

"Keys," Vic said again. Then he lowered the barrel so his target was the middle of the man's thigh.

"They're on the hook behind the door."

"Ghia, grab 'em."

Ghia moved the front door and swung it shut. A row of keys hung on hooks in a neat horizontal row. "Which is which, Danny?"

"The one on the left is the F-150, the middle one—the one with the fob—is the Celica, and the big ring has the Escape."

"When'd you get an Escape?" Ghia asked. "I hear the new ones are nice."

"Ghia, please," Vic said. Then to Mr. Clean, "Can we all fit in the Escape?"

"I told you, Vic. I ain't going nowhere with you."

"Take the F-150 then. Hit the road."

"Hit the road? I ain't leaving my house. Fuck that. You haven't even told me what's going on."

"You know Terry Naughton, right?"

Mr. Clean's face blanched a little when he heard the name of the BB's Nomad president. "Yeah, I know who he is. So what?"

"Well, in a couple of minutes, him and a bunch of his crew are gonna come burstin' through that door looking for me and these two kids, and they're gonna kill anything or anyone who stands between them and what they want."

Mr. Clean looked confused. He bunched his grey eyebrows together causing a ripple of wrinkles across his expansive forehead. Trinity understood what Vic was saying, though. She stood behind Mr. Clean, her chin knocking downward like a metronome. Vic couldn't tell if she was nodding yes, or slipping into shock. She believed what Vic said, she'd heard the stories about him, knew there was something dangerous behind his quiet demeanor. He was charming, funny in his own way, even kind of handsome, but she never thought the quiet man who lived in the messy house on the hill was anything less than the devil.

"It's not an option, it's not a request. We're leaving either way. You wanna live? Take my advice. You wanna roll the dice? Go ahead. But, I'm telling you, they ain't in no negotiating mood." Vic stepped across the room and squatted down in front of the bag of weapons and supplies Jerry had dropped on the floor. He tucked the .38 into his belt and pulled the Glock 19 from its holster and dropped out the magazine. He reached in the bag and lifted out a box of ammo to top-off what he'd spent on cover fire at Ghia's cabin.

And that's when a round cut through the front window.

"Did ya hit anything?"

Terry Naughton, Billy BB, and Meth Master Mike had gone to Mr. Clean's cabin, while Cardiff and Aaron were watching the more obvious escape route, the front side of the hill, which ran through the Merkels' property. Geographically, it made more sense, but Terry's gut told him Vic and the kid would be rolling through this fool Dan's backyard. Besides, the Merkels were not only unfriendly with the other growers on the hill, they were rumored to be armed to the teeth with a stockpile of weapons suitable for the apocalypse. Better that cheesedick Cardiff camp out in front of the Merkels', maybe they'd all get lucky and Cardiff would catch a stray round or two.

Terry's hunch paid off. From their hiding spot in the woods, they saw several shadows move past the windows of Dan Clean's place. He hated that fucker Mr. Clean too. He was one of the more recent transplants to Humboldt County, a Johnny-come-lately to the marijuana business. Guys like him were a dime a dozen nowadays on the hill. Guys who showed up after the danger had subsided, after CAMP chilled out on their helicopter raids, after the feds cleaned out a lot of the Mexican cartel farmers. Shit, six months before the shit'll go legal. They had nothing to worry about but the locals, the ones who were there first. The ones who planted a flag. The pioneers. Guys like Terry.

"I don't know, I can't tell." He peered through the branches at the cabin. The lights were still on, but a window had been smashed by the bullet. There was no movement now. Everyone must be on the floor. "I hit a window. I can't see nothing moving though."

"Can you hear anything?" Mike asked. "I can't hear nothing."

"Maybe," Terry said, "if you shut up." One solitary dog barked. A higher pitched yelping, steady in rhythm and volume.

"That's them, for sure," Billy said. "That baldheaded fucker only has little dogs. Listen to that. That's a pit all right."

Terry kept his pistol raised, swinging the Sig Sauer P224 from the door to the window. "Keep your fucking eyes peeled on the sides, they might try to jump out another window."

"What do you think we're doing?" Mike said. "Jeez Louise, Ter. You think I don't know that? You think I'm out here for a breath of fresh air. I'm wanting to get home to Betty, so the sooner you shoot who you gotta shoot, the better."

"Billy?"

"Yeah."

"If Mike doesn't shut up, shoot him."

"You kidding?"

"Of course he's kidding. C'mon. You guys wouldn't shoot me here. You need me. I mean not now, but in other ways. It would be what they call an unnecessary risk, leaving me here. Killing me is just another headache you don't want."

"Who you trying to convince, Mike? Us or you?"

"Serious," Terry said. "Shut the fuck up." The Sig had been outfitted with night sights and Terry's right eye began to water as he refused to blink, the fluorescent green dots started to blur. "Where are you, motherfucker?"

As the seconds hammered slowly, Billy got up from his haunches and raised his Glock 21 beside Terry. "What do you want to do? Go in while I cover? You wanna lay some down and I'll go?"

"Y'all should just smoke 'em out," Mike said. He was still down on his knees, crouched behind Terry and Billy. "Toss an incendiary device in there. That's how SWAT does it."

"What'd I tell you, Mike? Shut the fuck up."

Chapter Nineteen

Eric Tribban stood in his kitchen on the second story of the building he owned. He listened to Cardiff's tiny voice on the cell phone pressed to his ear. The two BBs who lived with Eric in the back of the building lounged on the couch in the living room. They were sponges as far as Eric was concerned, but they did what he asked. Besides, they were all brothers. Dead BBs shared what they had with each other, even if the balance wasn't always even. As president, he didn't expect it to be a two-way street. He was always going to have more to share with his brothers than they had for him.

Ollie buzzed around him, too, preparing another pot of coffee for Dmitri. Ollie was one brother who never asked for anything from Eric. He wished the BBs had ten more just like him. The only thing Ollie ever asked was what else could he do for you. He wasn't the brightest of the bunch, but the Dead BBs weren't MENSA either.

"I can barely fucking hear you, man. Where are you?" Eric pinched the cell between his shoulder and his head so he could light a cigarette. "Are you sure that's safe? What if they hear you?...Okay, sure. Yeah, I know him. You're in good hands... Who got shot?...I don't know any Doughboy...Is Aaron with you?...Put him on." He waited a moment until he heard Aaron's voice. "You got shit under control?...Who's this Doughboy he's talking about? He's one of ours?...Oh yeah, all right. I remember him, sort of. Is he okay?...Well, shit. He'll probably be fine then. Hang on a sec." Eric peeked into the living room and saw his two henchmen embroiled in a video game. He looked behind him and saw Ollie wiping up spilled coffee grounds with a handful of paper towels. He placed a palm over the cell and said, "Um…who the fuck is downstairs with Dmitri and our guest?"

The two BBs on the couch looked up, game controllers still knitted in their hands, but it was Ollie who dropped what he was doing and bolted down the stairs.

Eric clicked off the phone. He stepped out of the kitchen, through the living room and stood at the top of the stairs, listening.

From the first level, Ollie let out an angry, *"FUCK!"*

After she wrestled the bat from Dmitri, Barbara beat him with it till he was unconscious or dead, she wasn't sure which, and she didn't wait to find out. He'd wagged it in front of her, taunting her as though it were a giant wooden phallus. She reached out and yanked it toward her and the surprised Dmitri toppled forward. Like a lot of tough guys, she found out he wasn't so tough. It was only seconds before she was up and swinging, cracking the greasy bastard in the head.

As soon as he was down, she went straight out the side door they'd brought her through and found herself in a small parking lot bordered with a cyclone fence. Ollie's van sat in front of her. It was the first time she got a good look at the innocuous white van. She wondered if the keys were still inside but didn't want to risk the sound of opening the door. The lot was littered with vehicles—broken down cars, hot rods, trucks, and motorcycles. Barbara opted for the fence.

When she hit the sidewalk, she started running. She wasn't sure which way to go, but she needed to put as much distance between her and the house as possible. She hadn't even reached the end of the block when she heard a muffled voice yell, "Fuck!"

* * *

Aaron held the phone in his hand and looked at it.

"What happened?" Cardiff said.

"He hung up."

"What'd he say?"

"I don't know. He hung up." Aaron handed the cell back to Cardiff. "We'll call him back when we have good news."

Aaron stubbed out his cigarette, and they sat for a few more moments watching the silent house.

"You gonna pick that up?" Cardiff asked.

"What? The butt? No."

"If something happens here, then that's evidence. Use your head, Aaron. Pick it up in case a fucking gunfight breaks out and we don't have time to get it after."

"Gunfight? You think it's fine to leave shell casings everywhere, but a cigarette butt is a problem?"

Cardiff didn't take his eyes off the house of his hand off his gun. "You don't wipe down your shells before you put 'em in your gun?"

Aaron bent down and picked up the cigarette butt. As he got back up, a gunshot echoed through the forest.

"You hear that?" Cardiff said.

"Yeah, but it ain't that unusual out here."

Then they heard two more.

"Get 'em on the radio." Cardiff said.

As soon as the window broke, all of them hit the floor. Jerry lay there, the smell of dust and lint from Mr. Clean's filthy carpet tickling his nose to the point of sneezing. He reached across the floor and squeezed Piper's arm. She turned her head toward him.

"You okay?" he whispered.

She nodded, cheek pressed to the carpet.

Mr. Clean started saying, "Oh no, oh God. Oh no, oh no."

"Is anybody hit?" Vic asked. "Ghia, you okay?"

Mr. Clean kept repeating the same words over and over. Vic sat up so he could see everyone. And everyone was looking back at him, everyone but Dan and Trinity. Mr. Clean had crawled to Trinity and was kneeling over her.

"Dan," Vic said. But Dan didn't reply. "*Dan*," he repeated.

"She's dead."

"You sure? Move. Move so I can see her."

Mr. Clean's voice was choked with sobs now. "Fuck you, Vic. Fuck you."

Vic motioned for Ghia to check Trinity, but as soon as Dan moved out of the way, it was clear she was dead. A bullet had pierced the side of her skull and her eyes were wide and blank.

Jerry listened to Mr. Clean's rhythmic sobs, waiting for a break that wouldn't come. Finally, he asked Vic, "How many do you think are out there?"

"I got no idea. I don't know how many there are period." Vic looked around the room, trying to see what he could use. There was a lamp on an end table illuminating most of the room. He pushed his back up against the front wall near the lamp. On the back of the cabin there was a large mirror, the kind big enough to give a false sense of size to any room. He could see the shot-out window in its reflection. Vic peeled off his coat and slowly lifted it in front of the lamp, causing a murky shadow to splay across the back wall. Two shots rang out and their bullets pounded the drywall.

Vic had seen the muzzle flash in the mirror. He didn't know where all of them were, but now he knew where one of them was. The one with the gun.

Then they heard something else. The crackle of a radio. Jerry whispered that he thought they'd been cornered by the police.

But Vic shushed him. He knew better. No police came up here. Not unless they were ripping down people's grows. Vic knew it was them, the BBs. And if they needed a radio, they weren't all gathered outside. He also knew whoever was shooting at them—whoever killed Trinity—was calling for reinforcements.

Chapter Twenty

"The radio's going off."

Terry stayed his firing stance. "I know, dumbass, I can hear it."

"What do you want me to say?" Billy spoke in an unnecessary stage whisper. All of their ears rang from Terry firing the Sig Sauer.

"I'm fucking busy, Billy. Tell them to get their asses over here."

With his hand cupped over the radio, Billy said, "Roger, hello, over."

A static-filled voice crackled back. "What's going on down there? Are you firing? We hear gunshots. Was that you?"

"Roger. Ten-four."

Terry, still aiming at the cabin, interrupted. "Talk like a normal person, you're confusing them."

"Hello?" the radio said. "Hello?"

Billy took a moment to think before keying the mic again. "Yeah, that's us. Over. We're at Danny Clean's place. I think we got 'em pinned down."

"Who the fuck is Danny Clean?"

"It's the only other place they said they'd come down. Mike said it's a quarter to a half-mile down the gravel road off to the left here, remember?" Aaron pointed behind them at the road they'd come in.

Cardiff said, "This was a stupid plan. Why the fuck don't we have someone with us that knows the layout. I mean, shit, all three of those hillbillies are *from* here. They should be showing *us* how to get there. We're supposed to drive around this fucking mountain in the dark?"

Aaron turned to face Cardiff. "I'm going to tell you one more time, these guys are my brothers. Cool it with the hillbilly shit."

Cardiff snickered as he spun toward the car. "Or what?"

"Or we'll leave you here."

Cardiff stopped before he opened his door and looked at Aaron across the roof of the car. He knew what that meant. That meant leave him in a hole. "Aaron," he said. "Don't be so serious. Don't worry, I'm here to solve the problem, not become the problem. Besides, you haven't seen the worst of me yet. It can get quite…exhilarating."

Ollie leaned over Dmitri.

Eric asked, "Is he dead?"

"Fuck no, he's not dead." Ollie slapped him in the face, but Dmitri was out cold. A lump on his right temple grew and seemed to pulsate on its own. Two more contusions on his forehead had small cuts and thin lines of blood trickled into his hair.

"Then wake him the fuck up." Eric stepped closer and kicked Dmitri in the leg. "Actually, no. I'll wake him up. Ollie, you go find this bitch. And get those assholes upstairs to help you."

Barbara was on the move now. She knew she was in the East Bay, but she wasn't sure where. She was less convinced she was in Oakland. She loped along the street, a sharp pain driving up her leg into her hip. She wasn't sure what caused the pain; there were so many sore spots and bruises she'd received since that morning. She kept looking over her shoulder to check for headlights or people on foot. Finally, two beams of light broke over her shoulder. She spun around. It was a bus. Thank Christ, a goddamn city bus. She ran forward, searching for a stop ahead of her. As the bus neared, she turned and waved frantically. The driver pulled over and opened the door.

In a tired and flat voice, he said, "Stop's another half-block." He made a slight motion with his chin to indicate the upcoming stop.

Barbara was out of breath, panting as she spoke. "I...I know...I just need...need to get on." She grabbed the rail and climbed the steps and began to check her pockets for money.

The driver watched her, having seen this pantomime countless times before. After a few moments, a sigh, then a disgusted look, he hooked a thumb over his shoulder and told her to sit down. The hydraulics wheezed as the bus slipped into gear. It was the sweetest sound Barbara had heard all day.

She took a bench near the back. The vessel was empty, not one single rider. She recognized the bus now, its colors, the logo. She was in the city of Alameda. Or—more importantly—the island of Alameda. She knew Oakland pretty well, having spent plenty of time here in her forties, but Alameda not so much. For a brief period in her late twenties, she'd dated a guy who lived in Alameda, but that was a long time ago. The city had changed so much. The whole world had changed.

Alameda was an island city sitting in San Francisco Bay right beside Oakland. Separated by a rivulet of salt water and either the Webster Tunnel or one of two bridges, the city itself was nearly indistinguishable from Oakland. Same look, same feel, same style housing. Oakland was part of Alameda County, but Alameda had its own police department, city hall, and mayor.

Barbara wasn't sure which way she was heading on the island, north or south. She saw the street signs, knew she was on Santa Clara, but wasn't sure what the declining address numbers meant to her. "Excuse me," she called from the back. She saw the driver's eyes flick up in his rearview, but his head remained still. "How can I get back to Oakland?"

The driver returned his eyes to the road and said, "Webster, three stops."

There were two ends of Alameda, the south end attached with three bridges, or the north end with one tunnel running under a sliver of the bay directly to Downtown Oakland. The Webster Tube. Another bus might have taken her through the tunnel, but running the tube on foot would be a big risk. She knew they'd be looking for her and there were only a few places she could exit the island.

The Webster stop approached, the street was lit brighter than the others with its fast-food joints open late and all-night gas stations. Barbara stood as the bus slowed and asked the driver for a transfer for the next bus, but he ignored her. She shoved her way out the back door when the bus finally stopped, the cold night air biting into her exposed arms. She had no jacket, no purse, no money, no phone. She looked down at her feet. At least she got out of there with her shoes on.

Piper was biting into her lower lip trying to hold back her hysteria. Jerry couldn't help her. He didn't know how. Trinity's blood had spread across the floor, but the flow slowed now. Any life in her had completely drained out. The man who'd been introduced to them as Mr. Clean was covered in her blood as he sat cross-legged and cradled her head in his arms. Jerry felt helpless, his fear palpable, cold and tight in his throat, pressing on his chest. Even the dogs knew to stay silent, keeping their breaths as shallow as they could.

"Vic," Jerry whispered.

Vic sat with his back pressed to the front wall, right below the window that'd been shot out. He kept his eyes on the mirror on the opposite wall while he pressed his left index to his lips, signaling Jerry to keep quiet.

"What are we going to do?" Jerry pressed.

Vic ignored him, his focus acute, pinpointed on the reflection. He breathed through his nose, visualizing his next move, and waiting. Finally, a flicker of movement in the space he'd been watching. He leapt up, the Glock already cocked and extended, and fired twice into the darkness. He dropped back down the cabin's floor awaiting return fire. None came.

From outside, they heard a shout. "Holy fuck! Terry, Terry. You okay? Holy fuck!"

Vic returned Jerry's look now and shot him a wink. "One down," he mouthed.

They all sat quietly as they listened to someone call Terry's name over and over. He was dead or dying, for sure. Vic kept looking at the mirror, waiting for more movement but he saw nothing.

"Who the fuck is Terry?" Jerry asked.

Piper said, "I hope it's not who I think it is."

"Who?" Jerry said.

"The only Terry I know that's with the guys up here is president of the Nomad Chapter." Her voice quivered. It sounded thick and coated with mucus. "Mean fucker too."

Danny Clean looked up from his grief. "Great. We're fucked."

Vic didn't see it that way. He knew they were now without direction. A platoon without a leader. "Nah, we just cut off the head. They're gonna be scrambling. And when they do, we're making a break for it."

Ghia said, "Best thing I've heard all day."

The radio began to crackle as soon as Cardiff and Aaron were in the car. They'd heard two more shots echo in the distance and now the broken voice yelled at them through the radio's tiny speaker. Aaron grabbed the two-way because Cardiff was behind the wheel.

"I can't read you. Stop yelling."

What followed was an even more intense, higher volume burst.

"I can't make out a thing he's saying," Cardiff said. "How much farther is it?"

"I don't know, I've never been out here before. He said less than half a mile. There should be a mailbox or a driveway or something."

The radio kept squelching in Aaron's lap.

"Did he just say someone's dead?"

"I can't tell what the fuck he's saying. Keep your eyes open for this place."

The radio blasted again. "Terry's dead. That's what he's saying. I think it's Billy. Shit."

"Billy's dead?" Cardiff asked.

"No, Billy is the one talking. He's saying Terry's dead."

"Is he sure? Who else is with 'em. Tell him to put the tweaker on the line."

Aaron lifted the radio to his mouth. "Billy? You read me?"

There was an unintelligible response, the crackle so dense now it sounded like a buzzsaw.

"Billy? Is Mike there? Put Mike on."

After a moment, Mike's voice came on. It came through better than Billy's, but not by much. "Yello? You got me. Who's this?"

Cardiff snatched the radio from Aaron's hand. "Who the fuck do you think it is? Where are you idiots?"

"We're at Mr. Clean's. Terry caught one. A bad one. Real bad. How long till you guys are here?"

"We don't know where the fuck we are." Cardiff squinted at the dirt road and out the window at the sky above, as though the stars might pinpoint his location. "Can't you guys send up a flare or something?"

Aaron tried to interrupt. "Ask him how Terry looks. If he's

gonna be okay."

Cardiff ignored the request. "How're we supposed to find you?"

Mike looked at Billy and Terry, cloistered on the ground, and reached down for the Sig, plucking it from Terry's limp hand. "You ready?" he said into the radio.

Cardiff came back over. "Ready for what?"

Mike said, "Listen out your window."

Cardiff's window was already down, but he hit the brakes and killed the engine and hushed Aaron, who wasn't making any noise anyway. In the distance, they heard one clear shot. Then another.

"Fuck," Aaron said. "That's behind us. We fuckin' passed 'em."

Chapter Twenty-One

They'd split the arsenal inside the cabin. Ghia had the .38 and Dan cradled the shotgun while Vic still held up the Glock, ready to fire. Vic said, "This is it. Here's what we're gonna do. Dan, you let go a couple into the woods. Just get up and blast that thing, they'll lay down, don't worry. Jerry, you take the bag and Piper. Ghia's gonna follow with cover fire. We get our asses to the Ford and get the hell out. Okay? Dan, where're the keys?"

Dan didn't answer.

"Dan? The keys? We need the keys."

"They're on a hook by the fridge, beside the oven mitts."

Ghia reached up and pulled the Ford's key fob from its hook and tossed it to Jerry.

"What about Trinity?" Dan asked.

Vic looked at Trinity's body, now alone on the cabin's floor, her pallor gone from white to an inescapable light blue. "She's dead. We leave her."

"We can't leave her. This is my house. *My home.* This is a fucking homicide. I can't leave a body on my rug. I'll lose everything."

"Look," Vic said. "You gotta make a decision, whether you want to live or not. You want to die here? 'Cause that's what's gonna happen. You get your ass to safety, then you worry about the fucking fallout. You didn't fucking kill her, did you? No. You gotta snap out of it."

Dan stared down at Trinity's body.

"Dan? You hear me? We get out. There ain't nothing more we can do here. Now when I say go—"

He was cut off by the sound of a gunshot. The five of them looked at each other, their eyes bright, sober, and clear. Then came another shot. And another. They echoed upward, sounding almost distant. Nothing in the cabin was hit, no ricochets, as though the shooter was aiming elsewhere.

"Let's do it," Vic said. "Dan, let a few go into the woods. You guys ready?"

But Dan didn't move. The shotgun stayed cradled in his lap. He wouldn't look away from Trinity.

"Dan! Get the fuck up or hand the shotgun to Jerry."

Dan looked up. His face tightened and he leapt onto his feet, spinning with the Remington leveled near his hip. "Fuck you," he cried and he fired out the broken window, the flash off the barrel briefly illuminating the woods like a crack of lightning.

The other four sprang into action too. Each of them scrambling into a chaotic line, boots scuffing on the hardwood floor, breath wrung out of their lungs. Vic took the door first. As soon as it swung open, Mongo and the little dogs bolted. Vic saw them disappear out of his peripheral vision, but he couldn't call after them. He stayed in motion, his Glock held out in front of his face. Jerry followed with the bag of supplies slung over his shoulder and Piper's elbow pinched in his hand. She wore the leather pouch containing the cash from their score, it flopped at her back. And lastly, Ghia followed, clutching Vic's .38.

"Go, go, go," Vic cried. He paused outside the door to let the others file past, then he popped two shots into the thicket where he'd last fired.

Dan exited his cabin last, the shotgun's butt against his shoulder now. His fired again, the thunderous boom somehow crisper in the open air.

Vic heard the Ford Escape's doors opening and he began to sidestep to the vehicle. "Dan, let's go."

Dan stood with his feet planted apart as he pumped another

round into the chamber. Before he could raise the barrel to the woods, another shot rang out, accompanied by a flash in front of him. A slug tore through his chest, driving him backward into the front wall of his own house. He tried to yell, but the only sound he made was a grunt. The shotgun curdled back into its earlier position in his lap. Vic fired at the flash, but another shot rang out a split second later, this one hitting Dan in the head. Vic kept firing at the bushes till he reached the Escape.

Jerry was already in the driver's seat with the engine running. There was no way to cut the lights as they pulled out. They heard more shots tear into the car as the wheels found purchase on the gravel road.

Ollie gripped the wheel of Eric Tribban's Charger and wrung it with his hands. He knew he wouldn't be blamed for the woman escaping, but he somehow still felt guilty, responsible. It was the Russian, or whatever the fuck he was, it was his fault. Who lets themselves get overpowered by a woman? An old woman at that. Ollie couldn't understand how it happened, how Dmitri let himself get that close to her. What an amateur, he thought. When Ollie saw him lying there, unconscious and bleeding, he wanted to kick him in the face.

He'd already zig-zagged through the neighborhood, giving special attention to the park and corner store, but there were a million places for her to hide. She could hop a fence, wait it out till morning in someone's backyard, knock on a damn door and beg for help. If she believed her life was at stake, she'd be desperate enough to try anything. Unless, thought Ollie, unless she believed it wasn't *her* life at stake. If the woman thought she might still be able to save her son, then what would she do? He thought about it a moment, hooked a U-turn on Central, and started speeding back toward Webster. She'd want to get the hell off this island, that's what she'd do.

* * *

Barbara looked up Webster Street for an Oakland-bound bus, but the street was empty. No traffic, no people. Only two sets of headlights, and they both turned before they reached her. She had no idea what time it was and if the buses were even running at this hour. After another minute, she gave up and decided to run. She'd make it through the tube, she knew people in Oakland. An old boyfriend, Palo, lived near Chinatown. Jerry had a friend near there too, Richard, who lived on 7th and Alice for as long as she could remember. They'd help her. She'd get a hold of Vic, warn him, see if they'd already gotten to Jerry. No way she could go to the cops, they'd only fuck everything up. If those bikers were still holding her son up in Humboldt, they'd kill him the second they knew she brought in the authorities. This way, at least there was a chance. As long as she could talk to Vic, there'd always be a chance.

Her clip turned to a jog. She neared the entrance to the tunnel and slipped down the cement steps to the railed walkway, a raised sidewalk spanning the length of the Webster Tube. It bowed low in the middle as it ducked under the Bay's causeway above. As she started in, it was impossible to see the other side, there was only more tunnel. Her lungs burned while she fought back her exhaustion and pushed herself through the tube. Each step a hardship, but each step bringing her closer to the other side. That was her only goal, the next step. One after another till she saw the street lights of Oakland peeking down the end of the tunnel.

By the time Cardiff and Aaron found the driveway to Mr. Clean's cabin, their prey had long since gone. They found Mike and Billy kneeling over Terry Naughton in the parcel of light emanating through the shot-out window of the house. Dan Clean lay unattended a few feet away, on his back with his eyes wide and blank.

Cardiff leaned over Clean first. "Damn, I can see why they call him Mr. Clean. He looks just like him. Well, he ain't clean anymore. Nothing's gonna scrub that hole out, that's for sure. Look at him, Aaron, he's got the eyebrows and everything."

Aaron had already joined the other two. "How's he?"

"I dunno," Mike said. Billy was pumping on his chest and Mike kept pulling back his eyelids. Neither of them seemed to know what they were doing, but the mere pantomime of what they thought they should do stifled the reality of the situation.

Aaron grabbed Terry's wrist and felt the heaviness, the limp lifelessness. It wasn't cool, yet, but its warmth was dissipating. He knew as soon as his fingers made contact.

"That guy's dead," Cardiff said over their shoulders. He stood, bent over with his hands resting on his thighs. "C'mon, we better get outta here. Those fuckers are probably on the 101 by now."

Billy looked up at Cardiff, his eyes bloodshot with rage and grief. "We ain't leaving him. Where's the car?"

"Oh hell no. We're leaving him. We're leaving both of them. Fucking dogs can sort it out. We have to go."

The Dead BB stood up from his friend, his brother and leader, and puffed his chest out at Cardiff. "He's ours. We ain't leaving him, no matter what."

"Shit," Cardiff said.

Roland Mackie sat bolt upright in bed. He'd been dreaming again. Another bad one. His head pounded as he slapped the nightstand in search of the clock. Two-forty-seven. Goddamn it. He craved a cigarette. He hadn't thought about smoking one in years.

Roland tried to piece together the nightmare that'd startled him awake, but there was nothing. No shape, no form, only a face. However unfocused, he knew who'd invaded his dreams. Victor Thomas. Wasn't the first time either. He'd come to realize these dreams weren't premonitions, they weren't repressed memories, they weren't much of anything except a crystalized hatred of the man he'd come to view as his nemesis.

He got up, made his way to the bathroom, and pissed. After gulping some water from the tap, he glanced at his shadowy reflection in the dim light. Dawn would arrive soon. He'd have an earnest chance to catch up to Thomas. It'd been years since he'd popped up on the radar. Now Mackie might be able to take him out of his dreams and place him in an investigation, and, like a gift, he'd have a chance to start over. A chance to right some wrongs, to balance the scales of justice. He took a deep breath and wondered how the hell he was going to get back to sleep again.

Vic hunched over the wheel as he eased the Ford into Garberville. The four of them roughly in the same positions they held in the Rhino—Jerry and Piper in back, Ghia riding shotgun, and Vic behind the wheel. The tiny town seemed quiet, but he knew any open eyes would be upon them. He couldn't be sure if word was out, if the BBs had scouts out looking for them, but anybody who was awake at this hour would be curious. It was part of the town's suspicious makeup. He noticed some street kids peeking in a dumpster. They stopped what they were doing as soon as the headlights turned onto the street. Even though it was a tiny rural town, constant transient traffic forced most business owners to padlock their dumpsters. When Vic turned the corner, one kid had the dumpster lid pried as far as the chain would allow while the other reached inside for what he could with one arm. The Escape spooked them and the first kid dropped the steel lid on the other's arm. Both turned and squinted into the SUV's headlights like trapped raccoons.

"Jesus," Ghia said. "Ain't they pretty."

"Don't make eye contact," Vic said. "I don't want 'em to remember us."

Jerry leaned in from the back. "Fuck, this town is crawling with tweakers, man. I can feel their eyes on us."

"We're just getting gas," Vic said. "We'll be gone in a heartbeat."

Vic pulled into a Chevron station and up to the pump. He hopped out and started punching buttons on the automated payment kiosk.

From the rear, Piper said, "I fuckin' hate this town so much. What a shithole." She knew the place from riding up here with her father. Endless waiting and nothing else to do. For Piper, boredom was one of the worst fates.

"Didn't seem so bad the other day," Jerry said. He glanced at the closed Blue Moon Café, the rowdy bar where he met Ripper. "Lotta hippies, but not too bad."

"It's alright," Ghia said. "It's the biggest burg around when you're on the hill, so it's kind of a make-do situation." She powered down her window and called out to Vic. "What's the hang up?"

"It'll only take a card. No cash after hours."

She didn't need to ask him. She knew he had no bank account. Vic was as far off the grid as you can get. "How 'bout you two. Who's got a card?"

The two younger people stared back at her. Piper felt the useless pouch of cash pressing into the small of her back. "I don't have anything," she said. "I don't even have a bank card."

"Seriously? This is a life and death thing here." She waited another second, but knew no card was forthcoming. "I'm dealing with children," she said as she dug a card from a tiny billfold she kept in her back pocket and handed it out the window to Vic. "You're lucky," she told him. "You got a responsible grownup in the car."

"Oh yeah, I feel lucky." He returned to the pump and completed the transaction. Once the nozzle was in the car, he looked through the rear glass and saw someone standing across the street in a doorway. The figure was still as the dead, but there was no question, he was watching the car. Vic looked back at the digits flipping on the pump. Five gallons, six gallons, seven... Why the fuck didn't Danny Clean keep this thing full? Didn't he know that was the smartest thing to do? The figure watching reached into his pocket and pulled out a cell. Vic saw the phone's glow light up the man's face. Just another gaunt cretin. Then, without taking his eyes off Vic and the Ford, the man lifted the cell to his ear.

"Y'all heading south?"

The voice surprised Vic. It was reedy and Southern. The lazy twang of friendly conversation lolled behind him. Vic spun around, remembering his pistol was in the truck.

"Shit's stacking up if you go north. I mean, not Eureka, but the pass, in Oregon, I hear the weather's messed up the pass something awful."

Vic didn't say anything. He didn't move. He tried to get a read on the man, to gauge whether he was an annoying stranger or an agent of the club. The man was dressed well, for late night Garberville anyway.

"You heading that way? Or you heading south?"

"Neither. We're just going home." Vic spun the gas cap into place and walked to the driver's door without turning his back on the man. He climbed in, fired the engine, and drove away leaving the curious stranger standing by the pump.

Chapter Twenty-Two

Vlad walked into Eric's place and wrinkled his nose as though he smelled something bad.

"Where is he?"

The man who'd greeted him at the gate, the same man who'd waved him in and guided him into his parking spot like a he was guiding a jumbo jet into a terminal, pointed his finger at the staircase to the right. The man hadn't spoken since Vlad walked in. Vlad guessed big fuckups like this were solemn occasions for bikers. Silence being their way of saying sorry as they waited for the boom of blame to swing 'round to them. Rightly so.

Vlad took the stairs two at a time, noting there were no pictures on the scarred walls. The ancient green carpet on the stairs was stiff with crust and filth, an overpowering scent of cigarettes, mildew, and, of course, weed.

At the top of the stairs was a kitchen to the left and on the right was a living room with a long couch. Dmitri was on the couch with a pack of frozen vegetables on his forehead. He looked at Vlad with the one eye the packet of broccoli florets wasn't covering. "*Chto proiskhodit?*"

"English, please," Vlad said. "Our hosts don't like it when we don't speak English. It makes them think we are trying to hide something." Truth was, Vlad had all but abandoned his native tongue. There was something old world about it he wanted to leave behind; it wasn't part of the new Vladimir Lysenko—American entrepreneur. "Why don't you tell *me* what's going on?"

Dmitri removed the packet of frozen vegetables so Vlad could see his eye. It was swollen shut and the brow was split under a sizable divot of flesh on his forehead.

"Oh, my goodness. She really got you, huh?"

"It's worse on the back of my head. I think I have a concussion."

"Oh, you definitely have a concussion. Especially if she knocked you out."

"I should be at the doctor's."

"No. No doctor. I think you'll be fine. You want to smoke, maybe? It'll help with the pain."

"Fuck no. I hate that shit. What I need is a drink."

Vlad called over his shoulder to the kitchen. "Eric? You have something for Dmitri to drink? Some vodka maybe?"

Eric called out from the kitchen. "I already told him. Whiskey only. Or tequila. I think we got some tequila."

"Whiskey then," Vlad said. He sat down on the coffee table in front of Dmitri and did his best to look concerned for his friend, but it wasn't a concussion that worried him. "You want to tell me how a little old lady managed to overpower you, knock you out, and get away with our money?"

Dmitri groaned like he'd already been asked this question too many times. "She didn't have our money."

"Then where is it?"

"I don't know. She didn't tell us. I'm thinking she didn't know."

"But you don't know for sure."

"No, but I'm pretty sure."

"Pretty sure," Vlad repeated. "Not one hundred percent sure." He took his thumb and jammed it straight into the raw wound above Dmitri's eye. Dmitri cried out but didn't fight back. Vlad pulled back his thumb and said, "You know you put us in a bad spot here." He looked over his shoulder to see if anyone from the kitchen was listening and added, "I wanted you to finish the interview by yourself. I needed her to tell you what

153

she knows without all these ears in the room, you know? Now she's going to be back in their hands when—*if*—they find her. Do you understand the problem there?"

Dmitri didn't, but he nodded anyway.

Vlad leaned in close so he couldn't be heard in the kitchen. "Dmitri, what did she say about the money?"

Dmitri turned down his lower lip and shook his head. "Nothing, she didn't say nothing."

"Did she tell you how much the boy took?"

"I told you. She didn't say nothing."

"Nothing? Not how much? You couldn't get her to say an amount?"

"Nothing."

Vlad leaned back and studied his friend. He raised his eyebrows, halfway expecting Dmitri to part with a little more information, something he was holding back. Eric entered the room with three shot glasses pinched between his fingers and a bottle of Jack under one arm. Vlad looked at the whiskey and said, "That's it? You don't got nothing better?"

Eric didn't respond. He sat down the three glasses beside Vlad on the coffee table and filled each to the brim. They lifted their glasses and silently threw back the liquor.

While Eric refilled them, Vlad asked, "Can I talk to you in the kitchen for a moment?"

They both smiled at Dmitri in feigned condolence and carried their second shot into the kitchen, leaving Dmitri on the couch with his.

Vlad spoke first. "Look, no offense, but I don't give a shit about your daughter. I know family is important, but so is business. I just hope you understand we need to have that money back."

"What're you trying to say?"

"I'm saying I hope you're not holding back in the search, worried if she's going to get caught in the crossfire. I mean, she's the one who put herself there. In fact, as I understand it, she's the reason this whole fucking mess happened. Without her, I'd still be holding my two hundred grand, right?" When Vlad mentioned the amount, he peered into Eric's eyes, but the man stared straight back at him. No sign of guilt, no trace of dishonesty. Vlad couldn't read him. Maybe he was lying about the total, maybe not.

"We're going to get them. All of them. We're going to bring back Piper and that piece of shit alive, and we're going to peel their skin off inch by inch till you have your money. I give you my word."

Now Vlad was more confident he was being fed bullshit. Whenever someone "gave their word" he knew he was being lied to. He hated that phrase. It meant nothing to him.

"Even though this is your daughter?"

"Stepdaughter."

"Stepdaughter?"

"Yeah, what'd I just say?"

"What about the mother? Maybe she could help reach the child?"

"Forget it. The mother's long gone."

"What about this Vic I keep hearing about? Cardiff says he's a problem. Maybe *the* problem."

"Oh, we know who he is. We know all about him. Don't worry, we're gonna take care of Vic. He ain't coming back. He ain't even getting off the hill."

"I hope so," Vlad said.

"You don't have to hope, you can take that shit to the bank."

"That's what you said about my two hundred thousand."

As the 101 wound down and the space around the freeway opened up again, Vic's mind began to drift and he thought about Barbara. He thought of her eyes, warm and reassuring, her raspy but playful voice, and her laugh. Then, his memories shifted in the direction they usually did when he thought about her. Like the cat you're petting turning on you and hissing, the memories turned sour. They turned to Fulton Street.

When he thought about the night it happened, the memories boiled up as emotions. It wasn't like framing a picture in your mind's eye, or replaying a scene from a movie, it was visceral, gut-twisting. His stomach would clench and bile would rise and he knew he was back in that room, laid out on the floor, knowing he was going to die.

He'd gone to Fulton Street that night to get back something he felt was his. In the mid-nineties, Mexican cocaine had glutted the market and Vic and his partners began to move heroin by the pound. The problem with the drug business was being in the drug business. You couldn't count on anyone or anything going the way it was supposed to. You'd think—further up the food chain—the little headaches would disappear, but no, the stakes were only higher. There were still rip-offs and short shipments, late buyers and slow payers. There were cutthroat dealers, crooked and bumbling law enforcement, and, worst of all, addicts. The myth about not getting high off your own supply was just that, a myth. It was usually drug use that brought people into the business, so drug abuse was systemic. Especially at the top. The stress and pressure from making these kinds of deals eventually ate away at the player's resolve, and they succumbed to something or everything. And that was the problem with Fulton Street. The people they'd been dealing with were stone-cold junkies.

Ray and Shoshana Morillo had two kids, fifteen and nine. It turned out to be a blessing the older one was cursed with junkie parents. He couldn't stand being at home. The filth, the dirty needles, the constant parade of strangers. Ronny Morillo spent as much time as possible out of that house. And on August twenty-ninth, that's exactly where he was. Elsewhere. His sister, Alani, wasn't so lucky. Ronny didn't have to endure what his little sister and parents did. He didn't have to see what Vic saw.

Vic thought about that Thursday evening often. The inerasable August twenty-ninth of ninety-six. It remained vivid, all the details, even the unimportant ones. He'd stopped for a pork bun at his favorite Chinese bakery on Clement Street on his way over, but they were sold out and he proceeded to the Morillos' on an empty stomach. He was stalling. He didn't even want to go to the Morillos' that night. He was going to have to talk hard to Ray, maybe scare him a little. He didn't like playing hard ass. A shitty part of the job he didn't enjoy.

The sun was setting and the night was surprisingly clear. Usually by that time the fog had worked its way past Ocean Beach and pushed its way up Fulton Street and into the city. Vic parked, a few blocks away as was his precautionary habit, and he watched the sky down at the end of the Fulton—where Golden Gate Park met the Pacific Ocean—turn a postcard orange. He knew dealing with the Morillos was unpredictable, so he'd brought his snubnose .38. He felt good though, hopeful the most dysfunctional family in America had his money for the three pounds of black Mexican tar he'd dropped off nearly four weeks ago.

He jogged up the few marble steps to their front door and pounded hard with the side of his fist. No noise from inside. Usually there was music, a TV, one of their customers coming or going. This time, nothing. It occurred to Vic that he'd knocked too hard. Maybe the patented "cop knock" kicked in Ray Morillo's vague sense of caution and he didn't want to answer the door. Vic knocked again, this time in a more playful way. The ol' shave and a haircut. He listened and heard some feet padding across the hardwood toward the entrance. The door swung open. No one was there, the foyer was empty. Vic heard an anguished wail from deep inside the home. "Shoshana?" he said. More out of reflex than anything. He leaned in and called out her name again. That's when the hand came out from behind the door and pulled him inside. He reached for his .38, but the barrel of another gun was jammed into his forehead. A man with a thick Spanish accent said, "Get down on the ground. Lay flat. Spread you hands and you legs."

The .38 was yanked from Vic's jacket. He tried to speak, to ask where Ray Morillo was, and he was answered with the tip of an expensive-looking cowboy boot. He turned his head to avoid more blows and the same boot pressed down on top of his head, pushing his cheek to the floor.

Another voice asked in Spanish who the visitor was and the man with the pointed boots admitted he didn't know. The other man said something like, "Let him join the family." But Vic was never really sure.

They dragged him into the back room, the place where the Morillos did most of their business, and Vic saw what had been going on. Blood flecked on the walls, blood pooled on the floor. Ray Morillo sat with one eye swollen shut and a head wound bleeding into the other eye. His back was flat against the wall and he seemed to be weeping. Shoshana lay on the floor in front of him, curled up in a fetal position. Her cries were open and loud. It took a moment for Vic to see, but Shoshana appeared to be missing two fingers. She held her left wrist tightly with her right hand and her left hand bled so badly it was hard to assess the damage. It wasn't until Vic saw the two fingers near his feet he was actually sure that's what'd happened. She thrashed and convulsed with pain.

The man behind Vic shoved him down by the shoulders and whipped him once across the back of the head with his pistol barrel once he was down. Vic kept quiet, trying to calibrate what was happening. Ray appeared to be in shock and wouldn't lift his head. There were only the two of them. Ray and Shoshana. No kids. Where was Ronny? Where was Alani?

The man with the pointed boots repositioned himself in front of Vic and asked, slow and deliberate, first in Spanish, then in English, "Who are you?"

"I'm a friend."

The man slapped Vic so hard it felt like he loosened some

teeth. Then he asked the question again.

"No, motherfucker," Vic said. "Who are *you*?"

The man with the pointed boots sneered and lifted his pistol to Vic's head. It wasn't a threat.

"No, no, no, no, no," the other man said, holding out his hand. Then they spoke in Spanish, too quickly for Vic to grasp. But as best he could figure, they wanted more information before they killed him. The other man stepped in front of the man with the pointed boots and squatted down to meet Vic eye to eye.

"You have walked into a real mess, my friend. If these people are your friends, then I'm sorry for you. You must know what..." The man seemed to think for a moment, trying to find the right word. "...shits they are. We are going to kill them. I think you know that too. What we want to know is, who are you really? You are not a friend. People like this, they don't have friends. And if you are a customer, we want to know if you know about our business."

Another voice came from the back of the room. An American voice. "If you wanna know who he is, then take out the fucker's wallet and look at his goddamn driver's license."

Vic peered over the squatting man's shoulder to see where the voice was coming from, but what he first saw was Alani. A man's forearm snaked around her neck and held her tight. Her eyes were wide and lit up with fear. She was bruised, both her face and body. Vic could see, even from where he sat, her right arm was broken. An unnatural bend above the wrist looked inflamed and painful. The arm hung at her side.

The man holding her grinned at Vic.

At first Vic thought the man may be some kind of security guard. His navy blue uniform looked official. But as his eyes settled on the man, he realized it was no security guard—he was a cop. An SFPD officer. Badge, patch, and gun.

"Yeah, shitbird. You waking up?" The policeman reached down with his free hand and squeezed the young girl's wrist right above the break. She screeched in agony. "You coming to

Jesus yet, stranger? You ready to tell us just what the fuck you're doing here?"

He told them exactly what he was doing there. The pounds of tar, the owed money, everything. No point in not telling them. But they didn't believe him. They thought he concocted the story. Vic quickly assessed they weren't in the heroin business, they were in the coke business. Ray and Shoshana and been double dipping, selling through the front door and stealing out the back. Vic had no idea how they could've gone through all that money or all those drugs, but the two tortured zombies seem to have done it. They lay bleeding on the floor at his feet, looking at him as though he could do something. What could he do? These men, these narco-terrorists holding them prisoner, wouldn't buy his story. And he was telling truth.

What followed was a slow and horrific destruction of his will. They started on the Shoshana first—continuing where they left off with her fingers—then they worked a little more on Ray. By the time they got to Alani, Vic was worn down. He had nothing left to give. They held him down and made him watch.

"I gotta piss," Jerry said.

Vic was lost in his thoughts, he wasn't sure how many times Jerry had said it. Jerry leaned in from the back and whispered so he wouldn't wake Piper. Vic asked Ghia, "Where are we?"

"Jesus, Vic, aren't you paying attention? We're almost to Willits." Ghia checked her rearview again. There'd been almost no traffic at this hour. They passed the occasional eighteen-wheeler, but that was about it. "You sure you wanna stop? We got plenty of gas to keep going."

"You don't gotta stop in town," Jerry said. "Hell, just pull off the road, I'll piss on the back tire."

Ghia said, "Charming. Where'd you find this one again, Vic?"

Vic wasn't listening though. He said, "Does anybody have a signal yet?"

* * *

It was hopeless. There were no phones out on the street. Payphones were a thing of the past. Her plan to head straight to the BART station was quelled when she realized what time it was. The subway wouldn't open till the early morning commute. She was stuck on the street, too terrified to risk taking sidewalks across East Oakland while a pack of bikers and thugs hunted her down. She only had to stay awake and wait. As soon as the sky lightened a shade, she'd know BART would be open and she'd head for the payphones there. Until then, she had to hide like a scared cat. She found a wide hedge lining a walkway to an apartment building and crawled in and waited.

She recoiled into the shrub, pulling her entire body inward. Like a statue she waited, eyeing the sky from between the leaves and branches, urging it to lighten. In her mind, she measured out the steps back to the BART station, to the nearest phones. She was only alive in her mind now, her body stiff and numb, dead as stone to the nighttime world.

With her meditation, her mind began to drift. First to her son, Jerry. She searched the psychic universe for some sign he was all right, unharmed and moving to a safe place, then her mind moved to her son's protector, the man she at least hoped was his protector. She tried to envision what it was like up in Humboldt, what Vic looked like now. It'd been years since she'd seen him face to face, but she was sure he was the same. Men like that rarely changed. His outer shell evolved with age, but his core—his essence—would remain.

Her mind moved further down the timeline, to the day everything changed for the both of them. That day on Fulton Street.

After she left high school in the eighties, Barbara was wild—at least by the standards of her schoolmates in Sacramento. She bounced around a few minimum-wage jobs while her closest friends started makeshift families with surprise pregnancies. Seeing nothing but welfare checks ahead of her, she decided to attend a six-week government-sponsored program to become a nurse's assistant. Spotty attendance and late-night partying stunted her progress, but when she was finally handed a diploma, she enacted the second part of her plan: leaving Sacramento and moving to the Bay Area.

It took her a while after graduation, but she finally found a gig in Daly City, just south of San Francisco. Barbara worked as a nurse's assistant in a small doctor's office that dealt mostly with elderly patients—a job that allowed her access to a medicine cabinet larger than she'd ever seen. The gig also connected her with a registered nurse named Tony Tocci, a handsome bad boy and eventual boyfriend with a wicked habit and a pad full of blank scripts.

Convenience and opportunity conspired and Barbara and Tony fell in love. At least what they thought was love. Barbara was already stealing pills and forging scripts, but to feed Tony's needs, she broadened her fraud at work, using different doctors' names, even making some up. Soon she had a little sideline going—selling pills to Tony's ever-expanding circle of drug addicted friends. She wrote massive prescriptions for Diluadid, Demerol, morphine tablets, and even a new drug coming on the scene, Oxycontin.

With a passion for pills and each other, Barbara and Tony fell into the familiar pattern of complacency. Their lives were muted by drugs and an endless pattern of work, TV, and sleep—until they were finally interrupted by a pregnancy: Jerry.

After the baby was born, Tony disappeared for the most part, only showing up to offer excuses and break promises. He and Barbara officially split up when Jerry was about two. His addictions eventually brought him down, but—through Jerry—he and Barbara were entwined forever. The responsibility of being a single mother helped Barbara shed her taste for drugs and the wild life, but she was forever chasing down Jerry's father. Through methadone clinics, pawn shops, and drug dealers' houses.

The Morillos' was a favorite hangout for Tony. After he split from Barbara and Jerry, Tony's taste in drugs turned darker and soon he was shooting heroin with Ray Morillo. Ray and his wife were old customers of Barbara's, but Barbara eventually stopped selling to them because she couldn't meet their demands. The Morillos had a seemingly endless appetite for all things narcotic related.

After Jerry was born, her only connection to the Morillos was Tony. Barbara banged on their door for years, usually finding what she was looking for—a deadbeat dad with his chin on his chest and a burned out cigarette wedged between his fingers. The Morillo home was a place Jerry's father would hide from Barbara, responsibility, and the world.

On the evening of August twenty-ninth, 1996, Barbara listened before she knocked and heard screaming. It was Shoshana's voice, high and vibrant. She wasn't sure if Shoshana and Ray were having another of their epic domestic battles, but it sounded like one. Twice before she'd taken the children out of the house for fear they might witness their parents beating each other. It never happened, not as far as Barbara knew, but it always felt like an inevitability. Barbara tried the doorknob and found it unlocked. As she opened the front door, there was another scream, this one more pained and less angry. She heard men's voices too. Several of them. A few in Spanish and a couple in English. Barbara froze, not sure what she'd wandered into. Some of the company the Morillos kept went beyond strange and into dangerous. She stood still and quiet by the door, knowing that an exit would make more noise than her entry.

Then she heard a booming voice shout, "Shut up. What we did to her, we're going to do to the girl." It was followed by Alani's voice winding up like a siren. It was coated with sheer agony. The vibration of that voice so shook Barbara, she recoiled in the foyer, frozen, waiting.

The paralysis of fear locked her in place as she listened to scream after scream. But one unholy sound broke her spell: the sound of Alani dying. The finality of that last tortured yelp will be forever burned into her memory. She would never forgive herself for not acting sooner.

Barbara came into the room at full speed, tackling the man who held the child. She ignored the SFPD uniform the man wore and took him down from the midsection. Both he and Alani tumbled to the floor. The policeman broke his grip on the child and Alani tumbled away on the hardwood floor. But it was too late. Alani already was dead. Ray was dead. Shoshana was dead. The only captive left alive was Vic. He was broken and beaten, sliced and stabbed, but the second Barbara burst in the room, Vic sprang into action, attacking the man closest to him, the man committing most of the violent atrocities. Vic broke the man's grip on the knife and turned it into the sadist's stomach. The second man was unarmed, he was only there to keep the hostages in place. Vic made quick work of him while Barbara pummeled the cop. When the second man had been dispatched in the same method as the first, Vic and Barbara beat and stabbed the man in the cop's uniform till he was still. Everything was still.

Barbara and Vic sat on the blood-soaked floor trying to catch their breath. She now saw the extent of his wounds. He wasn't going to make it far without medical attention. She helped him out of the house on Fulton Street, took him home, helped him recover, helped him hide. What they endured that day created a bond more intimate than any love affair ever could. They were connected then, now, and forever.

Chapter Twenty-Three

Eric Tribban was the first one back to the house. He'd left after the others and limited his search to the surrounding blocks. He peeked over fences and peered into doorways till his eyes watered. The dark that felt so close minutes ago was now turning a pale blue, a shade that seemed anemic to Eric, like the color of sickness itself. He felt the creak of his bones as he got out of the truck. It'd been a while since he pulled an all-nighter. He looked up at his building, checking for lights. They joked and called it the compound, but it was really just a rickety two-story wrapped with asphalt. The BBs owned it outright, though, and they were lucky to have it. The house looked empty so he keyed the huge padlock hanging off the side door and went inside.

Vlad and Dmitri were gone, thank God. He wasn't sure he could look at Dmitri's pathetic swollen face another minute without punching it. The man sold himself as a gangster then let a woman get the jump on him and escape. He was quickly losing respect for both of them. Eric knew, like anyone who did business with the BBs, their time and usefulness had an expiration date. Sometimes they ended things with their temporary partners without trouble. Other times things got complicated. Ugly.

With his two house guests and Ollie still on the street, he figured someone should be coordinating from home base. Besides, he'd forgotten his cell. He bounded up the stairs and found it right where he left it next to the stove. He picked it up and saw four missed calls. No texts, no messages. He checked the incoming calls and saw they were all the same number. A seven-oh-seven area code. Humboldt.

He swiped the missed call and lifted the phone to his ear.

"Eric? That you? It's me, Doughboy. You remember me from the beer truck at the run?"

Eric did remember Doughboy, the brother Aaron told him was shot earlier in the day. He was a member of the Northern Chapter. He didn't know him well, but he recognized that strange twang of his, he'd seen him at a few of the larger club functions. "No, lemme call you back in two minutes." He didn't wait for a response. He hung up and went to his bedroom for a new phone. He always kept a couple of fresh burners charged and ready. He flipped one open, checked the signal, and walked back to his own phone. He punched in the number manually and waited.

Doughboy's voice came on the line. "Can you talk?"

Already annoyed, Eric said, "Yeah. Spit it."

"Terry's down."

"What? I can barely fucking hear you. What d'ya mean he's down? Who is? What're you talkin' about?"

"I mean he's down. Terry. They got him. He ain't getting back up."

Eric didn't understand. The only reason he called back on the burner was so he could avoid this cryptic shit. "What the *fuck* you talking about?"

"He's dead."

Eric still didn't believe Doughboy. Terry was one of Eric's closest brothers. They came up together in the nineties. He'd known him since the late eighties. He was president of his own chapter. Shit, him and Terry practically ran the show in Northern California.

"He was at this cabin down the hill, trying to, you know, fix our problem. And there was trouble and he took one."

Eric still couldn't believe what he was hearing. "What? Terry? Are you sure?"

"I wasn't there. I'm stuck up the hill with a hip full of buck-shot. But they brought him back up here. I was just fucking looking at him, brother." Doughboy's voice started to choke with emotion. "He's done. He's done."

Eric knew he wasn't being fucked with. This was a serious problem. This changed everything. "Where are you?"

"I'm standing outside the Big Man's shack."

"Call Big Man. You tell him I told you to call. Tell him to get out there and help you clean things up."

Cardiff and Aaron were on the 101 South with the awning of the pre-dawn sky opening up above them. A low ceiling of grey cloud pressed down and flattened the color of whatever the light touched. They hadn't even reached Garberville yet. It took them well over an hour to load up Terry's body and get it back up the hill to the shack where Doughboy was laid up with a bloody hip and more pot than any hippie could smoke in a life-time. They left him on the couch with a bottle of Jameson and Terry's body wrapped in a shower curtain on the floor. It wasn't a soldier's funeral, but it'd have to do for now.

They both sat silent now, exhausted, eyes burning, arms aching from lifting the body. Aaron was behind the wheel and Cardiff stared out his window.

"You ready for a bump?" Cardiff asked.

"Way past ready."

Cardiff produced a small baggie of coke from the glove box and shook some out onto the fleshy pad between his thumb and index finger.

"You ain't gonna chop that?" Aaron asked.

"Fuck no. There's plenty. I ain't got the patience." Cardiff lifted his hand under his nose and inhaled the pile of white pow-der. "Ugh," he said. "At least that's a little bit better." He shook some more onto his hand and held it out. Aaron vacuumed it up.

The coke didn't help. Not at this hour, not under these circumstances. But Cardiff tapped out another hit for himself anyway, then more for Aaron. After three solid blasts, Cardiff tasted that familiar bitter slick on the back of his throat. When he spoke, his voice felt tight and unused. "How long to the Bay, you figure?"

"From here? Five hours." The coke had tightened Aaron's vocal cords too and it was hard for him to be heard above the sound of the road.

The drugs had increased the static electricity in the car with the kind of false energy only drugs can create. They were still bone tired, but now their jaws were clamped tight. Their eyes were wide, but burned just as badly. Cardiff reached out and turned on the radio and began to scroll for stations. He'd hear a clip and scan to the next one. Spanish, pop, classic rock, none of them held his attention for more than a few seconds.

Aaron poked the power button and ended the selection.

"Hey, I'll find something," Cardiff said. "Just gimme a minute."

"Ssh." Aaron cocked his head. "What's that noise?"

They both listened as a metallic melody stopped and started. It sounded as though it came from the floorboards. They looked at each other, confused. Then Cardiff's eyes lit up and he frantically began searching under his seat using the flat of his palm. He located the object and pulled it out. Barbara Bertram's cell.

"Who is it? Who's calling?" Aaron asked.

Cardiff tilted the screen to show Aaron the caller ID: *Vic.* "It's him. The fucker from the cabin."

"Answer it. Tell him we're gonna kill him."

Cardiff held the phone until the ringing stopped.

"Why didn't you answer it?"

"If it's him, then he doesn't know we already got her," Cardiff said. "He thinks she's still out there, free and roaming. He's trying to send her a signal, a warning. We already know where he is. He's on the goddamn 101 South. If I answer, then he knows we got her because we got her phone. He'll know he's fucked.

This way, he don't know what the fuck is going on. I can call him back on another phone if I want, surprise him. Way I see it? He's probably doing the Prince Charming thing. Gonna save the damsel, gonna save the boy, gonna save everybody. Shit, not only do we know where he is, we know where he's going."

Vic held the phone in his hand. He stared at the black screen.

"You didn't leave a message?" Ghia asked.

"No. No point, I guess."

They were pulled over at a turnout, an unmarked patch of gravel at the side of the road. Both Jerry and Piper were relieving themselves in a nearby clutch of birch trees. Jerry was tucked out of sight, but Piper was squatting in front of the foliage in full view of anyone who may pass by in the dawn light.

"Man," Ghia said. "That girl ain't shy, huh?"

"Nope. I'd say her upbringing had something to do with that."

"Why? Who brought this one up? Circus folk?"

"Dead BBs."

Ghia blew out a gust of air. "You're kidding me."

"Nope. And not just any BB either. She's Eric Tribban's kid."

The name meant nothing to Ghia. She waited a moment to see if Vic would offer any more information. "Okay. I'll bite. Who's Eric Tribban?"

Vic tilted his head at her. "El presidente. The big cheese. Capo di tutti capi."

This time Ghia sucked in a breath and held it. Her brow leveled as the humor drained from her face. "Suddenly all this bullshit makes a lot more sense."

"The road ahead ain't gonna get any smoother. That's for sure."

Ghia didn't inquire as to what Vic meant. She watched him while he watched the two young people at the side of the road. She knew he wasn't seeing them. His mind was far off, somewhere else he needed to be, somewhere they were heading. "We're going to find her, aren't we?"

"Who?"

"Your friend, the woman. The one you told me about."

Vic didn't move his head or shift his field of vision when he answered. "Yep. Got to."

Ripper lay as still as he could. A thin layer of dew gathered. He knew he'd have to sit through the night. This far back in the bush, there was nothing you could do but wait. Trying to make it back down in the dark would be impossible. He got comfortable on his back and watched the mist from his mouth billow in the moonlight. His leg hurt, and the throb was steady, but he knew it wasn't life threatening, not yet. He folded his arms across his chest and listened to himself breathe. He never did get that beer he went back to the cabin for. He could have used one now. He could have used six of them. Ripper let himself drift off to sleep.

Tory Nagle couldn't sleep. He shouldn't have had those two beers when he got home last night. Any alcohol during the evening contorted his sleep pattern. He sat up in his bed, careful not to disturb his sleeping wife, and let his eyes adjust to the early dawn.

He slipped out of bed and walked to the front room, stopping to turn up the thermostat. The coffee machine had been filled the night before, a ritual he never tampered with, and he hit the brew button and settled down in front of the computer monitor. Their tiny apartment living room doubled as the dining room and his office, so he scrolled through the headlines while he waited for his coffee. After realizing not much had changed in the few hours he'd slept, Nagle decided to search for the Fulton Street Massacre. He clicked on the first article that came up. Its headline read: "Richmond District Bloodbath."

San Francisco Chronicle, August 30, 1996.

Six bodies were discovered yesterday at a home in San Francisco's Richmond District in a multiple homicide that officers at the scene described as "horrific."

Names or ages of the victims have not yet been released, but San Francisco Homicide Detective Frank Purcell said at least one of the deceased was a SFPD officer. Purcell said the officer was found at the scene in uniform, although it is not known whether the officer was on a call at the address or if he had some other relation to the victims.

The scene at 4014 Fulton was chaotic throughout the night as police and other officials tried to determine what happened there. Police have shut down Fulton Street from 15th to 17th avenues while the investigation continues. Purcell did not comment on the causes of death.

Neighbor Amanda Yee said she heard nothing last night. She added that the occupants of 4014 Fulton were longtime residents and there was a lot of "traffic" in and out of the apartment. SFPD is requesting that anyone who was in the vicinity of 16th Avenue and Fulton last night and may have heard or seen something, please contact SFPD Homicide Division at 415-553-0127.

Below the article were two pictures. One of the flat itself, roped off with crime scene tape, and the other of a distraught young officer with his arms crossed in front of him and his face twisted with grief. One of those award-winning shots brimming with emotion. Nagle looked closely and saw it was Roland in the photo.

Nagle hit *ctrl+* and blew up the photo till Mackie's pixilated face filled the monitor. He sat back in his chair and stared at the haunted image of his friend. Mackie looked impossibly young and completely shell-shocked.

Nagle clicked back to the search page and brought up another article. This one dated about two months after the initial crime.

There were more details by this time, a list of victims and their ages, including an unnamed nine-year-old minor. Four adults, one child, and the SFPD officer. There were vague descriptions about the way in which the victims died, the method of their executions. By this time it was clear that's what they were, executions. Torture followed by execution. There was some editorial speculation about what kind of culprit could have committed such a crime, but no real leads on who was responsible. Being in law enforcement, Nagle knew there were plenty of details left out of articles like this. He'd heard rumors, of course, but they were just that. Rumors. The crime had occurred years before he'd joined the bureau and its legendary status was opaque with myth.

The real facts of the case were now held close to the vest of those who were directly involved. Retirees who suppressed their memories, crime scene photographers with their negatives buried in cardboard boxes. And young patrolmen who were on the scene, who had to carry the weight of those memories while they kept the streets of the city safe.

He could only imagine how walking into the carnage on Fulton Street affected the young rookie Roland Mackie. No wonder it scarred him. If it were true—if this Victor Thomas was responsible—then he was also a child killer and a cop killer. No wonder Vic filled his friend's nightmares.

Nagle got up and filled his favorite mug, a gift his wife had bought him. FBI was stenciled on the side of the mug and below it was written Furry Beaver Inspector. It was an old and stupid gag, but it still made him smile every time he read it. He thought about the day ahead and part of him hoped he wouldn't hear from Roland Mackie. Not now. Not ever.

Sometimes Big Man's own snores woke him up. Other times it was his dog barking. But it was rarely an alarm. An old heavy metal song was set for his ringtone, and that's what was playing in his dreams. Over and over. He blinked open his eyes. The light creeping past his dark curtains was pale blue. He knew it wasn't quite daylight. He squeezed his eyes shut again.

He fumbled in the near dark and found his ringing phone. He wanted to say, What the fuck? Or, This better be important, but all he could do was clear his throat. There was so much phlegm clogging his windpipe, he couldn't articulate a single syllable.

"Big, is that you?" The voice on the phone said.

After a few more moments of gurgling, Big Man managed to get out, "Who's this?"

"It's Doughboy. I'm up on the hill. You better get up here."

"Why, what's up?"

"Just get up here, man. And you may want to bring someone you trust, somebody who can help out."

"What the fuck you talking about, Doughboy?"

But Doughboy wouldn't say anything more. He was cryptic and sounded scared. Big Man told him he'd be at the cabin in about an hour and a half.

Doughboy said, "Big?"

Big Man was sitting up now. Two feet on the floor, trying to shock his huge body into consciousness. "Yeah?"

"You may want to bring a shovel."

Chapter Twenty-Four

Vic tried to navigate the small phone in his hand. His fingers always seemed too fat and stiff when he tried to operate these gadgets. They sat in a Jack In The Box parking lot in Willits. The sun was mostly up now, but not high enough to warm the inside of the Ford. The adrenaline sweat and the lingering dirt of the forest gave the car an odd musk, like earthworms and vinegar. Vic had hoped to prove a point regarding their distance from Sacramento and the time it'd take to get there. Jerry and Piper were of the belief a ride straight down the 101 would be best, cutting across near San Rafael and rejoining Interstate 80. Vic knew from experience a path through Clear Lake would save them time.

"But the BBs have people in Clear Lake," Piper said.

"Shit," Vic said. "They got people everywhere. We're not stopping, we're only driving through."

Ghia ended the discussion. "It's Clear Lake. It's gotta be. Where do I turn onto Highway 20 again?"

Vic said hang on, he'd double-check, and he focused back on his cell. "These fucking things are a pain in the ass."

And, as if it were offended by such a remark, the phone started buzzing in his hand. An unidentified five-one-zero area code number flashed on the screen. The number meant nothing to Vic and his first instinct was to ignore it. Then something tightened in his gut and he swiped the screen to answer the call.

Barbara's voice came over the line, clear and bright. "Vic? Is that you?"

He lowered his voice in an attempt at keeping the conversation covert. "Jesus Christ, I thought I'd lost you. Are you all right?"

"I been better," Barbara said. "I'm in Oakland. At the Twelfth Street BART Station."

"What the hell are you doing there?"

"Long story, but I'm stuck."

"I'm on the way. I'm on the 101 now. I'll be there in about two and a half hours. You sit tight, okay?"

"I can't sit tight. It's not safe. I have to meet you somewhere."

"What do you mean, it's not safe? What's going on?"

Barbara glanced over her shoulder. "There's no time to talk, just meet me at Jerry's friend Richard's house."

"I don't even know who that is, but we're on the way."

"*We*? You have Jerry with you?"

Vic smiled and reached back to hand Jerry the cell. He wanted Barbara to hear her son's voice for herself.

"Hello?" Jerry said. "Hello?" He plugged a finger into one ear and tucked his head down. "Mom? Hello?" He checked the screen and saw the call had ended.

Barbara saw Ollie coming from across the station. His pace was direct, cutting through the morning commuters, slicing through the crowd directly toward her. His arms swung at his sides and he took long strides, the rhythm of his boot leather increasing in tempo. For a split second, she thought she was safe, watched by cameras and witnesses, no way he'd try to grab her. Not here, not with the BART police, not with the bright fluorescent lights exposing them all.

He was close now. Close enough for her to see his eyes. She saw determination. She saw a complete lack of caution. Ollie didn't care about cameras or cops. He only cared about his prey. Barbara turned and ran, pushing past slow moving commuters.

Behind her she heard the quickening pace of his boots pounding the floor of the station. Then a shout. By the time Barbara was skipping up the escalator two steps at a time, there was a full blown commotion on the station floor. Without slowing her pace, she turned her head and saw a uniformed man trying to impede Ollie, holding him back with the palm of his hand while he barked into his radio. An older man had been knocked to the floor and a woman was shouting at the officer and at Ollie. Several people circled the fallen man. One commuter had folded his overcoat into a makeshift pillow and stuck it under the man's head. Ollie stood still, ignoring the cop and the commuters. He'd resigned to the interruption, knowing the watchful eyes, electronic and otherwise, were too attentive to continue the chase. His own eyes, though, were focused on Barbara. Just as she reached the top of the escalator and felt the warming morning light wrap around her, Ollie stretched his arm out and pointed at her. Not shouting, not saying anything, just pointing.

Vic took the phone back from Jerry. "What'd ya mean, it's dead?" He held it to his ear. "Hello? Barbara? Hello?" They still sat in the Jack In The Box parking lot, somber and still.

"There's nobody there," Jerry said.

"Fuck. Maybe the call dropped. Maybe she'll call back."

The phone rang just as he said this, but it wasn't the Oakland number Barbara called from on the ID—it was Big Man. Vic didn't want to answer it for fear he'd miss the call back from Barbara. He let it ring. He knew Big Man wasn't the type to leave a voicemail, so it didn't surprise him when it started ringing again. This time, Vic answered it.

Big Man didn't wait for Vic to say hello. "What the fuck?"

"Big Man, how're you doing?"

"What the fuck have you done?"

"I'm dealing with problems as they arise. I don't know what you've heard, but—"

"Do you have any idea what kind of spot you're putting me in?"

"They have Barbara. Down in Oakland. They have her."

"I don't give a shit if they got the pope roped and trussed in the trunk of a car. You fucked me good on this one, Vic. You not only got me in Dutch with the fucking club, there's a good fucking chance I'll end up in a prison cell 'cause of you."

"Listen, I'm not gonna let that happen—"

"Are you fucking kidding me? How you gonna stop it? What're you? Superman? You think you got some sort of power the rest of us don't see? You're fucking delusional, man. You always were. Living up there on the hill like Kung Fu has just made you crazier. If I end up dead 'cause of this shit, whether it's in a cell or in a ditch, I'm going to come back from the dark side to fucking rip your head off."

Vic hit the end call button. The other three stared at him. They'd heard most of what Big Man had shouted into the phone.

"Change of plans," Vic said. He started the Escape and buckled his seatbelt. "Sacramento's out. We're heading to Oakland."

Chapter Twenty-Five

"You look like shit," Mackie said. "What'd you do? Stay up half the night drinking?"

Nagle smiled, but it was a forced smile, making a crescent of his lips that looked as though it may crack his face. He'd agreed to meet Mackie at a pastry shop across from the Hall of Justice. At seven a.m., he was two hours earlier than he normally showed up for work. He pulled a chair across the table from Mackie and sat down with the weight of a man exhausted. "I was up doing research."

"Research? On what?"

"Fulton Street. What else?"

The mention of Fulton Street quelled any morning cheer in Mackie. The everyday din of the coffee shop closed in around the two men. Serious and somber, Mackie asked, "What did you think?"

"I think it was fucked up. I think it was a pretty heinous crime."

"Unsolved crime."

"I don't know if I'd go that far. There're some unanswered questions, sure, but it looked to me like the guys responsible for most of that carnage were left dead on the floor with their victims."

"You weren't there. I know what it looks like from the reports, the photos, but what I saw was something different. Vic was never questioned about his role, what he knew about the cop, why he was there. We know he was there, his fucking wallet was lying on the floor. For all I know, Victor Thomas ordered the hit, had the whole family killed. Maybe he was just there to supervise. Maybe he was there because he wanted to watch. He's a cold sadistic sonofabitch, so it wouldn't surprise me. Nothing would."

Nagle sighed. He'd read the newspaper accounts, not the SFPD file, but from what he understood, his friend's zealousness was shaped by the traumatic impact the crime scene held. A cop sees plenty over the years, but there's something about the first time you see a child victim. It's something that works its way into you, settling in the brainpan like sand. And you can't wash it away. Not with liquor, not with the job. It sticks with you. And, maybe in Mackie's case, becomes you. "You think he killed the cop too?"

"Yeah, sure. Why not? It's as good an explanation as any, right?"

"But you don't think there's any other explanation. You think Thomas is the guy."

"Okay, it is the explanation."

"No. It's not. Not as far as I can tell. The cop was bad news. The file shows every indication he was knee-deep in narco shit."

"That's what I'm saying. If the cop was bad, if he was running shit, then maybe Vic killed him to escape. I mean, even if it was a him-or-me thing, he's still a cop killer."

Nagle regarded his friend, his tone, the desperation in his eyes. He knew Mackie was vacillating between fact and the fantasy he'd rationalized as fact years ago. "Look, let's just work the case we agreed to work, and see where it takes us, okay?"

"That's all I asked of you in the first place."

"I'm serious, Roland. You're gonna have to let go of some of that shit and concentrate on Juan Jiménez and what we know about OC involvement in the pot clubs. Whether it's the BBs or the Russians or MS-13 or whatever. It'll take us were we need to go. Not necessarily where you want to go."

"I get it," Mackie said. "You don't need to talk down to me. Let's get started."

Nagle stood up, pushing the chair back with his legs. "You had coffee?"

"Yep."

"You want some more?"

"Oh yeah."

Eric Tribban was drinking coffee. It was fortified with Bailey's Irish Cream, but that didn't give it much punch. He poured in the rest of the pot to heat up the remnants in his cup. This time he threw in a splash of Jameson for some extra bite. He was chain smoking too, lighting a fresh cigarette off the butt of another. He couldn't believe his friend, his comrade, his brother was gone. Eric wasn't one to show emotion and he prided himself on having an even keel, but he was very close to losing control now. Problem was, he wasn't sure where to direct his anger, how to avenge Terry. He knew Vlad wasn't directly responsible, but he couldn't help but feel the spear of vengeance would eventually be pointed at the Russian. He hated Vlad the Inhaler, hated doing business with him, hated having to kowtow to him. That's what drove him to steal Vlad's money. This last burn was only the tip of the iceberg. The BBs had been skimming off the pot clubs for years. He was sure the Russians assumed there was some sort of skim, but having the cash ripped off by Piper and her boyfriend might expose how much. With that kind of larceny out in the open, staring the Russian mob in the face, they'd have no choice but to retaliate.

He thought about his position, the BBs' position. When he came on board as a BB, the club was like most other outlaw motorcycle clubs. Sure there was criminal activity, and plenty of mayhem, but it was mostly about the brotherhood. The general public never believed it, but most of the members were there for the bikes. The bikes, the rides, the brotherhood. Even the biggest club in California, after years of being eroded by police harassment, had pulled back from its illegal activities. Too much surveillance, too much enthusiasm from law enforcement. What their absence created was a vacuum. A void Eric—with his newly found ambition—filled. Now, here he sat, fifteen years later, wondering why he'd dug a hole so deep. The money, the privilege, and the power were benefits, yeah, but at what cost?

The meditation helped focus his rage. Yes, he hated Vlad, and blamed him. Letting Vlad send his own emissary north with Aaron was a mistake. But he had to play nice and go along to see if the BBs could get to Jerry Bertram first. If they got rid of Jerry, there'd be no evidence of the money being short. Cardiff was just going to be collateral damage. Even in the world of outlaws and cutthroat criminals, Cardiff was a loose cannon. No doubt the slimy fucker escalated things. He hated Vic Thomas too. Vic was legendary. He was an OG from way back, with a reputation he probably didn't deserve. Nobody is that tough. He ain't fucking Cool Hand Luke. He'd only met Vic once as far as he could remember—and he wasn't too impressed. He was introduced to him in a crowded kitchen during a house party in Eureka after the Redwood Run. He didn't like how Vic played the strong silent type and figured he was just as scared as any other citizen who found themselves at a Dead BB party. After Vic left, some brothers whispered in his ear about Vic's reputation, but Eric wasn't buying it. He'd make sure that piece of shit paid the full freight for killing a Dead BB. He was angry at the whole Nomad chapter for fucking this up and letting Terry get caught in the crossfire. Eric thought some of the blame fell on Big Man's shoulders too. Him and his crew, the Cripplers. A bunch of old timers who should have helped in the fight or hung it up. You're with us or against us, Eric thought. They should have been able to screen this trouble. There should have been a barrier of guys on the front lines so Terry didn't have to be. He knew though, Terry was a man's man, a Patton of a leader. He'd never ask his crew to do anything he wouldn't do himself. Maybe that was his undoing.

But, when he thought about who he blamed the most, it was Jerry and his little girl, Piper. They were the ones who caused this mess. They stole the cash and ran for the hills. They pushed first domino. If he got a chance to lay his hands on Jerry Bertram, he wasn't going to let go till he peeled the kid's skin off, pulled the meat from his bones, and threw him in the hole himself. And, the way he was feeling right now, he'd consider tossing his stepchild in there with him. That little bitch caused him nothing but grief since she turned ten.

Eric heard the familiar crash of the metal gate downstairs and he moved to the top of the stairs. He watched Marcus kick open the inner door and push his way in. He dragged someone inside with him, someone in a headlock. Once the door was shut behind him, Marcus released the person. Eric saw who it was. No mistaking the heroic Barbara Bertram. The best bet he had for getting a bead on Jerry Bertram just been dragged through his front door.

"Nice job, Marcus. Where'd you find her?"

"Fucking BART station. Ollie went in and flushed her out. Caught her at the top of the escalator, trying to bolt. She wasn't even looking, practically ran into my arms."

"Where's Ollie?"

"He got hung up at the station. Caused a bit of a ruckus trying to get through the crowd. He'll be by in a few I'm sure."

Mackie asked, "Where are we going again?"

Mackie sat in the passenger seat of a federal vehicle, an unmarked Crown Victoria that ran on natural gas. He'd waited over an hour while Nagle made clandestine phone calls to his varied contacts at the FBI. He'd thrown back three large cups of coffee, two doughnuts, and a cream cheese bagel with all the fixings. Now they were on their way out of the city and his friend was acting obtuse about their destination.

"East Bay."

"I know we're going to the East Bay, we're on the goddamn Bay Bridge. I mean where in the East Bay."

"We're going to knock on some doors. I think the BBs' clubhouse is too obvious a place for them to be conducting this kind of business, so I thought we'd try something else."

"What kind of business?"

"I had some field agents in the Sacramento office roll by Barbara Bertram's place in Citrus Heights. Looks like she's been snatched. We're not a hundred percent sure, but, from all indications, she got pulled outta there. If not against her will, then certainly unexpectedly. Open front door, burned coffee in the pot, TV on, hungry cat, that kind of stuff. If what you say about her kid is true, then maybe the BBs, or even some friends of Vladimir Lysenko, stopped by to see if the kid showed up."

"And you were going to tell me this when?"

"I'm telling you now. That's who I've been on the phone with. Trying to find us a lead."

Mackie took a breath to process this information. "You think if they didn't find the kid, they took her as collateral instead?"

"Guessing, but yeah. That was enough for me to request a peek at her cell records."

"That's fucking great. Being a fed has its perks, huh?"

"Oh yeah, we're a twenty-four-hour operation. We deal with so many of these things, sometimes we subpoena the cell carrier in the middle of the night."

"Who's she been calling?"

"Oh no, we can't see that stuff. The subpoena was bare bones, cell tower only, just for location. The kind we use in emergencies for kidnappings, that kind of stuff. We'd need a title three for that other stuff. However, we can tell where she pinged last. The last tower that her cell bounced from was in Humboldt County, actually right on the Humboldt-Mendocino county line. As far as getting a real location, that's approximate

183

at best."

"So, the feds are calling it a kidnapping?"

"Of sorts, I guess. Kidnapping is federal and it gives it a little more juice. We got the tower ping, didn't we?"

"So why are we going to Oakland?"

"Not Oakland, exactly. Alameda. We're going to go see Eric Tribban."

"The BBs' president?"

"The one and only."

"Wait a sec. Why aren't we following the cell record?"

"Shit, Roland, you ever been up there? We can drive for five hours and find ourselves in a patch of redwoods. It's like a jungle up there. There's no doors to knock on. The bureau has next to no intelligence there either. It's a waste of man hours. But, I was thinking we could go to the source, talk to the man himself. You know, shake the tree a little, and see if we can't find something out."

"I don't get it. You want to do a cold call on the president of the BBs and ask if he has a woman tied up in his basement?"

"Pretty much, yeah. You got a better way to start our morning?"

"That doesn't make any sense. If her cell went up north, we should be going that way."

"Look, the investigation is here. Vlad is here, the hierarchy of the BBs are here, the pot clubs are here. And—" Nagle stopped talking a moment to check his phone, "—the crime was committed here. This is where we need to be. It'd be a goose chase to scramble up the 101. By the time we got our bearings up there, the players would all be back down in the Bay. Trust me."

"I think we're chasing our tails here. No way is Tribban even going to answer his door, let alone talk to us."

"Like I said, we're shaking the tree."

"Yeah, well, I hope something ripe doesn't fall out and hit us on the head."

* * *

The 101 South opened up again, like a movie playing backward, the scenery came at them in reverse. It was like being slowly woken from a nightmare. Vic knew better, he knew the horror wasn't over. Jerry watched the clear bright morning develop in front of them. He sat in the back seat smoking cigarettes while Piper slowly began to nod, her head bobbing with the rhythm of the road till it fell back onto the headrest. When she emitted a steady soft purr, Jerry leaned forward and asked Vic, "How you doing up there? You need me to drive?"

"No, but you can keep me company." He tilted his head toward Ghia. Like Piper, she was deep asleep, exhausted by a sleepless night, life-threatening stress, and the physical exertion that came with a hike down the mountain into a combat zone.

"I'll keep you awake."

"I'm not going to fall asleep." Vic wrung the steering wheel with his hands and asked Jerry to light him a cigarette.

Jerry shook out a couple of Camels and lit them both at the same time, passing one up to Vic. "I just meant that, you know, after last night, you must be wiped."

"You get what we're trying to do, right? Where we're going? These assholes have your mother."

"Yeah, but you said she got away, that's what she said when she called."

"She hung up. The line went dead. That don't seem strange to you? For all I know she's back with them. They snatched her."

"Or maybe she's fine."

Vic squinted at the young man in the rearview mirror. "If she was fine, she would've called back." What was wrong with this kid? His mother's welfare was on the line and he acted nonplussed. Had he misjudged him? He knew the kid was a fuckup. He wasn't the brightest kid either, but was he this selfish?

Vic had seen other people in the same spot as he was now,

where their trust and judgment were compromised by the assumption someone they counted on wasn't a fool. Where the judgment of that someone being a good person, of having hearty moral fiber, was based on the simple fact they knew them, or knew of them, or knew their loved ones. As if just knowing someone automatically creeded them with good character. Did Vic fall victim to the same mistake, thinking this kid could be even close to the pure-hearted hero his mother was? He watched Jerry contemplate his last comment, chewing on it, considering how it may affect him. Vic decided it didn't matter, the son's lack of conviction wasn't going to change what he had to do for the boy's mother. He owed Barbara. In this life, and probably in the next too. He owed Barbara Bertram a debt that could never be fully paid.

A few quiet miles went by. The wind whistled around the Ford. Vic didn't want to turn on the radio for fear of waking Piper and Ghia. After a while he asked Jerry, "What did you come up north for?"

"What'd you mean?"

"I mean, a kid like you, things aren't so bad. It looks to me like you sabotaged your own life. Why?"

"Shit, seemed like easy money. Piper said there'd be—"

"That's what I'm sayin', you're telling me you let your girlfriend steer you into this mess? You knew who she was, you knew who you were ripping off. Ipso fucking facto, you had to know the whole thing was going to go south." Vic glanced into the mirror again to see if Piper was still sleeping. "You really think the girl is going to turn her back on her family forever? For twenty fuckin' grand?"

Jerry gnawed his lower lip. He didn't like being painted into a corner like this. He hadn't given the big picture much thought. Not thinking too much about the consequences that rippled out from his actions was how Jerry got through life. He'd never worried about it. When the wheel of karma turned back around to him, he tried not to focus on why it returned. He dealt with it the best he could and he moved on to the next score. Jerry felt thinking too much wasn't so much a weakness, but a way to invite complications. Focus on what you wanted and keep your blinders on. He'd had a lifetime of compartmentalizing. The drugs and liquor helped. So did his willingness to settle things with his fists.

Still looking at Jerry in the rearview, Vic said, "All I'm sayin' is, it's time to start figuring out what's important. And it ain't money. I know you don't wanna hear this shit, but it's time for you to pull your head out of your ass and learn what it means to be a man. A real man."

"Come this way," Eric said.

"We're on to something, we got her phone. He called her. I mean, he called us, but he thought he was calling her. He still thinks she's in Sacramento."

Aaron's voice sounded scratchy and small through the burner's tiny speaker. There was excitement in his voice and Eric knew the younger brother wanted nothing more than to please him.

"No he doesn't," Eric said.

Aaron paused, confused. "How do you know?"

"She called him."

"You let her call?"

Eric took a deep breath. He didn't feel like explaining every detail. It wasn't only that repeating the whole story of Dmitri and Ollie and the BART station wasn't necessary, he was tired and relating the evening's events drained him. "She got out."

"What? How'd that happen?"

"Doesn't matter. Ollie and Marcus got her back. She was on the phone to this guy Vic when they found her. They are most definitely heading this way. Now reroute and get your asses down here."

There was a pounding on his front door. The cop knock. Every cop knocked the same way, loud and with the side of their fist. If they ever tried a lighter rap with their knuckles, they might get the jump on someone, but it was like they had to announce they were law enforcement with their banging. Eric wondered if the knock was something they taught at the academy. He trotted down the stairs as they pounded again.

Before opening the door, he stuck his head in the main room to the side of the stairs. "Marcus, keep her quiet."

It was easy for Marcus. They had Barbara trussed this time, and instead of keeping her quiet with a gun—which was an empty threat with police at the door, the sound of a shot would bring a SWAT team swarming—he held a polished buck knife to Barbara's throat. The point of the knife pressed into her trachea, just hard enough to draw blood.

Chapter Twenty-Six

"This is the place, huh?" Mackie wasn't impressed. The two-story corner building was run down. Peeling paint, dirty windows blocked with flags and sheets, a few dead cars parked in a makeshift parking lot fenced off by a cyclone fence. The decrepit state didn't surprise him, but he certainly wasn't impressed.

"Yep. We've had this joint on the radar for years. It's been under surveillance over and over, we've just never had cause to kick in the door. Lots of activity, just not enough of it criminal." Nagle stepped out from behind the Crown Vic and walked to the front door and rapped his fist against the metal gate.

They waited, keeping silent so they might be able to hear any movement inside. Nothing. Nagle hit the door again. No response.

"You think he's in there?" Mackie said.

"Your guess is as good as mine." Nagle drew his cell from his pocket and checked the time. "It's almost ten in the morning. He's probably still in bed."

Mackie stepped to the side of the building and surveyed the lot. Several cars were broken down, one was up on blocks. At least two vehicles looked road worthy. "No dog? I thought all these outlaw biker types had dogs."

"He's not a biker 'type,' he's president of the BBs. He's *the* outlaw biker. As far as the bureau is concerned, the number one target—" Nagle held up his hand and cocked his head toward the door. There was movement inside, footsteps down the stairs.

The inner door behind the heavy iron gate opened up. Eric Tribban stood behind the metal mesh, looking tired and annoyed. "What?"

"Mr. Tribban?"

Eric didn't say anything. He offered nothing. He kept his eyes, lidded and dead, focused on the man on the sidewalk.

"Mr. Tribban, I'm Special Agent Nagle and I'd like to ask you a couple of questions. May we come in?"

"We?" Eric hadn't seen the other man. A shorter, less clean-cut version of Agent Nagle appeared at his door. Eric looked both men up and down and said, "No."

Before Tribban could turn away, Nagle said, "Please, this is important. It won't take but a minute of your time. I assure you, this isn't part of any investigation involving you or the Dead BBs."

Eric smirked at the assurance and opened the gate, quickly stepping onto the sidewalk and shutting the gate behind him. "You got two minutes."

Once he was out in the morning light, Mackie noticed how bad he looked. His eyes were bloodshot and pinched with crow's feet. He was crusted with stubble and his hair hung lank and greasy. They hadn't woken him at all, this guy had been up all night.

Barbara couldn't even swallow her fear. Every time she moved her throat, Marcus' knife poked farther into her neck. She felt the warm trickle of her own blood drip toward her chest. She was relatively certain he wouldn't kill her, not with what sounded like the police at the door, but she couldn't be sure. She squinted in the darkness at his face and he seemed to be smiling.

Marcus lifted a finger to his lips and softly said, "Sssh."

Barbara listened as she heard the front door open and shut, then to the muffled voices outside. She hoped it was the cops calling. She hoped they brought backup. In fact, she hoped they brought the SWAT team.

Mackie opened with, "Do you know a woman named Barbara Bertram?"

Tribban stood before the two men with his arms folded across his chest and his back to his home. "No. Why? Who is she?"

"She's missing, and she's a relative of an associate of yours."

Tribban smirked. "I don't have associates. I do got a lotta friends though. Why don't you just cut to the chase and tell me what the fuck we're talking about."

"Barbara Bertram is the mother of Jerry Bertram. That name ring a bell?"

Eric shook his head.

"Really? No? Jerry is your daughter's boyfriend."

"Oh..." Eric nodded thoughtfully. "I still don't know him. Not really. The first name sounds familiar. I met him maybe once and I didn't like him. How many fathers you know pal around with their daughter's boyfriends?"

Mackie was about to say something more, but Nagle touched his arm to quiet him. No point in attempting an interrogation. Tribban was used to law enforcement trying to intimidate him. Mackie managed a thin smile. "You mind if we leave our number? Just in case you hear anything about her?"

Eric raised his eyebrows, noncommittal.

Nagle reached into his blazer and produced a card. Eric took it. "FBI? Fancy. What'd you say this woman did again?"

"She didn't do anything," Mackie said. "She's missing."

"Oh. Okay. If I happen to meet anyone by that name, I'll be sure to give you two a call." Eric waited till the two men retreated into their Crown Vic and pulled away before opening his gate again.

"Marcus?"

"Yeah, boss?"

Eric hated when one of the brothers called him that. "She all right?"

"She's still here. Still breathing."

"Good enough. I'm gonna scramble a few eggs and cut a couple of lines. You want anything?"

Without releasing any pressure from Barbara's neck, Marcus said, "That sounds great. I'll be right here with my new best friend."

When they were two blocks away, Mackie said, "Really, that's it? That's shakin' the tree?"

Nagle rounded a right. "No, that's not it. We're not going anywhere. We're circling around to see if any fruit falls from the tree."

"You gotta be kiddin'. He's already seen our car."

"Doesn't matter. We'll park far enough up the street. If they have her in there, maybe they'll try to move her before they think we'll come back. If not, we'll still be able to see who's coming and going."

"That's it?"

"For now. Until we figure out a solid move. I told you, I'm not pulling myself out of the fire to go sit in the woods. Trust me, Roland, I know you've been a cop longer than I've been an agent, but I know how these guys work. The players will come back to HQ. They always do. It's like the military. They need orders from the generals."

Vic leaned on the steering wheel. It was past ten o'clock. Ghia still slept beside him, Piper snored right behind his head. He peeked into the rearview and saw Jerry nodding off in the back. He played out his options in his head.

Barbara had mentioned going to a friend of Jerry's named Richard. A guy Jerry lovingly referred to as Dick. Jerry seemed to know where Dick lived but didn't know the exact address. It was pointless to chase down Jerry's friend. Vic knew in his gut the BBs had Barbara again. There was no reason for the phone call to have been cut short like it was. She would have found a way to call back if she was free. He reeled back the conversation in his mind. He was never able to tell her Jerry was with him. For all she knew, he was still on the hill with a gun to his head. If she'd known Vic had him, she probably would've gone straight to the police. But Barbara was nothing if not loyal. She wasn't going to risk her son's life to save her own. In truth, Vic didn't know if she knew anything about Jerry's score. He was beginning to distrust the kid more and more. For a son whose mother's life was on the line, he didn't seem very concerned. Jerry was a selfish asshole. It didn't take a lot of insight to figure that out. Anybody who lived score to score like he did was, by very design, a self-centered prick.

Vic knew he'd have to force a meeting. He wasn't sure how, or what he could offer. But he was going to have to walk into the fire before he could pull Barbara out.

Vic pulled out his cell and dialed Big Man.

Vlad and Dmitri sat in a diner on Webster Street. It was an old place that'd been remodeled and made to look even older. Dmitri pushed a wilted pile of hash browns around his plate while Vlad forked bite after bite of pancake into his mouth.

"What's wrong, *comaneci*? You still mad we're not going to the hospital?"

Dmitri shook his head.

"C'mon, you should know this job doesn't come with health benefits." Vlad mopped up some syrup with another fork-load of pancake. "We will, however, cover burial costs."

"Very funny," Dmitri said. "What are we doing now? We are waiting? For what?"

"We're having breakfast is what we're doing. At least I am.

I'm paying for this meal, the least you could do is eat it." Vlad waved at the waitress for more coffee. "After this I have to pick up my sister, check in again with the warehouse. Then...then we are going back to our biker friends to see if they've solved their problems."

"Our problems."

"Yes. Our problems." Vlad waited for the waitress to refill his cup before continuing. He gave a sickly sweet smile as she poured and retreated. "I get the distinct impression our friends aren't really our friends. I've had this impression for quite some time now. This is why it was so important you spoke to that woman by yourself."

"I told you, she didn't know anything."

"If she didn't know anything, then why did she feel it necessary to hit you on the head and run away."

"She was scared."

"Scared? Of what? You?"

Dmitri pursed his lips. He had an open gash on his forehead, his brain felt like it'd been slammed against a brick wall, he'd been humiliated as a man for letting a woman get the best of him. This was no time to tease. Vlad would do well to remember why he was hired, why he was trusted, who he was. "Listen to me, I was only doing what—"

"Okay, okay. I'll stop. I'm only trying to cheer you up. Look at you moping. What's done is done. The real problem is yet to be solved. We need that kid, we need the money, and—more than anything—we need to know, for true, how much money he took. Even if it means promising to let him live, we need to know if our friends are cheating us."

"Let him live?"

"*Promise* to let him live."

On his way up the hill, Big Man passed a strange sight. Old Meth Master Mike—looking as ragged as he'd ever seen him—

standing by the frontage road with his thumb out. Mike was only about a half-mile from his house, and Big Man wondered if Mike's tired brain was starting to show signs of dementia. He could have easily walked home from there. Big Man thought about giving the old tweaker a ride, but decided no. As many years as he'd known Mike, he was always annoyed by his endless rambling. Big Man was on a mission and didn't need to get sidetracked by whatever foolishness the man had going on. He decided to focus on the road ahead and prepare himself for the mess Vic had left him at his own cabin.

Big Man had just pulled into the driveway of the cabin when his phone started ringing. The cell was wedged in his back pocket, so there was no way he was going to reach it before it stopped ringing. Besides, the last call he got gave him nothing but bad news. He braked in the gravel behind the row of vehicles. The only cars left were the ones that'd sat here since he lived on the hill. It'd been three years since he'd let Vic move in and take over his operation. The isolation and boredom had been killing Big Man. There was nothing to do on the hill but eat, drink, and stare at the trees. The days were hard, filled with honest-to-God labor, but the nights, they were the worst. He'd never been so lonely. Not like Eureka was the big city or anything, but it beat the hell out of sitting in the jungle watching weed grow.

With a push on the steering wheel, Big Man shoved his way out of the truck. It took him a moment to straighten out. Climbing out of a vehicle was the simplest of tasks, yet he still broke into a sweat. He sucked in a lungful of the familiar clean air and started toward the house. Before he stepped on the porch, he remembered Doughboy's warning about what he might walk into and pulled his Glock 21 from the inside of his jacket. The old porch creaked loudly under his considerable weight.

"Doughboy?" He called to the open door.

"Yeah. Big Man, that you?"

Big Man hoisted the gun up in front of his face. "You alone?"

"Just me and the fucking ghosts."

Big Man stepped over the threshold and found Doughboy sprawled across the couch. He had two rolls of paper towels pushed against his thigh in an attempt to slow the bleeding. The couch itself was slick with blood. Doughboy looked pale and anemic.

"How you doing, Big Man?"

A half empty bottle of Jameson was clamped between his legs and a burning cigarette had just fallen to the wood floor.

"Fuck, Doughboy, you're gonna burn my place down." Big Man stepped in and ground out the smoke with the toe of his boot. "What the fuck happened?"

"Vic fucking Thomas. That's what happened."

"Did he shoot you?"

"No, one of his little piece of shit trolls did."

Big Man took a closer look at the thigh and winced. "That's not good, man. We gotta get you to a doctor or something."

"Oh, that ain't the half of it," Doughboy slurred. "Take a look behind you."

Big Man turned around as saw a heap of plastic. A form wrapped in a beige shower curtain. Blood marbled most of the curtain, but at the point farthest from Big Man, tucked near a small table, it was nearly all red. "Aww no."

"It's fuckin' Terry, man." Doughboy came close to choking on his words. "I don't know what to do. They brought him back just like that. I can't even barely walk, I don't know what I'm supposed to do."

Big Man put his hands on his hips and leaned in toward the body, titling his head left to right, as though a different perspective might change the ugly truth. Finally he said, "I'm not sure what we *can* do."

"Eric says to take care of it. I guess he means hide him. Bury him. What the fuck are we going to tell his wife and kid? I mean, shit, the guy just doesn't come home? Does he think the cops are never gonna come sniffing around?"

Big Man shrugged. "Not up here, it ain't likely. But, shit, no way, I can't be digging a hole that big. Fuck, when I was done, you'd have to put me in it too. You don't look like you're in any manual labor condition either. And trust me, digging a hole that deep is hard. Harder than it looks on TV, that's for goddamn sure."

"What do we do with him?"

Big Man rubbed his chin like he was trying to solve a math problem. "Honestly? I don't have a clue. How much meat you figure ol' Vic kept in the deep freeze?"

Chapter Twenty-Seven

Cardiff's phone lit up as soon as they hit Santa Rosa. He fumbled it on the first try, then managed to flip it open and answer the call.

"How're you doing?" Vlad didn't need to say his name. He preferred not to. It was one of those old gangster habits he liked to exercise, even though, these days, it didn't make much of a difference. If someone was listening in, they knew who they were listening to.

"We're okay. We're getting close to the Bay. How's it going down there?"

"Can you talk?"

Cardiff looked beside him at Aaron, who was bent over a CD case lined with blow. "No. He's wide awake, sipping a coffee. You want me to pull over?"

Vlad paused to choose his words carefully. "You think he can hear my voice?"

"I doubt it," Cardiff said.

"Piper?" Vic said her name softly, hoping not to disturb the others. Her head lolled from one side to the other. He saw her eyes flutter. He said it again, "Piper?"

Ghia woke beside him first, blinking at the light and wiping drool from her chin. "Holy shit, where are we?"

"Just south of Santa Rosa," Vic whispered.

"Why are you whispering?"

"I'm trying to wake up the girl."

"Try talking louder." Even in the first bleary moments of consciousness Ghia exhibited the witty charm that made Vic cherish her company.

"I don't want to wake *him*."

They both heard Jerry's snores from the back seat. They were deep, rolling, and luxuriously paced. It wasn't likely anything would wake him. His head was tilted back onto the headrest and his mouth was cocked open. Ghia turned in her seat and touched Piper on the knee. "Hey, wake up. Piper. Wake up."

The young girl snapped awake as though she'd been dreaming something terrible. "What? What is it? What happened?"

"I need to know where your father lives," Vic said.

She wrinkled her nose as though she didn't understand the question. When Vic repeated the request, she shook her head. Slowly at first, but then more rapidly as it dawned on her what he was asking. "Why?" she said. "Why would you want that?"

"I know he's in the East Bay. Just tell me where."

"Are you out of your mind? I'm not telling you. He wants to kill me." Her voice jumped up a half octave and Jerry stirred, blinking his eyes into consciousness. "Not just me either. He'll kill all of us."

"What's wrong, baby?" Jerry muttered. "What's a matter?"

"They want us to go to Pop's, Jerry. What the fuck? I thought you said this guy was looking out for us? I thought you said we'd be safe. He's driving me right back home?"

"Ssh, it's all right. Vic knows what he's doing."

She punched him in the arm. Everyone in the vehicle was wide awake now. "Wake the fuck up, Jerry. We're going *back*. Look around. We're going back home."

Jerry cleared his throat and leaned into the open space between the two front seats. "Vic, man. What's going on? We can't go back. You fuckin' traded fire with those motherfuckers. They'll be looking to kill all of us. Not just me and Piper."

"Nobody's gonna wanna kill Piper Tribban."

"You got that wrong. Her and the old man don't get along. Never have. You wouldn't believe the shit that's gone on between them."

"You're right. I probably wouldn't."

Ghia watched the exchange and kept quiet.

"Don't worry, Ghia," Vic said. "I'll be dropping you off when we get to a safe spot."

"Sounds like you have a plan. And dumping me off is my favorite part. Not that it ain't been fun, but this old lady wants to have a few more teatimes before she draws the curtain."

"You can let us all off," Piper said. "I don't want any part of this. You don't know what the hell you're doing."

Vic glared into the rearview. "You don't want any part of this? You two started this. All of it. If you weren't acting like greedy fucking junkie brats stealing from your own goddamn blood, I'd be sitting quiet on the hill right now, drinking coffee and thinking about my next shit. As it is, you got me and my very good friend here in a fucking firefight with some of the most dangerous assholes on the West Coast. Not to mention the very high probability that Jerry's mother—a woman I have not only enduring respect for, but owe a lifetime of gratitude to—fucking kidnapped. You get that? That innocent woman is sitting on the wrong end of a gun barrel thinking she's got to give up her life for you two pieces of shit. We're going to the East Bay. We're gonna figure this out. And nobody's gonna die. Not me, not Jerry's mother. None of us. Now...where the fuck does your old man live?"

"What do you remember about that day?" Nagle asked.

Mackie was unrolling a pack of antacid tablets. He offered Nagle one. "What day?"

Nagle shook his head, then said, "You know what day. Fulton Street." They were still in Nagle's car up the street from

Tribban's. It was a busy thoroughfare, but there was almost no foot traffic. They'd only been there for about an hour, but neither was used to sitting on any kind of stakeout.

"I remember everything about it. I remember I ate a bear claw for breakfast. I was a rookie and figured that's what cops ate. I remember the first call we went on was a skunk shooting."

"What?"

"Yeah, a skunk shooting. I was working Richmond Station and a call came in at Forty-fifth and Cabrillo, a two-sixteen. We get there to investigate and we find a skunk. Fucking bullet right through its head."

"People hate skunks."

"Yeah they do. Especially city skunks. There's a lot of 'em in SF too. More than you'd think."

As the two spoke, they both kept their eyes on Tribban's residence. At one and a half block's distance, it was hard to see anything other than a person or vehicle coming or going, but parking any closer risked too much exposure.

"Coyotes too," Mackie said.

"What?"

"There's a lot of coyotes in the park."

"I know. I live in the Sunset too. I know about the park. I got raccoons going through my garbage three times a week." Nagle tried to stretch but couldn't fully extend himself while stuck behind the steering wheel. "But tell me more about Fulton Street. What else do you remember?"

"I dunno. It was fucked up. It was like one of those Manson Family crime scene photos, but it was real. In color. It was my first big case. The amount of blood was incredible. I didn't know people had that much blood in them. Didn't realize it at the time, but all that blood meant those folks lived through most of it. They kept pumping it out as they were tortured. The kid was the worst. Jesus, I've never seen anything like it. Not in all my years since. I swore right then and there, I'd get the fuckers who were responsible. With the amount of bodies that have piled up because of the drug wars, there's never been..." Mackie trailed off because he knew Nagle wasn't listening. "What's up?"

"You see that?" Nagle pointed a finger at the windshield. "That white van making the corner there. It's the third time it's been by Tribban's. Twice from the right and once from the other side."

"Looking for parking?"

"There's plenty of parking. He's scouting the neighborhood, looking for surveillance before he lands."

"Can you make out a plate?"

"Not from here."

They waited as the white van made another trip around the block. This time, the van double-parked in front of Tribban's and a man hopped out of the front and circled 'round to open the gate. When the man turned to push open the gate, Nagle leaned over the dash and squinted.

"You know him?" Mackie asked.

"I think so. If I'm not mistaken, that's Ollie Jeffers."

"Ollie? That's his name? Sounds like a cartoon hillbilly."

"He's not a cartoon, but he is a hillbilly. And he's a march-in-step soldier of the BBs."

"He's patched in?"

"Oh, yeah. He's the kind of guy the club is made for. Does whatever they tell him, doesn't ask questions, excels at violence. He's got a brain the size of a pea, so there's no room for guilt or common sense. Closest thing to a robot killing machine these guys ever had."

"Why the fuck is he walking around free?"

"Oh, he's been investigated a few times. There're a few open cases against him now too."

"You said that more than once since we started this thing."

"What?"

"That they've been under investigation, or surveillance, or whatever. Do you guys actually ever go out and arrest anyone?"

They watched as Ollie got back into the van and pulled into

Tribban's makeshift parking lot.

"What now?" Mackie asked.

"What'd you mean, what now? We wait. We keep waiting. What else?"

"You know, for having the federal government at your disposal, you guys seem awfully short on intelligence."

"Feel free to contribute any time you're ready."

Mackie made a little snort and dug his phone out of his pocket.

"Here's the plan, we go to Richard's." Vic'd refused to exchange positions with Ghia or Jerry. He said he was fine behind the wheel. In truth, he didn't want to chance any diversions from the plan he was still formulating.

"You mean Dick's?" Jerry seemed pleased he was being brought in on the plan.

"Whatever. What's his deal anyway?"

"He thinks he's a gangster."

"What is he?"

"He's a dick."

Vic shrugged like that made sense. And, in a way, it did. Richard—or Dick—and his character also didn't matter. All he wanted was a launching point, an annex, somewhere to prepare his attack. He didn't think Barbara was going to be there. If she was, then hallelujah, they could all go home. But his gut told him it was going to take a lot more to secure his friend's safety. If Eric Tribban already knew about the BB Vic had taken out on the hill—and he mostly likely did—then Vic expected nothing less than all-out war.

Jerry asked, "You want me to call him, let him know we're coming?"

"No," Vic said.

"What if he's not there? You sure you don't want me to call?"

"I'm sure."

Vic looked into the rearview. His eyes flicked between Jerry and Piper. "You two set your phones up here on the console. Both of you, c'mon, let's have 'em."

Piper spoke first, her tone once again snide and petulant. "I'm not handing you my phone. Fuck that. I don't even know you."

Vic didn't say anything, he just tapped on the console sitting between the two front seats.

"Yeah, Vic. These are our lifelines," Jerry said. "What if we get separated or something. We may need to call for help."

"Besides, mine has no charge." Piper said, "I can't call anyone even if I wanted to."

"If there's no charge then they're useless as lifelines. Put 'em up."

"C'mon," Jerry said. "You're being unreasonable, why would we—"

Vic braked and yanked the Ford to the side of the freeway. Horns blared as cars flew by them. He threw the transmission into park and spun in his seat. He kept his voice low and even so he could be sure the two in back understood. "You two give me your phones. Right now. Or I'm going to shoot you both in the head with this gun." He held up the Glock to underscore his point. "First you, Jerry, because you're an asshole. Then you, sister, because you're the real reason we're in this mess. I'll take the next goddamn exit and kick both your dead bodies out and leave 'em on the side of the road for the cops to find. I don't give a shit. The gun is untraceable and half the West Coast wants to see you two dead."

Vic waited while Jerry and Piper looked at each other, both their eyes lit up, fearful with the impact of Vic's serious tone.

"What's it gonna be?" Vic said.

They both sat their cells on the console. Vic picked them up and put the car back in gear. They were less than an hour away from Oakland.

Chapter Twenty-Eight

"Ollie! That you?" Eric called out from his perch atop the stairs.

Ollie entered through the side door, the one reserved for friends and brothers. He walked past Marcus in the dim light of the downstairs area and almost didn't see Barbara trussed on the floor.

"Shit, she alive?"

"Yeah, but she just passed out."

"You sure she can breathe? You got her all roped up like that."

"Nah, she's fine. We didn't tie it to choke her, just to hold her. We don't want her slipping away again."

"You're not gonna fuck her, are you?"

"Fuck you, Ollie. She's an old lady. Get the fuck upstairs. Eric wants to talk to you."

Ollie squatted down to look at Barbara. Her eyes were rolled up into her head and veins bulged on her forehead, but she was breathing.

"She don't look too good."

"Neither do you," Marcus said.

Eric stood with his arms folded as Ollie ran up the stairs. "Where the fuck you been?"

"BART police, man. They ran my shit for an hour. Pain in the ass. I got a ticket on the van while they held me."

Eric cocked his head. He trusted Ollie, more than most of the brothers, but he still ran through protocol. "What happened?"

"I almost had her. She was a block ahead of me. I followed her down into the station. I saw her on the phone, so I started to run. I didn't give a fuck, I was gonna drag her ass outta there. What happens? A little old lady steps right in front of me. Bam! I mowed her down. People thought I was trying to rob her or somethin'. Suddenly it's a big commotion and I got the BART cops on me. Those guys are fuckin' morons. No wonder they're not real cops."

"You're lucky they didn't just shoot you."

"Me? She's lucky I didn't catch her."

"Not that lucky. Marcus caught her at the top of the escalator."

"Yeah, I just saw her downstairs. She tell you who she was calling?"

"Not sure. Marcus tried his little razor and lemon juice trick, but she passed out. I'm thinking of taking her to the warehouse or somewhere. We got heat on us here."

"How do you know? I circled for blocks looking for eyes but didn't see nobody."

"They came and knocked on the fucking door. Marcus had a knife to her throat in the next room while I talked to 'em." Eric turned and walked back toward the kitchen, letting Ollie follow. "Got no idea if they're still out there though. If we want to get her outta here we have to be careful. I'm glad you brought the van back. That'll help."

"Why the warehouse?"

"'Cause when this is done, we gotta chop her up, get rid of her."

"Oh." Ollie nodded. He'd dismembered bodies before, but not any women. He was sure it wouldn't be a problem. Too bad, he thought. He kind of liked Barbara. She certainly showed some balls kicking that Russian's ass. But then again, that's probably why he was going to be the one to kill her.

* * *

Big Man was winded. He couldn't remember the last time he'd exerted so much energy. Doughboy did the best he could, but with a thigh full of buckshot, Big Man didn't expect much from him. The deep freeze was a top-loading chest freezer meant to keep a winter's worth of food frozen and ready. Big Man bought it years ago, long before he let Vic stay at the cabin. In the appliance store he joked about it being big enough to fit a dead body. He never guessed it would one day house one. After taking all the meat and frozen dinners out of the freezer and stacking them on the floor, the two lugged Terry's considerable corpse into the storage room and upended the body into the deep freeze. It didn't have to be a perfect fit. They tucked and folded and shoved the best they could. Finally they were able to shut the door. Once they were sure it would close, they picked up the thawing steaks and frozen burritos and piled what they could on top of Terry.

"No sense in these going to waste," Big Man said. "You hungry? I can nuke us up some of these right quick."

Out of breath, Doughboy shook his head.

"You sure? You lost a lot of blood. You need them calories."

"I'm sure."

"Suit yourself," Big Man said, and he picked a box of frozen enchiladas and two frozen burritos and headed out of the storage, through the throngs of hanging marijuana plants, to the kitchen and the microwave.

He read the burrito instructions, stuck the packet in the oven and hit the time. While he waited, he heard a soft pinging sound. He reached back and drew his cell from his back pocket. Three missed calls. No messages. Two from Vic, that fucking asshole. And one from a four-one-five number. Vic had given him nothing but headaches in the past two days. He was looking at spending the rest of his days in prison because of the trouble Vic had brought to the hill. The other number though—

a San Francisco area code—could be the BBs. He swiped the missed call and lifted the phone to his ear. No reception. Same old shack. He waited till his burrito was heated, peeled back the wrapper, and took the snack out to the hooper, the one spot he knew he'd get a strong enough signal to hear and be heard.

Big Man winded himself on the short ascent to the fertilizer sack where everyone sat to talk on the phone. That sack had been there for years. It was the hill's version of a phone booth. He sat down heavy and tore off another sloppy bite of the burrito and swiped the missed call again. This time it rang through.

"You decided to call back."

The voice sounded familiar, but not in a good way. He knew right off it wasn't a BB, or even a friend. "Who's this?"

"You don't remember me? Big Man, I'm hurt. This is Detective Roland Mackie with the SFPD. Ring any bells now?"

With a mouth full of beef burrito, Big Man said, "Shit."

Big Man had crossed paths with Roland Mackie several years ago when he got busted moving stolen motorcycle parts through a bike shop in San Francisco. He knew it'd been a risky move, but he'd been paid with the parts in lieu of cash after a weed deal went south. He was only trying to cover his losses. SFPD was all over the case. They even had someone in the store working for them. But it wasn't Big Man they were after. Their target was a bigger bike club that specialized in stolen motorcycles, so they let Big Man slip out of the net. Mackie tried to lean on Big Man for information after that, but instead of an exchange, they sparked a tentative relationship, each knowing the other could be useful in the future. Mackie tried following up a few times after the case closed, but quickly learned Big Man would never become a CI. Instead, the two enjoyed some playful cat and mouse banter on the phone every couple of months till Mackie changed departments and disappeared from Big Man's life.

"How're things up there in the jungle?" Mackie continued. "You staying in shape?"

"Look, Mack, it's nice to hear from you and all, but I got shit to do up here. What'd you want?"

"You can sit down and talk to an old friend for just a minute, can't you? Sounds to me like you're having a lunch break anyway."

"So what ever happened to you after the bunco squad? You stopped calling. They bust you down to meter maid or somethin'?"

"Is that your way of asking if I'm in narcotics now? The answer is no. I'm sure you're relieved to hear."

"The only thing I'd be relieved to hear from you is goodbye."

"Don't worry, I won't keep you," Mackie said. "I just need a little help."

"Then you should call someone who can help you."

"Right...Listen, I'm trying to locate someone. Two people actually. Mother and son. Their names are—"

"What makes you think I would know anything about whoever the fuck it is you're looking for?"

"Word on the street, Big Man. You remember word on the street, don't you? Word is these two are up there in your neck of the woods."

"Who are they?"

"Woman's name is Barbara Bertram. She's in her mid-fifties. Handsome lady. Maybe you've seen her?"

"Doesn't ring no bells. Who's the kid?"

"Her son, Jerry. Jerry Bertram. Real asshole. Might have his girlfriend with him. That's why I thought you might know. Her name is Piper Tribban. Eric Tribban's daughter."

A moment of dead air passed between them.

Mackie added, "You know Eric Tribban, don't you?"

"Everybody knows Eric. I had no idea he even had a daughter."

"Well, we're looking hard for these folks. I'd be mighty appreciative if you get back in touch if you hear anything."

"What's that mean, mighty appreciative?"

"Like a get-out-of-jail-free card kind of appreciative."

Big Man snorted. He pushed the ragged end of the burrito into his mouth. "Hey, Mackie, where you really working now?"

"Still with SFPD."

"I mean, what department?"

"Gang task force."

Big Man looked back at the cabin. "You figure that was a promotion or a *de*motion?"

"You call me if you hear anything, all right?"

Big Man ended the call.

Dmitri and Vlad lingered after their late breakfast. While Dmitri's head throbbed, Vlad worked feverishly trying to figure out all the angles. Problem was, he couldn't see the whole picture. He was certain the BBs had been stealing from his clubs, but he had no idea how much. No evidence either. He needed the Bertram woman alive—but only if she knew something. He wasn't ready to risk a battle over a woman with useless information. Cardiff was supposed to grab the thieves who ripped off the San Francisco store, but it'd be their word against his about how much they stole. That's why Aaron, the thug the BBs sent along to babysit Cardiff, was up there. He was supposed to witness whatever truth was uncovered when they caught Jerry and Eric Tribban's stepdaughter, Piper.

The problem was Jerry and Piper were never caught. They were out there running around with as much—or as little—of Vlad's money they stole. Only they knew the real amount, and if the BBs got them before Vlad or Cardiff spoke to them, they'd be silenced. The amount they stole wasn't the issue, not the actual money anyway, it was the evidence of years of skimming. Hundreds upon hundreds of thousands of dollars.

"What did he say?" Dmitri asked.

"Who?" Vlad wasn't looking at Dmitri. He gazed out the window, figures and tallies running through his mind.

"Cardiff."

"He said they're on the way here."

"Where is here?"

"Here is here. Eric's most likely. He says this badass from up there, Vic, has the kids with him. He's some sort of cowboy. And he wants the woman. That's why he's coming. To get the woman. To save the woman."

"Sounds like we should take the woman. Not only can we see what she knows, but it sounds like she's a magnet. This guy will maybe come right to her. Especially if he knows where to find her."

"I don't know if we want to tangle with this Vic directly, you know? Cardiff says he already killed the BBs' bigshot up there."

Dmitri raised his eyebrows.

"Yes, this whole thing is heating up quicker than we thought."

"So what do we do?"

"First off, you go next door to the liquor store and get me one of those grape blunt wraps, I like. You know the ones. Then I roll a fat one and we sit and wait. Let's stay close to our friends here. Seems like they might be having a party."

Chapter Twenty-Nine

Big Man finished chewing and leaned his head back against the frame of the hooper and let the morning sun warm him. Getting a call from the cops was the least of his concerns. He had a dead body stuck in his freezer. His old friend and comrade had turned his world completely upside down. What started out as a good deed for a man he trusted turned into the worst mistake of his life.

He didn't want to call Vic back. He didn't want to deal with the Dead BBs when they came to fetch their leader. He didn't even want to get up off this sack of fertilizer. He was tired. More tired than he could remember. And not just from flipping Terry into his freezer. He was tired of the game, tired of the hustle. Being a marijuana wholesaler was nothing but a headache. He couldn't wait till the shit went legal. Most of the people he knew would vote against legalization, but Big Man was changing his vote on Prop 64 to yes. Let the fucking government experience the headaches of being a dealer. His own crew, The Cripplers, were nearly all retired. Self-sufficient good old boys who'd also grown weary of the criminal side of being an outlaw biker. He envied his brothers who'd had enough foresight to get real jobs, trades that allowed a parachute for the lean years ahead. Big Man felt trapped. Trapped by a lifetime of living outside the law, trapped by circumstances forced on him by guys like Vic Thomas.

Big Man squeezed the phone in his right hand and sighed.

"Goddamn you, Vic." He opened his eyes, blinked through the sunspots, let his vision settle on the screen, then swiped the missed call.

Vic was nearing the Bay. They were approaching the Richmond Bridge, linking the 101 with Interstate 80. On their right they passed San Quentin. He chuckled under his breath. After today, he'd be lucky to end up with a bunk there. There was no question in his mind he was walking into a potential suicide mission.

The cell phone cradled between his thighs started to buzz.

"Big, what's up?"

"What's up? You gotta be kidding me, Vic. Where the fuck are you?"

"On the highway to hell, my friend."

"Oh, you got that right. Thing is, you're taking me along with you."

"What're you talking about?"

"I'm sitting here with some of the mess you left behind."

"I'm sorry. None of that could be helped. I didn't want it to turn out this way."

"Fuck you, Vic. Where are you and where you going?"

"I'm going to do my best to straighten all this out."

"How's that even possible?"

"I'm glad you asked. That's why I called you in the first place. I need you to reach out for me."

"You want me to talk to the BBs for you? You're crazier than I thought."

Vic peeked at the rearview. He knew all ears were tuned into his conversation. Hopefully the others could only hear what he was saying, not what he was hearing. "No, I'll do the talking."

"What, you want a meet? You really are fucking crazy."

Vic stayed silent and listened to his friend wheeze into receiver.

"All right," Big Man said. "Stay by your phone. I'll see what

I can do."

"Thanks, brother."

"Don't call me that. Not no more. Not ever," Big Man said and hung up.

Barbara heard the heavy boots thunder down the stairs. With her weight on her stomach and chest and her legs and head trussed up together, blood flow had nearly come to a stop. She knew she'd lost consciousness, but couldn't say for how long. The biker with the knife sat in front of her. He was picking at the remnants of some scrambled eggs and toast on a paper plate and didn't seem to notice she was awake. Eric, her captor, the one in charge, came through the door at the far corner of the room.

"Cut her loose," he said.

The egg-eating biker said, "We're lettin' her go?"

"No, I mean cut the rope so she can get up and move around. That piece of shit Vic called Big. He wants to do a trade."

"Big Man wants to trade?"

"Holy fuck, Marcus, what's the matter with you? *Vic*. The guy we've been talking about. He wants to trade Piper for the old lady here."

"Then that's good right? We get her back, maybe her boyfriend too."

"Yeah, something like that."

Barbara knew the instant Eric said it, his plan was to kill them all. She didn't know the whole story, but she'd heard enough. They'd gone too far down this road. She knew one of the members of the BBs had been killed, maybe two. They weren't forgiving anybody. The details of what got her there didn't matter anymore, and she hoped Vic knew it.

* * *

Seventh Street and Alice was on the edge of Chinatown on the south end of Downtown Oakland. It looked like a quiet neighborhood, one and two-story dwellings mixed in with some small warehouses. Vic circled the surrounding blocks, noting the BART station at 8th and Oak. He wondered if this is where Barbara had run to. The thought of her being pulled from the phone quickened his pulse.

"You ever been here before?"

"Yeah, of course. Dick's lived here forever. That's why my mom knew it too."

"Not you," Vic said into the rearview, "her."

Piper shook her head and Vic squinted into the mirror, trying to guess if she was telling the truth. He pulled the Escape into a loading zone. When the car had stopped, he looked at Ghia in the passenger seat. "You got enough money to get you out of here?"

"What? This's it? The end of the road?"

"Yeah, the ride is gonna get too bumpy from here on out."

"Not for nothing, Vic, but it's been pretty damn bumpy all the way so far."

"I know. That's why it's best if you step out now, while you still can. You saved our lives. And that's no exaggeration. I don't know what kind of fallout there's gonna be after today, who's going to come knocking on your door. All I can ask is that you be mindful of the truth, and do the right thing."

Ghia chuckled. "Oh, I'm not complaining. My good deed is definitely done. I love you, Vic. You know I do. But if it comes to me getting hauled in or getting caught in the crossfire, I'll choose the former." She cracked the door and stepped onto the sidewalk. Before she stepped away, she leaned in and looked at Jerry and Piper. "This here is the bravest, strongest, smartest man I know. If you listen and do what he says, chances are you'll come out the other side safe and sound." And without another word, she shut the door and started walking to the BART station.

When she'd turned the corner, Vic put the Ford in drive and circled around the block.

"What are you doing?" Jerry said. "There's a parking spot right there?"

"I'm being careful, that's what I'm doing."

"Nobody knows Dick. He's a knucklehead, someone I met in high school. He's harmless."

"Kid, I think it's you that doesn't know dick."

"What?"

"Nothing. Lemme go 'round one more time and then I'll park."

After they'd parked and carefully removed all the firearms from the Ford, the three of them trod the short distance to Dick's front door. The house was a small Victorian with an unused garage underneath. Any realtor would have described the place as cute and cozy, but to Vic, it was a shithole. He understood real estate in Oakland was on the rise, and from the looks of the surrounding properties, the whole block was fixed up to flip, but Dick's place had a sheen of dirt, a layer of neglect it'd take more than a coat of paint to cover. Torn curtains hung in the windows and orange paint was peeling off the front door. Jerry stepped around Vic and pounded his fist on the front door, squaring his fist on a sticker for a skateboard company that'd been defunct since the nineties.

"Dick? It's me, Jerr. You in there?"

The three waited and listened, but the sound of the street washed over any stirrings inside.

Piper asked, "You sure he still lives here?"

"Yeah, baby, I'm sure. Look at this shithole, who else is going to live here?"

Before she could answer, the door opened a crack and a voice said, "Hang on a sec."

Jerry pushed open the front door to reveal a thin shirtless

man in cutoff corduroy shorts trying to balance on one leg while he pulled a shoe on his left foot.

"What the fuck, Jerry? Who's this? Where you been?" Dick pointed to Jerry's purple eyelid. "Whoa, nice shiner."

"This is my girl, Piper. I told you about her. And this, this is Vic. We gotta use your facilities for a minute."

"You came all this way to use my bathroom?"

"No," Vic said. "He means your house." He ushered Piper in ahead of him and shut the door. The stale musty air closed in on them immediately. Dust, stale cigarette smoke, and stubbed out roaches. Vic wasted no time and stepped through the main room into the kitchen, making sure no one else was there.

"Nice to meet cha, Dick," Piper said. "Speaking of bathrooms though, can I use yours? We been on the road a while."

Dick dropped his other shoe and pointed down a dim hall. "Second door on your right."

"Hold on a second," Vic said.

"Jesus, dude, what do you think I'm going to do in there?"

Vic didn't answer. He looked inside the bathroom and saw the only window was too small for Piper to attempt an escape. He waved her in with a welcoming palm. "Gives new meaning to the term shithole, huh?"

After looking into the bedroom to make sure it was also empty, he took the few short steps back to the living room where Jerry was trying to explain their presence to Dick with a string of lies and half-truths. Vic dropped the bag with the weapons onto the carpet and clapped his hands together once, saying, "Okay, Dick, here's what I need you to do."

Ripper knew the woods on the hill. He spent his days trekking across them from patch to patch, sometimes on the ATV, but mostly on foot. After he escaped the melee at the cabin, he high-tailed it straight upward, hopping rocks across the creek and working his way into the bramble where he knew no one would follow. But he couldn't stay there forever. His injuries weren't life threatening, but without basic first aid, they were going to get infected. He needed a bottle of alcohol and a pair of tweezers to pick out the buckshot. It'd hurt like hell, but it beat leaving them in there to fester. If he could get back to town, maybe he could convince a doctor that it happened in a gun cleaning accident and get the wounds properly treated with a side order of antibiotics. If he could get back.

He couldn't see the road, so he had no idea who was coming or going, and the rush of the creek's whitewater blanketed any sound drifting up from Big Man's cabin. Eventually, he was going to have to go back down to the shack and view the fallout. The fat biker was hit with the shotgun, that was for sure. Odds were he was still laid out on the couch. And the biker took more buckshot than Ripper. He couldn't sit there all day, he needed medical attention too. But there was no way for Ripper to know if the injured biker and his cohort were still there. Ripper had been up the hill overnight, but he had no idea how late in the morning it was. The pain was making it tough to measure time. Every minute ticked by slower and slower. And although the sting of the pellets buried in his flesh had begun to grow numb, he knew it was time to climb back down the hill.

Chapter Thirty

Dick collected what Vic asked of him. Tape, rope, cell chargers, cold beer. And he stacked the items on the dining room table. There wasn't actually a dining room, but Dick explained giving it such a title distinguished it from the kitchenette table.

"That's fine. Just pile 'em there."

Dick went on explaining things that didn't need to be explained. Vic saw it as an involuntary reaction to fear. There was no reason to be afraid. Jerry, nor Piper, nor himself had mentioned anything about why they were there. Dick sensed it. He knew he was in danger the second Vic walked through his front door.

When Dick was finished, Vic cracked one of the cold beers and found a spot to plug in his phone. He straightened up, stretching his lower back and letting the spine crack. "Oh, Richard, one last thing. My cell is dead, can I make a quick call on yours?"

Dick wrinkled his nose, letting his eyes dart to Vic's charging phone, but didn't hesitate and handed the older man his cell. Vic slipped it into his pocket.

"I thought you said you needed to make a call?"

"I do. Sit down, Dick."

"Look, man," Dick said to Jerry. "I don't know what you and your friends have going on here, but the last time you showed—"

"Dick," Jerry said. "Just fucking relax."

"Relax? Fuck you, Jerry. Every time you show up there's

trouble. And there's something going on now that you're not telling me. Your fucking girlfriend has..." Dick paused, searching for the right word. "...flecks of blood all over her."

Piper looked down at her shirt. Her left shoulder was spotted with blood. She'd been sitting too close when Trinity caught a bullet back in Mr. Clean's cabin.

Jerry wet his thumb and tried to wipe off a few freckles of blood from Piper's face. Neither of them had noticed the blood splatter till now. They were exhausted. "Just sit down, dude. We don't wanna hear this shit."

"Not right now, at least," Vic said. "Right now we have to focus on the task at hand." Vic picked the heavy bag off the floor and sat it on the table with a heavy metallic *thunk*. The sound was enough to make Dick sit down. Vic took out the Glock and dropped the magazine. He pulled out a box of ammo and punched in the remaining rounds. Then he did the same for the .38, spinning the chamber and holding it up to the light before adding the extra shells.

"Somebody want to tell me what the fuck is going on here?"

Without taking his eyes off the weapons, Vic explained. "We're here to pick up Jerry's mom. You know Barbara, don't you? She's being held by some Dead BBs here in town and we're going bust her out. Cowboy style."

Dick blanched. "Dead BBs. You gotta be kidding, right?"

"Of course, I'm kidding. Nobody's busting her out cowboy style. Jerry here is going to sit down and talk with the people he stole from, tell them where their money is, and we're gonna let them settle it like men, do the right thing so they let his mother go."

Jerry said, "Stop fucking with him."

"Who's fucking with him? You gotta talk to these guys, let 'em know what's going on. They've got your mother, for Christ's sakes. Don't you want to help her?"

"Yeah, I wanna help her." Jerry's voice shot up in pitch and he sat on the edge of the sofa. "Of course I do. Fuck, Vic.

That's why I'm here. That's why I didn't jump out of the fucking car on the way."

Piper started to join in, but Vic held his hand up, telling her to wait. "Stand up," he said to Jerry.

"What?"

"Stand up."

Jerry got up and straightened himself, standing between the couch and coffee table. Vic stepped to him and punched him hard in the eye socket. Jerry fell back onto the couch, the surprise leveling him as much as the blow.

"The reason you didn't jump out of the car is because you know I'd have shot you in the back."

Piper yelled at Vic, but moved to Jerry and wrapped her arms him, cradling his head to her chest.

Vic stepped back to the table and opened the bag and pulled out the stun gun he'd been lugging around since he left the cabin. "I knew this would come in handy." He turned back to the couch and pressed it into Piper's neck while he thumbed the trigger. The loud crackle silenced any other sound in the room. Piper kicked her legs out, smashing them into the coffee table, as her spine flattened and her eyes lit up with the shock.

With a hand over his left eye, Jerry said, "What the fuck? What're you doing?"

Vic reached over and zapped him on the hand covering his eye. "Two million volts. That's what the package said. That feel like two million to you? With two million volts, I think you'd flop around a bit more." Before Jerry could say no, Vic gave him another crack with the stun gun. Jerry cried out while his body convulsed.

Dick sat still, watching the display. He knew better than to run or fight. His best option was to do whatever Vic told him. He watched the older man return to the table and pick up the Glock and walk back to the couch.

"Dick, set three chairs in the middle of the room."

"What kind of chairs?"

"Chairs, Dick. Fucking chairs. I want to remind you three—especially you, Jerry—you are not bargaining chips. The best way I could ingratiate myself with those assholes is to serve you up dead. That's the kind of peace offering they'd like. You get that, right?"

Dick had dragged three of the chairs from the kitchenette and placed them facing each other in front of the couch.

"Perfect. Thank you. Now face them outward and sit down with your friend on the couch."

It wasn't his own snores that woke Big Man, it was the sun warming his face. Sweat ran down his forehead. When he blinked, the salty perspiration stung his eyes. He shielded his face with his hand and focused on the familiar terrain around him. He was still there, on the hill, at the shack, Terry's body in the freezer. It wasn't a dream. It was all still happening. He wished he was still asleep.

His cell buzzed in his hand. He looked at the caller ID. An Oakland number. Probably Eric.

"Hello?"

Big Man was surprised to hear Vic's voice on the other end. He held the phone out in front of him, wishing he hadn't answered.

"I can hear you fuckin' breathing, Big Man. Talk to me."

"What do you want? You've already fucked shit up as far as you can fuck it up, there's nothing left to be done. You want to make it easy on yourself? Throw back a few whiskeys and stick the barrel of that damn .38 you love so much right in your mouth."

In Dick's living room, Vic stood with the .38 in his hand. He looked down at it and smiled. He did love that gun. "You're a smart feller, Big, but that may be the worst advice you've ever given me."

"What do you want me to do?"

Vic stood between the three chairs in the middle of Dick's living room. The chairs all pointed outward. In each chair sat Jerry, Piper, and Dick. They were duct-taped, roped, blindfolded, and gagged. Completely immobilized. After Vic initially secured them, he ransacked Dick's house for more tape, more rope. He hammered the legs of the chairs to the floor with four-inch nails. He considered hammering Jerry's feet to the floor too, but he decided against it. If Jerry was in too much pain, he may wiggle loose. This way, the nails at least slowed down their ability to topple over and try to help each other. "I want you to do what I asked. I want you to call 'em. Tell 'em I got the kids with me. Set up a meet so I can get Barbara the hell out of there."

"What do you think this is, a fuckin' TV show? You're gonna meet out in the desert and swap hostages? I don't think they give a shit about those two brats. Terry's dead, brother. There's no coming back from that. I know the girl is Eric's daughter, but you don't know that son of a bitch Tribban. I think at this point he'd rather bury everybody. And you on the bottom of the pile. You should do what you do best, my friend. Get in the wind. Go back down south and when you get there, keep going."

Vic hadn't noticed he'd begun to pace while Big Man spoke. He waited till there was a pause in the conversation. "Big?"

"Yeah, what?"

"Do as I say and set up the meet."

"I already did."

Eric Tribban stood in the middle of the open space on the first floor of his building. He had a bottle of tequila in one hand and a Bass beer in the other. He was distracted, staring into the empty space before his eyes. "This beer tastes like shit."

Marcus said, "Yeah, it's a Bass. You want me to run upstairs and get you something else?"

"Nah," Eric said. "Stay here, keep an eye on her." He stepped backward to the table he and Dmitri shared coffee at hours before. He leaned back and crossed his legs at the ankle. There was no grace left in his movements, the tequila starting to show its effects. His clarity was fueled by anger but simultaneously quelled by alcohol and exhaustion. "I'll get myself a fresh one. You keep the knife pointed at her."

Marcus smiled and held up the blade to underscore his position of power.

"And, Marcus?" Eric said. "If she gives you any trouble, just fucking stab her. I never promised I'd deliver her alive."

Marcus had cut Barbara loose and let her stand. She tried to stretch so her numb limbs would tingle again. She didn't buy the idea she was about to be killed. But she knew she was still in danger. The mere action of her ropes being cut told her there was something happening. Her captor's mood had changed too. The man in charge, Eric, seemed energized, excited. Barbara only felt more dread.

Mackie was restless. He tried to stretch his legs by pushing his feet against the floorboards of the Crown Vic, but only frustrated himself. He stifled a yawn and said, "How long we gonna stay here?"

"What, you made your play with your deadbeat informant and got nothing. We got everything we need right here. Salt 'n vinegar chips, your energy drink, a bush to piss on in the church parking lot over there. This is it," Nagle said. "This is how we're working it for now. The subject is in the house, and this's where we're staying."

"*Your* subject is in the house. Tribban is the focus of your investigation, not mine, not ours. For all we know, he's back in bed jerking off. We're wasting a day sitting on the sidewalk."

Nagle didn't answer him, his head was spun round toward the street. "Holy mother of God."

"What?" Mackie said.

"I think that's him. In the BMW. Get that plate."

"Who?"

"Lysenko. He just drove past. At least I'm pretty sure it was him. He was in the passenger seat. Look." Nagle pointed at the metallic BMW on the block ahead of them. "They're slowing down in front of Tribban's."

Mackie squinted at the car. He caught the first few digits of the plate, but that was all. He'd never seen Lysenko, he had no idea if that was him in the car. "We gonna follow him or what?"

"I don't think so. He's circling the block. I think he's either looking for parking or checking for surveillance."

"Christ, you almost wet your pants when you saw him. You think he saw us?"

"I don't think so. If they made us, they would've just kept going. They're slowing down. They're going to visit Tribban."

Mackie sighed, knowing he wasn't getting out of that car anytime soon. These meets could last hours. His cell sitting between his thighs buzzed. It was his deadbeat informant.

As Ripper crawled up the bank on the other side of the creek, he saw the crest of the shack. He thought it'd be best not to creep up directly to the rear, where he may be heard or seen, but instead flank high above the hoopers and come in at the driveway. His hip stung with buckshot. Ripper tried not to imagine the lead pellets poisoning him—he wasn't even sure they put lead in buckshot anymore. He knew his lightheadedness was born of exhaustion and pain, maybe even blood loss, but the thought of lead pellets floating in his flesh wouldn't leave him.

The closer he got to the shack, the more amplified any sound became. Every twig breaking under his feet sounded like the crack of a tree trunk. His heavy, hollow panting was louder than birds singing high above his head. He heard something over the noise he was making. A voice. Ripper held fast, grabbing a redwood trunk to steady himself. No mistaking the nasal tone of the voice. It was Big Man. He was outside, calling from the signal spot in front of the hooper, about fifty yards in front of Ripper.

"Yes, I know it for a fact. I told you, I just talked to him." Big Man started coughing.

Ripper listened to the death rattle of Big Man's near choking. Then there was silence, followed by the familiar blue note of tobacco smoke drifting up the hill. Ripper visualized Big Man on the fertilizer sack sucking as hard on the cigarette as his wind would allow. After another thirty seconds, Big Man resumed speaking.

"I know they're there, I told you I just talked to him. But you're not listening. Vic is in Oakland. He's going to meet with them. He said he's got Eric's kid and Jerry."

Another pause.

"Because Vic called me to set up the meet, that's how."

Ripper crept closer. He could see the hooper now and make out the round back of Big Man sitting on the sack. He waited till Big Man spoke before taking another step.

"Yes, I do. I'll give it to you, but you gotta promise me you're going to arrest him. I don't want fuckin' Vic Thomas finding out it was me who dimed him out."

Ripper was close enough now to hear the crackle of the voice on the other end of the line.

"I told you, Mack, I set it up. Of course I fucking know. It's at a warehouse near Jack London Square. It's a place owned by the BBs...Yeah, he knows. I fuckin' told him." Big Man paused to drop his butt on the ground and stub it out. He shook out a fresh one and lit it. "Before I tell you, I want to remind you what you promised."

There was a brief crackle in the cell's receiver.

"A get out of jail free card. That's what you called it...Okay, okay. I guess I have to trust you...You known me awhile, Mackie, don't fuck me over."

Ripper was close now. Right behind Big Man.

"The meet's at four-eighty-five Third Street. Right behind the place where they do those rock shows...Yep. Use your fucking GPS, Officer." Big Man laughed and hung up.

"Did you see an unmarked car back there?" Vlad asked.

"Back where?" Dmitri was more focused on parallel parking the BMW than what Vlad was saying.

"Back there on the main street. We drove right by it."

"No. I didn't see anything. It's fine. There's no one watching."

"What's the point of checking the perimeter if we're not going to be thorough."

"We are thorough. We looked, didn't see nothing, and now we're parked. We pull out of here and it's going to be fifteen minutes before we find another spot. We can't leave it double parked in front of his house."

"Why not?"

Dmitri frowned at his boss. "You're not thinking straight. We don't know what we're walking into, or what we're going to do in there. Be smart."

Vlad winced, his gut churned. He couldn't tell if it was nerves or instincts twisting his stomach. "Leave the car here. We'll walk around the block. That way." He pointed behind them, away from Eric's house. "That way we can make sure. If they are cops, we'll come back the same way and get in the car and drive away."

Dmitri sighed, but acquiesced. They got out of the car, pulled their pistols from under their respective seats, and walked in the opposite direction from Eric's. It only took a few minutes to make it around the long city block, and when they got to the spot Vlad thought he'd seen the Crown Vic, there was only an empty parking spot.

"See?" Dmitri said. "No cops. Only us gangsters."

Chapter Thirty-One

"Where the hell are you?" Eric dumped the Bass in the sink and opened his fridge to fetch a fresh beer. He peeked into the living room and saw Ollie sleeping on the couch.

"We're stuck on the fucking eighty," Aaron said. "There's an accident in Richmond and we're just sitting here. Can't fuckin' move."

"Shit. The meet is set. I need you two to get over there and take care of business."

"Where's it at?"

"Our place on Third. You know the one? By Jack London?"

"Yeah, I know it. We'll make it, don't worry."

Eric asked to speak to Cardiff, who was behind the wheel with his head leaning out the window. Cardiff took the phone and pressed it to his ear.

"Aaron knows where to go," Eric told him. "I need you two there in less than an hour."

"We'll do what we can. What else?"

"You still got this bitch's phone?"

"Yes, sir."

"I want to make sure he's going to show up at the warehouse, you know? So I want you to call him from her phone, remind him we got her. Tell him to come alone, all that bullshit."

"Sure, sure."

"I want you two to get there before he does. It's got a numbered lock. Aaron knows the combination. And when he walks in, kill him and whoever is with him. Then call me and I'll send a cleanup crew. Okay?"

"Okay," Cardiff said with sing-songy cheer.

Cardiff did as he was told. He used Barbara's phone and called Vic. Traffic loosened a little and they moved a few yards, stopped, and moved again.

Vic picked up on the second ring. He stayed silent, listening for any clue on the other end.

"Hello? Hello—o?" Cardiff said.

"Yeah?"

"We've got your friend. Have you got our friends?"

"Yeah."

"Okay. We wanted to make sure. I don't want to do anything unnecessary to Miss Barbara here."

"Let me talk to her."

"No, no. I'm sorry, she can't come to the phone. How about we all just get together and we'll talk then?"

"Sure."

"You know the rules, right? Just bring yourself and our two friends, that's it. Be on time, that's important. We get mean when we wait."

"That's a strange accent you have. You Russian?"

"I'm actually Welsh, but it's a long story."

"You work for the Russian?"

"Okay, okay. That's enough. Just you, our two friends, and the money. Don't forget the money."

"You tell your boss, the kids only took twenty grand. Not two hundred. That's all they got, and they got it with 'em."

"Excuse me?"

"You heard me. There was only twenty in the safe. Not the windfall you and your boss were looking for, is it?"

Cardiff lowered his voice. "Are you sure?"

"I'm sure. I've seen the dough. He didn't hide nothing, he's been running with the whole score. There's only twenty, not *two hundred*. You got that?"

Cardiff looked over at Aaron to see if he was listening. "Yeah, I got that." He ended the call and started to force his way out of traffic and toward the nearest exit.

"What's going on?" Aaron asked.

"We're getting off. We're in a rush, right? We can take surface streets, it'll be quicker than this shit."

Aaron didn't argue. After hours of flying on the 101, the traffic jam was giving him claustrophobia. He knew they'd make the warehouse in time and he began to focus on the task ahead.

Once they were off, Cardiff pulled over at the first spot he found, hopped out of the car with his own phone, and called Vlad.

"Motherfucker." Vlad stopped on the sidewalk, his head bowed to the ground. "You believe him?" Vlad and Dmitri were a half block from Eric's house. They looked out of place on the empty residential street.

"Fuck yes, I believe him. That's what you were thinking all along, yes? Besides, why's he going to lie now?"

"To turn us against one another."

Cardiff laughed and said, "If that's the case, then I'd say it's working."

Vlad ignored the comment. "And you're going to the meeting, yes?"

"Of course. What do you want me to do?"

"When they show up, kill all of them. Leave the fucking door open. Let the BBs worry about the mess. Get me whatever money they *do* have, and bring it to me. I don't care if it's only twenty dollars, take what they got and bring it to me."

* * *

Vic checked the time on Dick's microwave. Less than forty minutes till the meet. He went over the three taped to their chairs. They looked like silver mummies wrapped in duct tape. They were silent, only the loud breath from their nostrils made any sound. Vic lifted his .38 to Jerry's forehead. The kid was blindfolded, oblivious. No way could he see the barrel inches from his skull. Knowing the kid now, knowing how he'd put his mother in the jackpot and didn't give a shit, Vic wanted to shoot him. Execute him right there. But there was no way Barbara would ever forgive him. She loved the kid. He was her son. Vic lowered the gun and picked up the heavy bag of weapons and headed for the door. He thought about taking the bag with the money, but decided to leave it. If those kids managed to escape, they were going to need it.

He started driving toward the warehouse where the meet was supposed to be held, but his gut told him that was what they wanted. Instead he drove straight to the address Piper had given him. Eric Tribban's house in Alameda.

The loud rapping on the metal gate startled Eric. It'd been a long night and an even longer day and his nerves were frayed. He held up a finger to shush Barbara, nodded at Marcus to watch her. The banging on the gate started again. Eric wondered if it was loud enough to wake up Ollie on the couch upstairs.

"Yeah," he shouted through the door that blocked the gate.

"It's me. Open up."

Eric recognized Vlad's accent and opened the door, then the gate.

"Motherfucker. You going to leave us on the street all day? You having a little fun with our guest?"

Eric was surprised to see Vlad and Dmitri. More surprised to see the guns in their hands. "I thought you were going straight to the meet?"

"That's not for another half hour. I think maybe we should have a little pow-wow, you know? Like a game plan."

Eric nodded thoughtfully, but didn't move.

"Eh, you going to let us in, or what?"

Eric pushed the gate the rest of the way open, but when Vlad and Dmitri stepped over the threshold, instead of going up the stairs, they moved right, into the main room downstairs.

"There she is," Vlad sang. "The guest of honor. How are you doing, my love?"

Barbara knew this was the man they'd been waiting for earlier. She saw that slug, Dmitri, flanking his left side. Both had guns hanging from their hands. Vlad's tone wasn't cautious, it was brash. Something was wrong. There was friction between the men.

"It's such a pleasure to finally meet you, the mother of this boy who stole *so much money* from me. You must be very proud of him."

Barbara recognized the sickly sarcasm, and noticed Eric wince ever so slightly when Vlad mentioned the word money. "I don't know where he is."

"Oh, I believe you," Vlad said. "Trust me, I believe you. More than anyone in this room."

Eric and Marcus moved out on either side of Barbara. The five of them now formed a loose circle.

"You know why they call me Vlad the Inhaler, Barbara?" Vlad reached into his breast pocket and pulled out a cigarette pack, flipped it open, and pulled out a fat joint. "Because I love to smoke weed. I *love* it. I always have. It helps center me, you know?" He stopped and tucked his pistol under one arm while he dug a lighter out of his pants pocket. He lit the joint and drew deeply and held the smoke in his lungs. When he blew it out, he offered the joint to Barbara. "No? You don't partake? At your age it could ease a lot of those aches and pains."

"All right, that's enough with the bullshit," Eric said.

With the joint pinched between his lips, Vlad took the gun

from under his arm and said, "Enough bullshit? Yes, I'd say so. Enough with the bullshit, enough with the lies."

Someone banging on the front gate woke up Ollie. He listened as Eric answered it and as voices receded into the main room downstairs. First he flopped back down, ready to return to sleep, but as he lay there, the events of the last twenty-four hours reeled through his head. He sat up again, trying to remember where the closest gun was hidden. He sat back again, crossing his arms over his chest. He was ready, on call. And his eyes fluttered shut.

"There's one fat fuck I never thought I'd see ratting out his friends."

The voice was so close, it startled Big Man, but his size and immobility didn't allow him to turn his head enough to see who was behind him.

"For a guy who talks a good game, you ain't shit."

Big Man tried to swing his large frame around without getting up. "Motherfuck—"

Ripper hopped to the opposite side of the biker. "I ought to kick your ass, fat man."

Big Man turned back quickly enough to catch sight of Ripper. "Try and it'll be the last thing you do."

Ripper side-stepped to get in front of the hulk, ignoring the pain of the buckshot panging up his leg. "Fuck you, Big Man. The only thing that made us fear you was the backup, who you were connected to. But without them, you ain't shit. I would kick your ass, but you can barely carry yourself on your own legs."

"Fuck you, punk, I'll fucking kill you."

"You won't do shit. After what I just heard gets out, you ain't gonna have a friend left on the hill."

Ripper had his fists up. He hopped on his toes, as though he was ready to spar.

Big Man didn't move. "Listen, kid, I don't know what you think you heard, but don't take this out of context."

Ripper hopped forward and landed a right to Big Man's left eye.

"Ouch. Fuck you, Ripper. Back off."

Ripper hopped forward again and hit Big Man with two quick left jabs. Big Man tried to get up, but Ripper kicked him hard in the belly and he collapsed onto the fertilizer bag. "Gimme that phone, fat man."

"Fuck you, Ripper."

Ripper laughed. "You can't even get up, you rat piece of shit. Gimme that phone and let's see who you're calling."

When Mackie and Nagle got to the warehouse, there were no signs of life. A red brick box in the middle of the block, the BBs' warehouse looked like it hadn't been used for anything but parties since the seventies. Huge metal roller doors marked the front, but they'd been painted over and were out of use. The bays sat above broken concrete loading docks that'd been removed when the sidewalks had been expanded. As far as Mackie could tell, the only working entrance was on the left side, so they positioned themselves up the block where they could see the entrance and surveille any persons coming or going.

"What a shithole," Mackie said.

"Yeah, but these days, even the shitholes are worth a ton of money."

"What do they do with it? Grow weed in there?"

"Nah, they throw parties, heavy metal shows, punk rock, that kind of thing. No liquor license, obviously, but they sell beer. I'm sure they do all right. Maybe they'll grow pot in there after it goes legal. Not many people know the BBs actually own it."

"You stop by, get your headbangin' on?"

"No, we've had this place—"

"I know, I know, under surveillance."

"It's a pretty big asset. When the eventual RICO case comes down—and it *will* come down—it'll be Uncle Sam who's gonna own this building."

"The other kind of gentrification."

"Exactly," Nagle said, without any sense of irony. "Hello, who's that?" He pointed at two men walking briskly up the street. One wiry, the other thick. Both men gave quick glances over their shoulders before eyeballing the outside of the warehouse. "Think that's the welcoming committee?"

"I definitely do," Mackie said. "The big one looks like he might be a BB, but the scrawny one, who knows."

"I don't recognize either, but it's safe to say they're on the BB side of the fence. You'd know if that was your boy, right?"

"Hell, yes. I'd spot his mug at a thousand yards. That ain't Vic. Not old enough."

The two cops waited while the two men found their way inside the building. The men they were watching seemed just as unfamiliar with the property as they were.

"What now?" Mackie asked.

"I think we need to wait and see who else shows up."

A couple more moments ticked by. Mackie said, "If we sit here and wait, there's going to be a bloodbath when the next people show up. This is an ambush we're watching. I think we need to get in there and secure them. Otherwise, whoever walks in that door is going to catch a bullet in the head."

"So you're suggesting we walk through the door next? Into their ambush."

"It's not an ambush if you know it's coming."

Chapter Thirty-Two

"Twenty grand."

"What?" Eric looked at Vlad as though a deep insult had just been leveled.

"Twen-ty grand. That's what your kid and her boyfriend got from the safe. Not two hundred, just twenty."

"Bullshit. How would you know?"

"That's what they said."

Barbara interrupted. "You talked to them? You spoke with Jerry?"

From his position behind her, Marcus hit Barbara in the side of the head with the knuckles of his open hand. He didn't tell her to shut up, didn't admonish her. The action spoke for itself. She bit her lip and stayed quiet.

Vlad didn't flinch when Marcus struck Barbara. Neither did Dmitri, who was standing outside the loose circle with a Walther PPK still hanging from his hand.

"Where you hearing this?" Eric asked again.

"The kid."

"You spoke to him directly?"

"I didn't have to."

"Oh, you heard this from that sadist pervert you got chasing them up there? I wouldn't go to war just yet. Not on his word."

Vlad raised his voice. "You do understand I'm not alone in this world, right? I have friends, many friends. People who have an interest in the clubs, people who count on that money. Peo-

236

ple who don't want to hear excuses. People who want to know where their money is. *All their money*. You understand what I'm telling you?"

"Yeah, I know how it works."

"Do you? I don't think so. Because if you understood whose money you were stealing, you wouldn't steal it."

"I didn't steal *any* money. Those kids did. And, yeah, that's my stepdaughter, but that ain't me. We're going to get back what they took and straighten this shit out. I don't burn my partners."

Vlad's voice slid back down in volume and intensity. "And yet, here we are."

"Why don't you wait and ask this Jerry kid yourself before you start talking shit and diggin' yourself a hole?"

"Sure, why not? Where is he? Upstairs brewing tea?"

"I got the meet set up with him in less than half an hour. That's why we're having it. We can all go see him. See what's what."

"Why would I wait to talk to Jerry?" Vlad spat the name as though it tasted sour. "You have the mother right here. Let's talk to her."

"We told you," Marcus said. "She doesn't know anything."

Vlad took a half step forward. "If she didn't know anything, why did she hit Dmitri and run away?"

Marcus took a step closer to Eric, staying about three feet behind him to his right. Vlad felt Dmitri tensing up behind him.

"You think this is a game? You think because you're biker boys you're going to get away with cheating us? You think those vests you wear are bulletproof? Are you that stupid?"

"Nobody's cheating anybody," Eric said, holding his ground physically, but at this point he was only placating, stalling. "We're going to settle this today."

"No." Vlad's volume was back up to a yelling pitch. "Let's ask her. You let her answer, with me here, in my presence." Vlad thrust a finger into the air to underscore his demand, his decree.

The gunshot silenced the room. There was nothing but ringing. Eric held a hand to his right ear and bent at the waist. Marcus stood behind Eric, his Glock leveled, arms extended. It took a second for anyone to realize what'd happened. Then Barbara dropped to the floor.

When Vic pulled up, the house was silent. He slowed down enough for a quick assessment, but didn't stop the vehicle. He'd gambled going to Eric Tribban's first. For a quick moment he second-guessed himself, wondering if he'd gone to the wrong spot. What if they were already at the meeting place, guns loaded and ready to take him out? He checked the time on the dashboard. Still a full half-hour till the meet. He circled the block, found a spot, and parked. He sat in Mr. Clean's Escape for several minutes, going over the game plan in his head and making sure both his guns were loaded and ready to shoot.

When he was ready, Vic got out of the car and walked the elm-shaded side street toward Eric's house. Now that he was on foot, he saw how different Eric's house looked in comparison to the ones surrounding it. It was boxy and weathered and lacked any of the Victorian style of the surrounding homes. No stoop, no porch, no arched roof, no bay windows—just a big square two-story block. Vic guessed it'd been commercial property at one point. There're more exits, Vic thought. He moved around the front, the side facing the main street. The windows were all blocked with something. He couldn't see in, but they couldn't see out either.

He moved to the short gate that opened up into the parking lot. He spotted the second entrance to the house. A side door he had no idea whether or not it was locked. The front door, side door, or straight through the plate-glass front window. Those were his options. He hopped the fence and walked straight to the side door.

Shave and a haircut. Two bits. It was the time-honored

friendly knock he hoped was casual enough for someone to open the door without thinking. He'd tried the knob first, but it was locked. But the moment he reached up to deliver the knock, a gunshot bellowed within the walls.

The sound of the gunshot froze Vic. He was helpless, the weapon in his hand inert. The gentle knock was pointless now. He pounded on the side door and yanked on the doorknob.

The three of them were still, the adrenaline crystalizing in their blood. The split second it took for each of them to realize what was happening was broken by a pounding on the side door.

Dmitri instinctually raised his Walther PPK at the immediate threat: Marcus. He fired twice, both rounds catching the man in the chest.

As Marcus took the impact of Dmitri's gunshots, Eric rolled to the left. Vlad, too, hit the floor, spread-eagled with his arms wide and his cheek pressed against the dirty carpet. The pounding on the door continued.

Ollie heard the shot and leapt off the couch and started running to the stairs. No weapon, no thought, just running. By the time he got to the top of the staircase, two more shots went off. He started bounding down the stairs, two and three at a time. He'd almost reached the bottom when he overstepped, his legs separated and his body crashed down. He flailed at the bottom of the staircase, crumpled against the front door. There were shouts from the main room as he tried to get up.

The first thing Barbara knew: She was in pain. The bullet hit her hard, like a haymaker punch to the chest. The second thing she realized: She was alive. The pain being the brightest indicator of her luck and strongest reminder her she was still breathing.

Two more booming shots rang out, the sound shocking her back to reality. Without thought, she rose and ran. The pain acute, but somehow not affecting her. The will to live somehow sharpening the pain and compartmentalizing it. Survival drove her forward as she jumped over Marcus and ran toward the only door she saw, the threshold to the stairs.

She turned the corner and stepped into the passage. It was blocked by a person lying upside-down with their feet pointing up the stairs. At first she thought the man was dead and she tried jumping over him, but then she felt his hand grab her ankle. She was yanked down like a ragdoll, crashing to the stairs and on top of the man. She recognized his voice instantly.

"Where you going?" Ollie said.

Helpless as he shuffled alongside the square building, Vic searched in vain for another entry point. The only windows were on the second story. The front gate, he knew, was locked. There was only the side door. He scanned the debris in the parking lot for a ladder, rope, anything.

After a couple punches to her head, Ollie had once again secured Barbara. He shouted to the main room, "I got her, I got her." But there was no response.

Eric had rolled over to Marcus, taking the dead man's gun into his own hands. Although Vlad was still splayed out on the floor, Dmitri was on his feet, his Walther pointed at Eric and Marcus' corpse.

"Hold on, hold on," Vlad shouted. His own voice hard to recognize through the ringing in his ears. "No more shooting. Nobody shoot."

Dmitri had his sights pointed down at Eric, and Eric finally had Marcus' gun pointed up at Dmitri. The clumsy struggle of two people could be heard on the staircase. Meaty thumps and wrestling bodies.

"Enough," Vlad said. "I'm getting up. Nobody fucking shoot anything." With Dmitri trained on Eric, and Eric trained on Dmitri, Vlad pushed himself to his hands and knees, then got up from the floor. "Listen, you motherfucker. We're done here. All this, what happened, it only means it's true. You've been stealing from us. You get to bury one more of your boys, but I hope you stole enough for your minions to buy *you* a nice coffin too. You're going to be next, my friend."

As he said this, he and Dmitri backed toward the side door, neither taking their eyes off the silent, calculating Eric Tribban, who lay on the floor with his gun resting on his dead brother's chest, pointed at the two men.

When they got close enough, Dmitri kicked at the door with his heel, but it didn't open. He turned and used the knob, doing his best to keep his barrel focused on Eric. The door opened and sunlight burst behind them, the day beckoning them to escape.

Vic was ready for them. He stood at the side of the door and smiled as the short, fat fucker backed out, gun stretched in front of him like a cowboy. The man was so focused on the inside of the building, he never noticed Vic standing there. Vic shot him once in the temple and watched him drop like a bag of charcoal briquettes. The other man in the doorway now held up his hands. Vic didn't need to ask who he was—it was Vlad the Inhaler. Vic shot him in the forehead. Vlad exhaled his last breath as he crumpled at Vic's feet.

Vic didn't step over the threshold, he held fast at the door. Lifting the Glock barrel to his face, he could feel the heat and smell the scorched gunpowder.

"Who's that?" a voice shouted from within. "Who's there? It's me. It's all right. I'm okay."

Vic didn't move. He was listening for sounds from Barbara. A whimper, a breath, anything. All he heard was the heavy breathing of the man on the floor calling out to him. The man assumed Vic was a friend, someone there to save him. Vic heard movement. He counted to three and swung around the door frame, his gun searching for anyone to kill.

He saw no one. A dead body in an empty room. That was all. No Barbara, no Eric Tribban.

Upstairs, Ollie shoved Barbara into the sofa and shushed her. She writhed before him, clutching at the gunshot wound in her clavicle. She was oblivious to his instructions, but she remained quiet, whimpering and making a combination grunt and moan. He heard a gunshot, then another. There was no way for him to tell what was going on. The last two shots echoed in the street, as though they were outside. It wouldn't be long till the police showed up.

Footsteps on the stairs. Eric's voice, "Ollie, what the fuck?"

"I got her. What do you want me to do?"

"Cover her, cover the stairs. I gotta get some shit." He ran past the two and down the hall but continued shouting from his bedroom. "I don't know how many are out there, but we gotta get out of here quick."

Ollie stood between the couch and stairs, his arms spread out as though they could affect any outcome. He glared at Barbara.

Eric came down the hall with a pistol in one hand and a shotgun in the other. He called to Ollie and threw him the shotgun, a Mossberg Maverick. Ollie caught the gun and pumped a shell into the chamber.

"Get down there and fuckin' clean house," Eric said.

Chapter Thirty-Three

Jerry strained against the sensory deprivation. The first sense he needed to overcome was time. It'd seemed like a long while since they'd heard the door of Dick's tiny house slam shut, but it may have been only a few minutes. No way to guess when Vic was coming back, or *if* he was coming back. He strained against the duct tape bindings, trying to shift his weight and rock the chair. Vic had nailed the chair legs to the floor, but Jerry figured if he rocked back and forth enough, he'd loosen the nails and tip the chair. Dick or Piper must've been thinking the same thing, because he heard the rhythmic creaking of someone else in the room.

His hearing was the only sense Vic hadn't diminished. A gag stuffed his mouth, tape on his eyes, and his hands and feet were lashed together. He had a vague sense of where the other two were in the room. He heard breathing and sensed their presence. He wondered if they were as thirsty as he was, if they were even conscious. Jerry continued to shift his weight and rock the chair and the nails in the floor began to creak. Soon the legs of the chair began to rise then clack on the hardwood floor. He heard another chair making the same progress. By the sound of the grunting, he figured it was Piper somewhere behind him and to his right.

After focusing all his inertia, Jerry felt the chair topple. It tipped and sent him crashing to the floor. He hit the floor hard. The taste of blood bloomed in his mouth. He was so certain the

243

chair hitting the floor would free him, he didn't give much thought to what he'd do after he hit the floor. He lay there a moment, wondering if the fall had loosened any of the tape, but realized as soon as he tried to move, he was just as immobilized as when he was sitting upright. Only now he was in more pain.

Beyond his physical limitations—the inability to suck in oxygen and the impossibility of moving that much weight with any kind of force or speed—Big Man was still a tough son of a bitch. Ripper took his time subduing the huge biker. Punching and kicking him and leaping out of the way before the man could return any blows. Ripper had his own disability to overcome: the hip full of buckshot rapidly becoming infected. He stuck with the pecking method, slowly wearing down the angry biker. Big Man would raise himself off the fertilizer sack and Ripper would kick him in the belly, knocking the wind out of him. Over and over.

Finally, when Big Man was on the ground, he held up a hand at Ripper's oncoming boot and said, "Enough, enough, you little shit. You win."

Ripper kept on kicking him. "You better get used to it, fat man. This is how they do rats in prison."

"Hey!" a voice called from the house.

Ripper turned to find Doughboy swaying uneasily with a shotgun in his hand. The shotgun was pointed toward Ripper, but the barrel kept dropping, like the gun itself was on the nod. "Whoa, slow down there, bud. I caught your boy here on the phone to the police."

"Bullshit." Doughboy's voice was slurred and muddy.

"Check his phone if you want. Dial that last number."

Doughboy said something else, but Ripper couldn't make out what he said. Ripper took a step toward Doughboy and held up his palms. "Look, man, I would've had trouble believing it myself—I mean, I've worked for this guy—but I heard him with my own ears."

"'Sup, Big? You want me to shoot him."

Big Man wheezed. It was all he could do.

Ripper took another step toward Doughboy. He pointed to the ground. "His phone is right there, check it and see." As soon as Doughboy's eyes flicked in the direction of the cell, Ripper reached forward and grabbed the barrel of the shotgun, yanking to the side. Doughboy was caught by surprise and didn't have the reflex to pull the trigger. With the shotgun barrel in his right hand, Ripper gave Doughboy a direct jab with his left, catching him right on the chin. Doughboy let go of the gun and melted.

Ollie stopped on the top stair. He held the Mossberg across his chest. He turned his head back to Eric and said, "Wait, where's Marcus?"

Eric said, "He's dead."

Ollie looked confused.

"On the floor, down there." Eric pointed at his feet to the floor below them. "Don't trip on him."

"Who else's down there?"

"I told you, I don't know. So be careful."

With the butt of the Mossberg tucked under one elbow, Ollie took the stairs one at a time, trying not to let the creaking steps telegraph his arrival. When he reached the bottom step he listened hard to the empty room. There was nothing. The sound from the street was strong because the side door had been left open. Ollie wondered if it was left open after someone ran out. He hoped that was the reason. He lifted the shotgun up, then swung it around the doorjamb. Still nothing. He curled back into the hall for safety. The room was dark except for the shaft of light streaming from the open side door. During the split second he surveyed the room, he thought he saw Marcus' body. Did he see another body too? He tried to get his breathing under control. Was there a shell in the chamber? Yes, there was. Was he ready to storm the room and start blasting? Yes, he was. Was he ready to die? Yes, he was.

Ollie swung around the corner again, this time not spinning back. He stepped into the big empty room, his shotgun trained ahead. He saw now there were two bodies. Marcus on his stomach—definitely dead—and the lanky Russian who was there earlier. Vlad lay flat on his back, a meaty gunshot wound in his forehead. Beyond him, in the light of the doorway, Ollie saw the lanky Russian's friend, the stubby man in the track suit who'd gotten his ass kicked by Barbara. He was crumpled in an unnatural way, so Ollie assumed he too was dead. Three bodies, no cops. Yet.

Ollie focused all of his intuition, bouncing it like radar across the room, trying to get a reading for signs of life. He got none. Death permeated the room. That's what he sensed: the stillness of death. Each step he took, his eyes adjusted. Behind the furniture, near the small bathroom at the back, he sensed nothing. The gunmen, whoever they were, must have left through the side door. Careful not to turn his back on any unchecked area, Ollie stepped toward the door.

Vic had been waiting behind a couch. It was a fairly obvious hiding spot in a nearly barren room, but as soon as he saw the man panning the room with the shotgun, he knew he hadn't been seen. Vic waited till the man stepped toward the door.

The first shot caught Ollie in the back, right below his shoulder blade. He spun around with the shotgun and managed to squeeze the trigger, but the spray of pellets hit the floor between him and Vic. Before Ollie could lift the barrel up, Vic fired again, this time catching Ollie in the chest, right above the exit wound from the first shot. The shock of pain caused the man to drop his weapon.

"Where's Barbara?" Vic said, holding the Glock at eye level.

Ollie drew a deep breath, listening to the sick whistle coming from the holes in his chest. He began to pant, then growl at Vic. Ollie held his arms out, like some real-life version of Frankenstein's monster and stepped toward Vic. "Fuck you."

"Okay," Vic said, and shot Ollie once in the head.

The big biker stopped. A look of surprise frozen on his face. His eyes didn't move, his mouth locked in place, yet he still took another step forward. Vic fired again, this time dropping Ollie, first to his knees, then flat on his face on top of his weapon. The near dead biker tried to crawl, pulling at the floor with his fingers, then lay motionless.

Upstairs, Eric said, "Get up."

Barbara hadn't heard him at first. Like Eric, she was focused on counting the shots, guessing whose weapon was fired.

"Get up," he repeated, this time waving the semi-automatic at her.

She didn't move. Wouldn't move.

Eric yanked her off the couch with his free hand. To him, the older woman seemed light, like her bones were hollow. He shoved her to the top of the staircase and pressed the muzzle to her temple. "Tell him you're up here."

Mackie's first thought was to walk through those warehouse doors and start blasting. Just like a walking concussion grenade, a human flash bang. His second thought was to wait for backup.

"Backup isn't going to help," Nagle said. "If Vic and Tribban show up and there's a ring of OPD cars around the block, they're not even going to slow down."

Vic. Hearing the name made Mackie second-guess his common sense. It was unfair too, because Nagle knew Vic was a carrot Mackie was helpless to reach for. If there was a chance to catch Vic Thomas, Mackie was willing to bend or even break the rules to do it. Mackie knew it, and so did Nagle.

"Let's get in there, secure the building, and see what kind of intel we can gather."

Mackie stopped and grabbed Nagle's forearm. "Did you just say 'intel'?"

Nagle turned on the sidewalk, not wanting to break his stride. "Yeah, so? C'mon. Don't stand out here, you're going to get us made."

"I want to know why the fuck you're not calling for backup, why we're doing everything ass-backward."

Nagle didn't respond. He stopped walking though. He looked Mackie in the eye and tightened his lips.

Mackie said, "You never got the okay, did you? You're out here trying to bring in the big fish, but you're not—*we're not*—sanctioned, are we?"

"Look, it was a tough sell. I mean, Forrester knows I'm out here. He knows what I'm working on, more or less."

"More or less."

"It's you that's got a hard-on for this Vic motherfucker. C'mon, you were ready to toss the rulebook aside to do it too."

Mackie turned away from his de facto partner and stepped toward the side of the brick warehouse.

"Where you going?"

Mackie drew his sidearm and said, "To collect some *intel*."

Mackie strode to the warehouse's entrance and kicked open the metal door. It was loud; he wanted it to be loud. He was first over the threshold with his service gun held up. He saw one figure in the middle of the empty concrete space. The man's back was to him. He thought he saw a shadow move in his peripheral too, but the thicker man was in his sights and on the move. Mackie pointed his gun toward the roof and fired off three shots. The reports echoed loud off the concrete and the man spread his hands out above his head. Nagle was behind Mackie now, gun raised, panning the space. No sign of the thinner man.

"Don't fuckin' move," Mackie shouted.

"Get down on your knees," Nagle yelled.

"Which is it?" Aaron called out.

"Where're the rest of 'em?" Mackie spoke as he strode toward Aaron, still with his gun up and his sights set on the man's back.

"There's no one else here."

"Where's the other one, the guy you walked in here with?"

"There ain't nobody else."

Mackie shot the man in the thigh. A scream sounded, an agonizing wail that filled the air. Mackie ran up to his victim, keeping the gun trained on the man. Nagle flanked out to the left, searching for the other man.

"Why the fuck you shoot, man? What the fuck?"

Mackie said, "Stop resisting."

"Fuck you."

"Where's the rest of 'em? Don't bullshit me this time or I'll pop you in the other leg."

Aaron held his wounded thigh with both hands, alternately yelping and cursing. Blood flowed free from his leg onto the dirty cement floor.

"Where are they?"

The man didn't answer. Mackie stepped on his injured leg. "I asked you a question."

"There's no one here. I told you. Nobody."

Mackie winced.

Nagle trotted back. He looked at Mackie, trying to understand what light bulb just went off in his friend's head.

The man on the ground still squirmed in pain.

Mackie said, "There's no one here."

"I know. I heard him say it. But what about the skinny guy?"

"I mean, there's no one coming."

Nagle moved to subdue and secure the man. He drew handcuffs from his belt and slapped them on the man's wrists.

"You stay here," Mackie said. "Call for backup for this guy.

And keep your eye out for his friend." Mackie started for the door.

"Mack," Nagle called. "Where you going?"

"Alameda. There's no fucking meet. It was a trap and Vic Thomas didn't fall for it. He's at Eric's. Call the APD and get them the hell over there."

After the goon with the shotgun went down, Vic knew the bottom floor was empty, except for the ghosts. He also knew he didn't have much time left to rescue Barbara. Maybe in Oakland you could get away with this many shots being fired, but in Alameda, someone was bound to call the cops.

As Vic moved to the doorjamb at the mouth of the stairwell, he heard the commotion upstairs. Not sure now how many shots he fired, he swapped the Glock for his Smith & Wesson .38. The gun felt small in his hand after working with the Glock, but he knew the caliber had more kick than the 9mm. He squeezed the grip and looked down at his hand. It'd all come down to this.

"I'm here."

Her voice was weak. Vic barely heard the words.

"I'm up here."

She sounded close, but scared. Vic had no way to know for sure how many BBs were upstairs, but he knew there was at least one: Eric Tribban.

He started up the steps, .38 arced upward, sites on the open space in front of him. When he hit the fifth stair, he heard a gunshot. He leapt forward, three steps at a time. He reached the second floor and barged into the main room, ready to fire.

Eric Tribban was splayed flat on the floor, arms and legs spread out like a snow angel. Behind him, Barbara stood, a gun hung loosely in her hand. She looked tired, beaten, ruined, but a thin smile cracked her face. "Looks like you got here just in time for me to save you...again."

Chapter Thirty-Four

By the time Mackie got back to Eric Tribban's house, a blockade prevented him from getting close. The whole block was shut down. Patrol cars acted as barriers and a uniformed officer stood in front of the cars diverting traffic. Mackie double-parked the FBI's car and was about to step out when his cell went off. It was Nagle.

"What's going on over there? I called nine-one-one and they said there was already two calls in for that address."

Mackie spoke into the phone while he walked toward the house. "It looks like a cop convention down here. I can't tell if they got anybody in custody or not."

"Whoa," the officer said, holding up his hands. "Go the other way."

Mackie worked his badge out of his back pocket and flipped it open for the officer. The officer squinted at it, unimpressed, and said, "San Francisco? You got a reason to be here?"

Surprised by the callous response, Mackie played the seniority card. "Yeah, I'm on the job."

The APD officer hooked a thumb over his shoulder. "Lead is Chang. He's over there on the side of the house."

Mackie pocketed the badge and bee-lined for the officer in charge. As he got close to the man barking orders at his under-lings, he was once again stopped by a flat palm.

"I don't know who you are or who you're with, but you have to leave this area now. Any statements will be given at a press conference later tonight. You guys know this."

It took a moment before Mackie realized he was being mistaken for a reporter. "I'm SFPD. My name is Roland Mackie. I've got a personal interest in this crime scene. What happened?"

"Personal interest? What in the hell does that mean? Are you part of an active investigation into..." Chang trailed off as he tried to pick his words. He wanted to be careful about what he said next.

"Tribban?" Mackie offered. "Yes. But more specifically some of the associates who were surveilled at this address earlier today."

"Earlier today? What was your name again?"

"Mackie. Detective Roland Mackie. SFPD, Gang Task Force."

"Well, Detective Roland Mackie, what we have here is a shitshow. And if you know anything about what went on here earlier today, then we need to have a serious talk."

"I just need to know if you apprehended a guy named Victor Thomas. Or Barbara or Jerry Bertram. Thomas is probably using an alias, so if I could—"

Chang stepped into Mackie, close enough so the heat of his aftershave fouled Mackie's nose. "Look, Detective, what we apprehended in there is a pile of bodies. We've got five victims in this house and no clue who did what. It's a goddamn daisy chain of dead bodies. You're not going anywhere till you've given us a full and complete statement."

"I'll talk to you, of course I will, but I'm going to have to wait for my partner. He's over near Jack London Square."

Chang's face puffed with anger. "Damn, how many of you SFPD are creeping around on our turf?"

"Oh, he's not SFPD, he's FBI."

Chang looked more confused than angry. "FBI? You gotta be shitting me. Way to keep the locals in the loop, guys." He blew out a quick sigh and pointed to the inside of the house. "All right, let's take a quick tour, shall we?"

Mackie nodded, but he felt the weight in his chest. He'd been here before. The bloody crime scene with no survivors, no witnesses. His prey had slipped from the snare once again. He followed Chang through the side door, knowing nothing he was about to see would put him in the same room as Vic Thomas.

Familiar now with the address, Vic trotted ahead of Barbara up the stoop and into Dick's house on Alice Street. He knew something was wrong when he saw the door. It was open. He knocked it fully ajar with his foot. No need to be cautious, they were gone. So was the bag with the money. Three chairs lay knocked to the floor. Scraps of silver duct tape and rope were strewn across the room.

"Where are they?" Barbara asked as she watched Vic inspect the house. But she already knew the answer. He didn't know. They were gone.

Vic checked the bathroom to see if any personal items were missing, trying to determine if they left in a rush, or even of their own accord. He was trying to be thorough, but his gut told him they simply escaped. He came back into the living room to find Barbara. She'd turned up one of the chairs and sat on it. The bleeding in her clavicle had slowed, the bullet holes— both entry and exit—clotted. She was a nurse. She knew it wasn't life-threatening. But it wasn't the gunshot that caused her greatest pain. She stared at the blank space before her eyes.

"I'm sorry," Vic said.

She looked up, eyes brimming with tears. "I don't know...I just thought this would end it. That he'd be forced to stand back and look at his life. That he would...somehow change. Grow up. Become the man I thought he could be."

Vic let her finish, watched her stifle herself into almost imperceptible sobs. He knelt down so their eye level was even. "He ain't never going to change. Not for you, not for Piper, not even for him. That kid is hardwired, I've seen him in action."

"No, no, Vic. You don't know him. You've only seen him in

trouble, you don't know the boy who—"

Vic held a finger to Barbara's lips. "Stop. You're not hearing what I'm saying. I know he's a nice kid. I know he can be a good boy, that he was a good boy. But he's selfish, selfish to the core. That's all I'm going to say. He may not be a grownup, but he's an adult. There's not a lot more you can do for him. Now, I didn't want things to turn out this way. We were forced into this, with only a few options, and we had to do what we had to do to survive. But it's on him now. He's not going to be reaching out for us—not where we're going. You need to trust that same selfishness of his is going to keep his smart ass alive out there. It's about us now. We're the ones who need to survive. I've done it before, and I'll do it again. The choices I've made, the things I've done, I can't undo them. No more than either of us can take back that day on Fulton Street. But the shit I did today...I didn't do it for him. I did it for you."

"I know you felt like—" she reached up and touched the wound on her shoulder, "—you owed a debt to me. You don't. It's done. What you did for Jerry, getting him out of there, that's enough. Thank you. I'll always be thinking of you. Always."

"But you can't stay. You'll get tracked down. If you're not picked up by law enforcement, you'll get found by the BBs. They're connected with people everywhere, believe me."

She squeezed his hand. She knew he was right. For a woman as tough as she was, she spent a lifetime apologizing for her son, cleaning up messes, and beating back bullies. Now she was doing it again, trying to fix the world for her baby.

"They got our names, fingerprints," Vic said, "the whole nine yards. Fake IDs ain't going to cut it. We need to slowly work our way out of the country. And when we're out—never look back."

"I can't. You know I can't. Look at my shoulder. I'm going to need treatment."

"You know as well as I do you can't go to a hospital. And that wound ain't that bad."

"No, I can't leave because I can't leave him. He's my son. I love you, you know that. I've loved you in a way I can love no other, but he's my son. He's my son."

Jerry and Piper and Dick were at a bar in Pacifica, a small beach community south of San Francisco. The three of them crowded into a booth in back, far away from the sunlight streaming through the front doors.

They finally were able to breathe after their escape, the adrenalin slowly subsiding. Jerry felt strong. The liquor helped. Vic wasn't there now. He was the alpha dog. He'd won. In the end he made it out, he outsmarted Vic. They even had the money.

They had no way of knowing what happened. News reports were just starting to filter in. The TV news played mutely behind the jukebox at the bar. Things like *BB Bloodbath* and *Alameda Massacre* kept flashing above the news anchor's head. No reports of any of the victims being women. Jerry had to assume his mother escaped. Maybe Vic did too. Maybe not.

It was going to be a big story, with an even bigger investigation. They had to get gone and stay gone.

"I say we go out East," Dick said, "My uncle lives just outside of New York, and he'd help us. I know he would."

Piper looked at him with distain. "You know what they call 'just outside of New York'?"

"What?"

"New Jersey."

"It's better than fucking Mexico. *That's* crazy. White people are getting kidnapped and cut up down there every day."

"There's no way we can stay in the states, Dick. There's gonna be too many eyes on us." Piper took a dry hit off an unlit cigarette. "I need to have a smoke. Jerry, can we go outside so I can smoke?"

Jerry wasn't listening. His eyes were focused on the back of a man leaning into the bar. "Is that guy serious?"

"What are you talking about? You're drunk. C'mon, let's go smoke."

Jerry didn't break his gaze. "That guy, right there, in the blue shirt. See how he's looking over at us in the mirror?"

"It's nothing. Maybe he wants to suck Dick's cock."

"What guy?" Dick said.

Piper sneered at Dick. "Why don't you go up there and buy us another round, maybe he'll give you his number."

"Fuck you, Piper. You two are the ones with the fat sack of cash. I'd still be in my house watching fucking *Jeopardy* if it wasn't for you two. You can buy the drinks."

"Fuck this prick," Jerry said.

"What prick?" Dick asked. "Who're you talking about?"

"That guy. Fuck, look, he's doing it again." His words slurred a little, sliding off their tracking.

"He's looking now because you're staring at him," Piper said. "Leave it alone, Jerry. Last thing we need is to draw the cops out here."

Jerry tossed back the rest of a shot, took a deep foamy pull off his pint, and grunted. He pushed his chair back and stood up, filling his chest with air. "No way. I'm not letting this one slide. I'm gonna straighten this motherfucker out."

ACKNOWLEDGMENTS

There's quite a few people I'd like to thank but can't, so let me at least acknowledge the folks up in the hills of Humboldt County who were kind enough to pull back the curtain on the weed business and show me how things work. Also, thank you to Eric B, my number one source for all things biker related. Thanks to Joe S, for the hospitality. And to Monterey Mark for the Cripplers. Thank you to Eric Beetner, once again, for the cover and Chris Rhatigan and Rob Pierce for their eagle-eye edits. And, as always, thank you to Eric Campbell and Lance Wright at Down & Out Books for their complete support. Also, David Ivester, Rory Costello, Pam Stack, and my brother Bob, thank you for all your help. And a special thank you to my boys, Dane and Logan, who in their own way helped shape this novel. And lastly, thank you to my wife Cheryl, who puts up with all my nonsense.

Tom Pitts received his education on the streets of San Francisco. He remains there, working, writing, and trying to survive.

On the following pages are a few
more great titles from the
Down & Out Books publishing family.

For a complete list of books and to
sign up for our newsletter,
go to DownAndOutBooks.com.

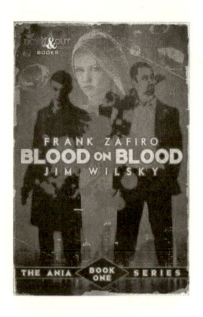

Blood on Blood
The Ania Trilogy Book One
Frank Zafiro and Jim Wilsky

Down & Out Books
978-1-946502-71-1

Estranged half-brothers Mick and Jerzy Sawyer are summoned to their father's prison deathbed. The spiteful old man tells them about missing diamonds, setting them on a path of cooperation and competition to recover them.

Along the way, Jerzy, the quintessential career criminal and Mick, the failed cop and tainted hero, encounter the mysterious, blonde Ania, resulting in a hardboiled Hardy Boys meets Cain and Abel.

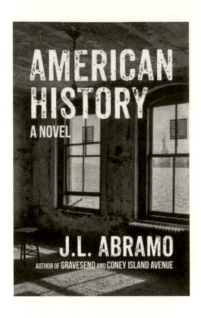

American History
J.L. Abramo

Down & Out Books
September 2018
978-1-946502-70-4

A panoramic tale, as uniquely American as Franklin Roosevelt and Al Capone...

Crossing the Atlantic Ocean and the American continent, from Sicily to New York City and San Francisco, the fierce hostility and mistrust between the Agnello and Leone families parallel the turbulent events of the twentieth century in a nation struggling to find its identity in the wake of two world wars.

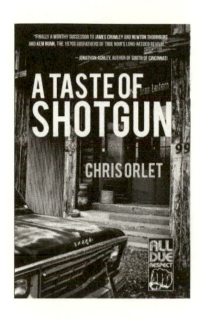

A Taste of Shotgun
Chris Orlet

All Due Respect, an imprint of
Down & Out Books
July 2018
978-1-946502-92-6

A local drug dealer has the goods on Denis Carroll. That shooting at his tavern five years ago? Turns out the cops got it all wrong. Now, after five years of blackmail, the Carrolls have had enough. When the drug dealer turns up dead, Denis is the prime suspect. As more bodies pile up, they too appear to have Denis' name all over them. Is Denis really a cold-blooded killer or could this be the work of someone with a grudge of her own?

In this darkly humorous small-town noir everyone has something to hide and nothing is at seems.

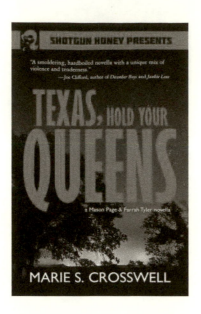

Texas, Hold Your Queens
A Mason Page & Farrah Tyler Novella
Marie S. Crosswell

Shotgun Honey, an imprint of
Down & Out Books
978-1-943402-74-8

When the body of an undocumented Mexican immigrant is found abandoned on a roadside, Detectives Mason Page and Farrah Tyler have no clue how a throwaway case that neither wants to let go will affect their lives.

On the job, Page and Tyler are the only two female detectives in El Paso CID's Crimes Against Persons unit. Off the clock, the two have developed an intimate friendship, one that will be jeopardized when the murder case puts them on the suspect's trail.